The Philosopher's Tale

J A Stevens

Published in 2008 by YouWriteOn.com

Published by YouWriteOn.com

Sold in aid of Sightsavers

and

Cancer Research UK

Copies may be purchased through any good bookshop or

online at:

http://www.amazon.co.uk/Philosophers-Tale-J-

Stevens/dp/1849230927/ref=sr=8-1

Chapter One

He woke early that morning with a stinking headache - like someone was using a pneumatic drill on the back of his eyeballs - and a mouth so dry it felt like his lips had been welded to his teeth. He lay on the bed, still fully clothed, gently moaning from time to time, and earnestly wishing he was dead. He'd have killed for a glass - or preferably a gallon - of water. But even if movement had been possible, it hardly seemed advisable, while his stomach was busy churning its contents like a demented dairymaid.

By the time he'd managed to crawl off the bed and down half a gallon of black coffee and a fistful of painkillers, he felt confident the worst was over. He knew all about hangovers - it was the rarest of rare mornings he woke without one - so he wasn't expecting any nasty surprises. But, just then, he remembered his briefcase.

He wasn't particularly alarmed, when he couldn't immediately locate it amidst the chaotic jumble that passed for the contents of his flat. But at the end of half-an-hour's frantic searching - when he'd looked everywhere it could possibly be and quite a number of places it couldn't - he was compelled to the hideous but inescapable conclusion that, at some point during the blank that constituted the previous evening, he'd lost it. For the briefcase itself, he cared not a damn. But at the thought of what was inside it, he suddenly lurched into the bathroom and finally surrendered that morning's battle to retain the contents of his stomach.

'You look awful,' Vanessa assured him, when he slunk into the staff room an hour or so later. 'Even worse than usual. Anything particular the matter?'

He sank down into the seat next to her and regarded her, with the expression of one on whom sentence of death has just been passed. 'You know Genghis gave us the exam papers, yesterday?'

'Uh-huh.'

'You know we were meant to keep them under lock and key, on pain of death?'

'Uh-huh.'

'Well, I forgot. I mean, I meant to put them in my locker but...'

'You forgot?'

'Right. So, last night, they were still in my briefcase. Only, now -'

'You've lost it.'

He felt his eyes bulge. Van was always perspicacious but this was ridiculous. What was she, telepathic?

'How did you know?'

'It's called putting two and two together, Tom. But don't worry, it's a grown-up thing. No one's going to expect you to do it.'

'You've got to help me, Van. Genghis is going to kill me.'

'Congratulations! You just put two and two together all by yourself.'

Tom scowled; if he didn't know better, he'd think she was enjoying this. 'Why are you being such a - bitch?' he demanded. Why was he asking that? Wasn't she always? When did she ever do anything, except take the piss out of him? He couldn't think why on earth he put up with it. 'Are you going to help me, or not?'

'I strongly suspect you're beyond any merely human help, my friend. But let's consider the options. You could resign. Or leave the country. Or save Genghis the trouble of killing you and commit suicide. Or -'

'Van, please! This is serious.'

She heaved a long-suffering sigh. Beyond doubt, Tom was his own worst enemy (even Genghis couldn't beat him to that particular accolade) and most days she could cheerfully - nay, gleefully - have wrung his neck. But refusing to help him was a bit like turning your back on a spaniel with a thorn in its paw and a particularly doleful expression. Theoretically, it could be done but it required a harder heart than she possessed.

'All right,' she said, 'you're the philosopher, let's look

at the problem rationally. A briefcase doesn't just disappear into thin air, does it? Even yours. So, where did you have it last?'

'If I knew that,' Tom groaned, only just mastering the impulse to throttle her, 'I'd know where to find it, wouldn't I? It's no good, Van. I've racked my brains but I was just too far-gone to remember. The bloody thing could be anywhere. Timbuktu for all I know.'

'Then what do you expect me to do about it? Honestly, Tom! You know Genghis hates you; you're already on a final warning; you're told to keep the exam papers under lock and key; so what do you do? You lose them. And hand Genghis your balls. On a plate. With your compliments.'

Visualising that image, Tom winced. 'Thanks for that, Van. You're such a comfort. Ever thought of joining the Samaritans?'

'Look, if you really want my advice, your best bet's to get pissed.'

Ordinarily, Tom wouldn't have taken much persuading but his hangover was still too recent a memory for that particular suggestion to prove attractive. Fighting down a renewed wave of nausea, he said, 'Did I mention you're supposed to be getting me *out* of this mess, not *into* a bigger one?'

'I'm serious. If you lose something when you're drunk, you're more likely to find it when you're drunk than when you're sober. I'm serious,' she said again, in response to his withering look. 'The research proves it.'

'Do all psychologists talk such unadulterated crap? Or is it just you?'

'Suit yourself,' she told him, with a shrug. 'It's your funeral. Any last requests, by the way?'

Tom spent a more-than-usually stressful morning trying to avoid Genghis, who seemed more-than-usually omnipresent. He appeared to be waiting for Tom round every corner - almost, Tom thought, as if the vicious little bastard could already scent his blood on the air.

Genghis (real name, Ian Xavier McPherson) had taken over as head of Claremont a couple of years ago and was as unlike Tom as it was possible to get. He was organised, ambitious, disciplined and pedantically correct. So it wasn't surprising he'd taken an instant and lasting dislike to Tom, who was then (as now) the head (because the only member) of the school's philosophy department.

All in all, Genghis had come as quite a shock to the system - Tom's at any rate. The old head, Max Wainwright, had had a soft spot for Tom - otherwise he'd never have survived, even in a second-rate private school like Claremont, or have landed the job in the first place. No one else in their right mind would have hired him but with the recommendation of Tom's professor (who just happened to be Max's oldest friend) the old man had been willing to give Tom a chance. He'd seen burnout before and he thought - not without some justice - that Claremont might be just the sort of backwater Tom needed, at least for a time. He hadn't expected the boy (as he always thought of him) to finish his career there but, over the years, he'd grown too fond of him to do more than give him the occasional, very gentle reminder that there was a whole world out there. Tom knew - which was precisely why he was staying put.

When Max died, Tom had experienced a further, unwarranted period of grace, while Vanessa was acting head; she'd the same soft spot for him that Max had always had. It was only when the school governors experienced a sudden, unaccountable rush of blood to the head and appointed Genghis, as Max Wainwright's permanent replacement, that Tom was finally landed in the real world, with a resounding thump.

It was the opinion of the new headmaster that Tom had had an easy ride of it for far too long. Genghis didn't like freeloaders - especially the kind who, having demonstrated an inability to hack it in the real world, were handed a cushy job, on a plate, by the friend of a friend. As far as he was concerned, Tom wasn't fit to be doing the job he'd been doing for the last twenty years and he considered it no less than his duty to ensure he wouldn't be doing it much longer.

From the moment he took over, Genghis made it his business to make Tom's life a misery and it didn't take Tom long to get the message - loud and clear - that the new head didn't like him or anything about him. Genghis didn't like his background, his politics, his teaching-style, his drinking, his smoking, his swearing, or the way he dressed. And so, a couple of years down the line, Tom had somehow acquired two written warnings on his previously unblemished personnel record (not that he could, or did, claim they were undeserved) and now all Genghis needed for the jackpot was one more. Just one more fiasco, one more cock-up and he'd have Tom out. On his miserable, freeloading ear.

Tom wasn't especially fond of his job - in point of fact, since Genghis had taken over, he'd more or less grown to hate it - but he did want to keep it. If the headmaster did manage to oust him, Tom was only too well aware that, as a middle-aged, disgruntled alcoholic, with at least one nervous breakdown (hopefully) behind him, he wasn't going to find himself top of any prospective employer's wish list and modest though his needs were (a daily bottle of whisky was hardly *extravagant*, in anyone's language) they couldn't be supplied out of thin air. Some form of income - and, consequently, some form of employment - was therefore an unavoidable, if highly regrettable, necessity.

So, whilst expounding Plato's theory of Forms to a group of frankly incredulous sixteen year olds, Tom was frantically inventing even more unlikely explanations for the disappearance of his exam papers. He was seriously warming to the idea of being mugged, until he remembered he shouldn't have had the papers in his briefcase, in the first place; they were supposed to have been safely under lock and key. Regretfully dismissing that idea, he considered staging a break-in of the school premises and claiming the papers had been stolen from his locker. But that was going to look decidedly suspicious, if nothing else was taken. Genghis might be - he *was* - a grade-one moron but even he had a sporting chance of seeing through that one.

By the afternoon, Tom had more or less settled on a plan to burn the school down - and the missing exam papers with it. As solutions went, he recognised it was a tad extreme but he was clean out of options and getting desperate. Anyway, he reasoned, if he was going to lose his job, he might as well do it in style. And at least they feed you in prison.

As he was dismissing his last class of the day, Vanessa dropped by.

'Mists cleared any?' she enquired.

'No. But your advice sounds a lot more attractive now, than it did this morning. I'm off to get pissed. Fancy joining me?'

'Tom,' Vanessa replied, reproachfully, 'do I look that sad, lonely and pathetic? Besides, you don't know it yet, but you've got a date. You don't want me tagging along, playing gooseberry.'

'Come again?'

'Takes some believing, doesn't it? But unlikely though it sounds, it's true. I forgot to tell you but I took a message for you earlier.' She handed him a note.

'Susannah Barton. Red Lion, Wellington Road. Half past eight,' Tom read. He looked back at Vanessa, with a scowl. 'What's this? Who's this Susannah Barton character?' He didn't know what the hell Van had been up to but he was in no mood for a blind date. Didn't she realise he had more important things on his mind? Like living to see the end of the week.

'She, Tom, is the woman who's saved your miserable, good-for-nothing hide. She phoned earlier to say she's found your briefcase and - if you meet her at half past eight this evening, in the Red Lion on Wellington Road, opposite St Luke's hospital - she'll give it back to you.'

There was a pause.

Then Tom said, dully, 'Of course, you're joking. You're taking the piss. *Again*. I wish you wouldn't, Van.'

'I'm not, Tom. Really. I promise you. It's true.'

He regarded her, narrowly. He'd been taken in by her

so-called promises before. More times than he cared to remember. But, seeing she really *did* mean it, he suddenly leapt to his feet, grabbed her by the ears and planted a hearty smacker of a kiss right on her lips.

'Ugh! Get off, you oaf!' She scrubbed her mouth with the back of her hand, her face the very picture of disgust.

'What a wonderful woman!' Tom exclaimed, ignoring Vanessa's histrionics.

'I do my best.'

'Not *you*! This Susannah Barton. Susannah Barton,' he repeated, rolling the name around his tongue, like a fine wine. 'I like the sound of her already.'

'I wouldn't get too excited, Tom. Judging by her voice, she's got to be eighty, if she's a day.'

'Oh.'

Tom was, undeniably, crestfallen. Sad, lonely and pathetic he might be but for him hope still sprang if not quite eternal, then at least with greater constancy than the event ever justified.

'Still, never mind,' he said, recovering. (One got used to taking these knocks on the chin.) 'She's got the briefcase, that's the main thing. What time did she ring?'

'Oh, quite early. About eight o'clock, this morning.'

There was a pause, while Tom's mind registered first the fact and then its significance.

'Eight o'clock! This *morning*! Then you knew all along. You've known all day!'

Vanessa grinned.

'I don't believe it! You evil, sadistic, vicious, twisted _'

'Careful, Tom. I am deputy head, remember.'

So she was. Not that she wielded any power; Genghis took care to keep all that to himself.

'I ought to kill you! I've been going out of my mind! Why didn't you tell me, for Christ's sake?'

'For the sheer joy of watching you suffer, Tom. It's just about the only pleasure I get in this miserable, God-forsaken hole.'

By half past eight in the evening, Tom was usually well on his way. But in honour of the occasion - and in deference to his saviour's advanced years - he restricted himself to a couple of doubles, before repairing to the appointed meeting place. He didn't want to shock the old dear, by turning up half pissed.

He was rather surprised by her choice of venue. The Red Lion was smart, trendy (and so not Tom's kind of place, at all) and invariably packed to the rafters. He couldn't imagine they got that many geriatric customers. This Susannah Barton must be a bit of an odd ball.

He'd been a bit concerned as to how he was going to pick her out in the crowd. But, as always, Vanessa had had the answer.

'Did she say how I'd know her?' he'd asked, when he'd finally run out of expletives to hurl at her.

'You mean apart from the Zimmer frame and the blue rinse?' Vanessa had replied. 'Well, here's a thing Tom. Guess what? She'll be carrying your briefcase.'

Tom hadn't thought of that.

As soon as he opened the door of the Red Lion, there it was. His briefcase. It leapt out at him, several times larger than life, as if it was on the other end of a zoom lens. In an ecstasy of relief, he fell on it, tore it open and virtually thrust his head inside, in his eagerness to be reassured the exam papers were still there. They were; still safely sealed in their manila envelope. God loved him, after all. He wrenched the envelope out, waved it triumphantly aloft and fell to kissing it with gusto. In the midst of this public display of passionate (if unrequited) regard, he noticed a pair of bemused grey eyes, watching him.

'You're pleased to have it back, then?' their owner enquired, hazarding a wild guess.

He looked at her - for it was a she. Very decidedly so, he thought, on second glance. She was youngish - thirty-something, at a guess - fair, grey-eyed (as he'd already observed) and with a kind, intelligent-looking face. The sort, Tom thought, that might well grow on a man, after a while.

'I take it you're Mr Lewis,' she said, recalling him to his senses - or at least what passed for them.

'Yes.' But how did *she* know? 'And you are...?'

She frowned, as if she thought that ought to have been obvious to him. 'I'm Susannah Barton.'

'*You* are? But I thought -' He craned his neck looking for the Zimmer frame - which was nowhere to be found. 'Vanessa said -' But, of course, she would have, wouldn't she? The twisted bitch. When was he ever going to learn, he couldn't trust a word that bloody woman said? Just wait till he got his hands on her.

'I'm not what you were expecting, then?'

'No,' Tom agreed. 'Not quite.'

Of necessity, his expectations were always low, particularly where women were concerned. So, even without Vanessa's attempt to wrong foot him, he'd never have expected anything half as enticing as the feast that was currently before his eyes. But of course, she'd be married. Or living with someone. Or gay. Or just sane. And therefore not prepared to waste her time with him.

'Can I get you a drink?' he asked, thinking - nothing ventured, nothing gained.

'OK. Thanks.'

He double-checked with his ears but that was, definitely, what she said. There was a long pause, while he stared at her, in disbelief.

'Orange juice would be nice,' she prompted, at last.

'Right. Of course,' he said, rousing his faculties. 'Sure you wouldn't prefer something stronger?' He couldn't help feeling a certain degree of intoxication would be indispensable, certainly for her and probably for both of them. After all, no sane woman was going to let him, not if she was stone-cold sober.

'I can't, I'm afraid. I'm on duty, in ten minutes.'

On duty? What was she, a policewoman? He might have known there'd be a catch. Still, that probably meant she'd have one of those uniforms you saw them wearing and possibly even handcuffs...

'I'm a doctor,' she added, breaking into his developing fantasy.

That was a relief - although he'd definitely been warming to the idea of a policewoman. 'What sort of doctor?'

'A paediatrician. I work across the road, at St Luke's. In the neonatal unit. You know, with premature babies.'

'Yes, of course.'

Despite his vacant look, he had known what she meant. He'd just been pondering why everything in medicine had to be made to sound like a disease, even when it wasn't one. "I've got a terrible case of the paediatrics." "I was up all last night with the most excruciating neonatal cramps."

'So, paediatrics. That must be…'

What must it be, he wondered, frantically groping for a suitable epithet. Satisfying? Interesting? Harrowing?

'Challenging,' he found, at last.

'Yes, it is. What about you? I've guessed you teach but what's your subject?'

'Philosophy.'

'That must be -'

'Harrowing? Yes, it is. Very.'

With a rather perplexed smile, she stole a surreptitious glance at her watch.

'I'll get those drinks,' he said, taking the hint, and shot off to the bar.

Contrary to all expectations, she was still there when he got back.

'Your health,' he said, tossing off his fourth double of the evening - he'd fitted in a quick one at the bar. It was at the back of his throat, before he realised he should have taken his time with it. He didn't want her getting the impression (albeit an accurate one) that he was some kind of drunk. Still, short of spitting it back into his glass, there wasn't much he could do about it now. He swallowed.

'I meant to thank you, of course,' he said, realising he'd forgotten his manners. 'For returning my briefcase. Where did you find it?'

'Here.'

'You mean, here in the Red Lion?'

She nodded, looking as if she couldn't imagine quite how many meanings of the word "here" he supposed there were.

Tom gulped. He had absolutely no recollection of being in the Red Lion last night or, for that matter, *ever* before. What had he even been doing on Wellington Road? It was miles out of his way. Jesus, he must be in a worse state than he'd thought. He really must get a grip and start cutting down. Seriously. Starting tomorrow.

The worst of it was that to have found his briefcase, *she* must have been in here last night too and, in that case, his cover was blown. There wasn't much point in trying to pretend he was just a "social" drinker, if she'd seen him in here last night, so pissed he couldn't remember the first thing about it now.

'Sorry to seem so dense,' he said. 'It's just I didn't notice you. In here. Last night.' Well, he wouldn't have, would he? He wouldn't have noticed Lady Godiva, if she'd been wearing nothing but a neon light.

'I think you must have left before I arrived. I came in with a friend - quite late - and found your briefcase under my chair.'

'Thank Christ for that!' Tom breathed.

'Sorry?'

'Thank Ch - I mean, thank goodness you found it. You just about saved my life.'

'No problem,' she said, finishing her drink. 'I'm sorry but I really must go. Thanks for the drink.'

Shit. She was leaving. If he was going to get to see her again, he was going to have to ask her. Now. But what was he going to say?

'Let me walk you,' he blurted.

'Where? St Luke's? But it's only across the road. You can see it from here.'

'Yes but it's dark. And...you never know.' Tom wasn't sure what it was you never knew but it was the best he could come up with at short notice.

'All right,' she said, looking as if she thought he was crazy but was prepared to indulge him. 'If you insist.'

He followed her, as she made her way through the crowd. At the door, she turned and looked back at him with a frown.

'Haven't you forgotten something, Mr Lewis?'

He checked his flies, found them securely fastened, looked up at her blankly - and spread his arms in defeat.

'Your briefcase,' she reminded him.

He clapped his hand to his forehead and scurried off to fetch it from underneath the table they'd just vacated. What must she think of him? He'd a mind like a sieve. Even sober. Still, he reflected, she ought to be flattered really; she was the one playing havoc with his concentration.

As she'd predicted, it didn't take long to walk her to St Luke's. About thirty seconds, to be precise. At any rate, it wasn't long enough for Tom to work out how he was going to get to see her again - short of having himself admitted to the neonatal unit, which was possibly a feat beyond even his ingenuity.

He did manage to establish, by means of a fairly hasty and unsubtle cross-examination, that she wasn't married and didn't have a boyfriend. He tried but he couldn't quite bring himself to ask if she was gay. Instead, he asked her what her favourite film was but, as she didn't say *The Wizard of Oz*, he was really none the wiser.

'Well, goodnight, Mr Lewis,' she said, preparing to leave him outside the main entrance.

She held out her hand for him to shake. On impulse - throwing all caution to the winds - he ignored it, bent his head and planted a quick, chaste kiss on her lips.

To his astonishment, instead of slapping his face, she pulled him down to her and kissed him back. Only hers was a real kiss: soft, warm and sensuous. Their tongues touched and he groaned, as his whole body was suddenly flooded with the most exquisite pleasure. He'd never felt anything like it. It was as if he'd never been touched before, in his whole life. Not once. Until now. And, God, it felt good. It felt *really* good.

When she finally released him, he opened his eyes and looked back at her, like one amazed.

She smiled. 'Pretty good, eh?'

He nodded - open-mouthed, breathless, too overwhelmed to speak.

Much later, he realised that had been his cue to ask her for a date - she'd probably wanted, even expected him to - but he'd just stood there like an idiot, gawping at her, eyes and crotch bulging, until she'd wished him a cool, 'Goodnight,' for the second time and gone inside.

What a total arsehole he must have looked.

'Bloody hell, Van,' he said, the next morning. 'That Susannah Barton. Bloody hell.'

'What's up? Did the nasty lady frighten you?'

'Bloody hell, Van. She's...Well, I mean...Bloody hell.'

Vanessa looked back at his awestricken, ecstatic face, in some surprise. He had all the appearance of having pulled but she wasn't prepared to believe something as unlikely as *that,* without some pretty compelling evidence to support it. She knew that - if only from lack of opportunity, rather than choice or virtue - Tom's sex life would have done credit to a monk. He was such a shambles, so utterly hopeless with women, that to believe *he'd* scored required a more-than-usually-willing suspension of disbelief. And she wasn't known for her credulity.

'She was your type, then?'

'She was...bloody hell.'

'If you say that just one more time, Tom, I'm going to kill you.'

'Sorry. But she was.'

'I realise you can't afford to be choosy but don't you think she might be a tiny bit *old* for you?'

Tom had been so bowled over by last night, it was only now he realised he'd quite forgotten to strangle Vanessa, in repayment for her latest little "joke".

'She isn't old. She's young. Younger than me, anyway.'

'Well, that's not difficult, is it? Anyway, I'm very pleased for you. I hope you'll both be very happy. When's The Big Day?'

'Look, Van, just stop taking the piss for five minutes, will you? I want to ask her out.'

'You mean you haven't already? Then what's all the fuss about? I thought you were engaged to be married, at the very least.'

'You don't understand. She - she kissed me.'

'Well, bloody hell - to coin your favourite phrase - that settles it. She'll *have* to marry you now.'

'Seriously, Van, I want to see her again but...well, what am I going to say? You must have got some tips - some chat-up lines - you can give me.'

'*Chat-up lines!* Exactly which century do you think you're living in, Tom?'

'You see? That's just what I mean. I'm out of practice.' That, he had to admit, was putting it mildly. 'But you can help me. You must know what women want. I mean, Christ, if *you* don't, who does?'

'Do I owe that dubious compliment to my gender, or my sexual orientation?'

'I don't know - either, both - take your pick. Just tell me how to get a date with Susannah.'

Vanessa sighed. She really didn't want to get involved. If she did, she knew only too well, from bitter experience, that she'd be made to regret it. Anything that had the words "Tom" and "help" in the same sentence was guaranteed to be an unmitigated disaster. On the other hand, he was undeniably such a God-awful mess that if he was going to get anywhere with this Susannah Barton - even assuming her to be desperate - he was going to need all the help he could get.

'Please, Van,' he said, as she showed no signs of relenting. 'I really want this.'

'Oh, all right. Look, the best advice I can give you is be yourself. Tell her how you feel and ask her out to dinner or for a drink or something.'

'Be myself? Are you crazy? I'm trying to get a date with her, for Christ's sake, not drive her into a nunnery!'

Vanessa glared at him. Tom had seen that look before and, all of a sudden, he had an overwhelming urge to dive for cover. If he'd known it was what he called her "time of the month", he'd never have asked. He'd have kept out of her way. In fact, leaving the country would probably have been favourite.

'That's just typical of you, Tom!' she exclaimed. 'You ask for my advice, then throw it straight back in my face. Why, in Christ's name, do I bother with you?'

Tom couldn't imagine. He opened his mouth, with the intention of doing the only (relatively) safe thing and apologising for his entire existence from birth onwards, but Vanessa was in no mood to listen. Besides, she'd heard it all before.

'Whatever it is, Tom, don't say it. Just clear off, before I do something we'll both regret. I've had more than enough of you for one week. And besides, it may have escaped your notice but some of us have *work* to do!'

Tom was quite wrong in supposing it was Vanessa's "time of the month". It wasn't her hormones that (occasionally) made her murderous; it was him. It was week after week, month after month, year after year of covering for him, of doing half his job as well as her own, of extricating him from his latest, self-generated crisis and of trying to stop him smoking and drinking himself to death at quite such an alarming rate. In short, it was caring about him and being forced to stand by and watch, while he systematically destroyed himself.

Fond as she was of him, Van had no faith he would ever get a relationship off the ground with Susannah Barton or anyone else. Untried and untested though it was, she was confident Tom's love life would prove about as aerodynamic as a block of flats. It was bound to come to grief and, when it did, she didn't want to be the one left to rescue him from the rubble.

For his part, though he had no doubt he deserved it, Tom hated it when - without rhyme or reason, let alone warning - Vanessa took it into her head to give him a bollocking. She was his best friend, his mainstay, his lifeline. Of course, he knew she'd come round in the end (she always did) but, in the meantime, it was hell - a sort of hideous, unexpected agony, like being savaged in the crotch by Winnie the Pooh.

He moped around for the next couple of days, occasionally gazing at Vanessa with his doleful, spaniel's eyes but generally making sure to keep well out of arm's reach - experience having taught him that was wise, if he wanted to live.

In the meantime, he couldn't - and didn't - stop thinking about Susannah. Not for a moment. For once, he'd been right; her face, or at least the memory of it, had grown on him. And as for that kiss...*that* had acted on him like a kind of drug. Whatever was in it, he was addicted to it already; he could get a hard-on, fit to chisel concrete, just thinking about it. He wanted more and he wanted it now. With or without Vanessa's help, he'd just got to see Susannah again. The question was, how?

To anyone else, the answer would have been simple. Anyone else would have picked up the phone. And Tom did pick it up - and he put it down again, countless times a day, without ever managing to call her. But, he told himself, the phone was a bloody stupid invention, anyway. It had always made him nervous. If he was going to talk to someone, he wanted to see the whites of their eyes.

Having decided against risking any new-fangled nonsense like the telephone, he thought he'd try writing her a letter - and he covered an entire ream of notepaper, in a fruitless struggle for self-expression. The beginning was easy. He could write "Dear Susannah" with the best of them. It was immediately after that he got stuck. Why was it that, as soon as it was committed to paper, everything he wanted to say to her made him cringe with embarrassment? He could make himself turn puce, in the privacy of his own bedroom, just thinking about it.

So, he couldn't write and he couldn't phone. So, what was he going to do? Try carrier pigeon? Or Morse code? Or maybe he should just do the sensible thing and abandon the whole idea. After all, it was pretty much bound to end in grief. It always did.

It was at this point, as the last of the glow that Susannah had lit in him finally died, that Vanessa - certain it was a mistake, certain she'd regret it - nonetheless relented.

Dropping into the seat next to him in the staff room, as if nothing had happened, she said, 'Well? Have you asked her yet?'

He shook his head.

'Why not?'

He shrugged. 'Too scared.'

'Idiot. Well, if you don't ask her, I will.'

'She's not your type.'

'Don't bet on it. I have very catholic tastes.'

'So I've heard.'

He looked back at her and, by now, they were both smiling. In fact, Tom was grinning from ear to ear, he was so grateful to be forgiven. If he'd had a tail, he'd have been wagging it. Not that he'd the foggiest idea what he'd done, in the first place. But then you never had with women.

'So, are you going to ask her?'

'I can't. I've tried. It just comes out all wrong.'

'For God's sake, Tom, get a grip! Look, just walk up to her and say, "Hello, Susannah. I wondered if you'd like to come out with me sometime." Now, what's so difficult about that?'

Put like that, Tom found it hard to say.

'I mean, what's the worst that could happen? She says "no" - and you're totally crushed and humiliated. So, what? I mean, it's not as if you've got any pride or self-respect left, anyway. Ergo, you've nothing to lose.'

'How on earth have I managed this last couple of days, without you to bolster my ego?'

'You haven't managed. At any rate, you haven't

managed to get yourself a date. Did it ever occur to you, Tom, that if you *just asked* she might say "yes"?'

'I suppose it's possible,' he admitted. 'Theoretically.'

'You don't think she might even be quite keen? I mean, after all, you did say *she* kissed *you*. Passing over the inevitable doubt that casts on her sanity - not to mention her eyesight - it does give you *some* grounds for hope, doesn't it?'

In the end, concluding Vanessa was right and he'd got nothing to lose that wasn't long gone already, he went to St Luke's and asked for her.

They seemed pretty dubious about him at first - no doubt they got their fair share of lunatics - but eventually directed him to the neonatal unit.

He walked in and she was the first thing he saw. She was standing there, sharing a joke with a couple of nurses, and he froze. He felt like someone had just grabbed him by the balls - and none too gently at that. He very nearly lost his nerve and bolted. But imagining what Vanessa would say, let alone *do* to him, if he chickened out now, stiffened his spine no end.

Taking a couple of deep breaths, he forced himself to say her name.

She looked up with a frown, not placing him at first. Then, recognising him, she smiled - and Tom's heart soared at the sight.

He left the hospital ten minutes later, with a date for the following evening, walking on air - and wondering how even he had managed to make quite such a meal out of something so simple.

Chapter 2

The next morning, he woke feeling his heart was somehow beating faster and stronger and the blood was coursing through his veins with new life and new energy. He felt younger than he'd felt in years. It might be absurd - he knew it *was* absurd - but he didn't care. So, he was a fool. So, it was bound to end in pain and disappointment. So what? Right now, his senses were on fire and he was revelling in a lust he hadn't felt, for just about as long as he could remember.

It was so long, he'd long ago stopped caring about how he looked. Looking in the mirror now was a rather sobering experience, even in his current mood. He despised all outdoor pursuits and never exposed himself to sunlight, if he could possibly avoid it. In consequence, with the exception of his face, neck and hands, his skin was the colour of bleached flour. He especially despised all sports - whether indoor or outdoor - and never took any exercise, which (by any amount of effort) could be avoided. In consequence, though he wasn't exactly overweight, he had the beginnings of a paunch and the muscle tone he thought, eyeing himself critically, of a bedridden octogenarian. His hair (mercifully thick) was greying and unkempt; his face (unshaven and so far unwashed) was lined and tired-looking; his eyes were dull and bleary with drink and his teeth were stained with too much coffee and tobacco.

What could she possibly see in him? How (not to put too fine a point on it) could she possibly want to go to bed with *that*?

Pulling down his shorts, he cast an appraising eye over his manhood. To his everlasting regret, Lazarus (as Tom had christened his dick, in the forlorn hope it might one day be called upon to rise from the dead) wasn't the sort of specimen calculated to leave the average female agog. It was a pity - in fact, it was the central sorrow of Tom's life - but there it was. He pulled his shorts back up again, now thoroughly depressed.

He could take a shower, get a shave, a haircut and a scale and polish but (short of booking himself in for a whole-body transplant - or, at the very least, penile enhancement) there wasn't much more he could do, before eight o'clock that evening. Maybe he should just phone and cancel.

Then there was the flat. If possible, it was in even worse shape than he was. He glanced around at the filth and chaos - undisturbed for months at a time - that was his habitual habitat. The carpet was encrusted with old food and discarded cigarette butts; half-eaten take-aways, dirty glasses and empty wine and whisky bottles were strewn everywhere. Normally, it didn't matter - he was the only one who ever saw it - but how could he ask her back here, to *this*? And if he didn't, how was he going to get his leg over? He couldn't bank on getting an invitation back to her place. It was a truly appalling prospect but there was nothing for it: he was going to have to clean up.

Holding himself firmly by the nose, in order to sound as nasally congested as possible, he picked up the phone to Brunhilde (real name, Catherine Zelda Frost), the school secretary and a woman after Genghis's own heart (in more ways than one, Tom suspected). It wasn't exactly unusual for Tom to call in sick and one day soon Genghis was bound to call his bluff but this was an emergency.

'Terrible cold. Sore throat. Couldn't possibly come in today,' he lied.

He had the distinct impression Brunhilde didn't believe him but maybe that was just guilt. Tom's conscience could be an inconvenient bugger, at times.

'I'll let the headmaster know,' she snapped. 'Is there *any* chance you'll be in tomorrow?'

'Can't say,' Tom croaked, adding a pathetic little cough for effect. 'Have to see how I feel.'

Bloody old crone, he thought, hanging up. What skin was it off her gigantic proboscis? Anybody'd think she paid his salary out of her own pocket. Tight-fisted old bag.

By six thirty that evening, he'd got everything under control. His flat was now so uncharacteristically clean and tidy even his own mother might have approved, if she'd been alive to see it. He'd had a haircut, had visited the dentist (who'd insisted on giving him three fillings, to go with his scale and polish), had bought a brand new razor and, consequently, now had the better part of half a toilet roll stuck to his face, in an attempt to staunch the bleeding. In addition, he'd given himself the most excruciating backache, with the effort of holding his stomach in all day. In other words, everything was ready and just about perfect. Then the phone rang.

'Tom?'

It was Susannah. He could guess what was coming. He didn't need to hear her say it.

'Sorry, Tom. I can't make it, after all. Something's come up. An emergency.'

Yeah, right. So she was a doctor. So she probably had to deal with the occasional emergency. He knew when he was being dumped. Why did she bother stringing him along like that, making a date and *pretending* she was going to keep it? Why didn't she just say "no" in the first place, if that was what she meant? Bloody women. They were all the same. To hell with the lot of them. Who needed them, anyway?

'Don't worry about it,' he told her, through gritted teeth. 'Some other time.'

He hung up and, deciding there was absolutely no point in sobriety now, poured himself a drink. A large one. He tried but, somehow, he didn't have the heart to wish she'd get run over by a bus on the way home. Trouble was, despite being dumped, he still liked her.

But what the hell. He'd get over it.

Some while later, he woke with a start. The doorbell was ringing. Fuck. He hauled himself up off the sofa, where he'd fallen asleep over a bottle of whisky, and staggered to the intercom.

It was bound to be someone he didn't want to talk to - like a double-glazing salesman or a Jehovah's Witness - so he didn't bother to be polite. 'For Christ's sake, *what*? Can't a man get five minutes' peace in his own home? Even at this hour?' What time was it anyway, he wondered? He glanced at his watch. Nearly ten. Didn't these people have homes to go to? 'Don't you people have homes to go to?'

'Sorry, Tom,' she said. 'I know it's late. Did I wake you?'

Susannah! *Fuck!*

'I - er - yes. I mean, no! Come up!'

Shit. *Shit!*

He ran round the flat like a madman with his arse on fire - the habitual chaos had already begun to reassert itself - emptying ashtrays, hurling dirty plates into the sink and stuffing his half-empty, tell-tale bottle of whisky down the back of the sofa.

In the bathroom, he threw cold water on his face, flattened his dishevelled hair with his hands and, noticing he was out of toothpaste, gargled furiously with some foul-tasting liquid he found stuffed at the back of the medicine cabinet, having half an idea it might once have been a mouthwash.

By that time, she was at the front door.

He opened to her, breathless and smiling.

She looked like shit. Really, truly wretched. In comparison, he thought, he positively glowed.

'Sorry, Tom,' she said again. 'I shouldn't have come but...I didn't feel like going straight home.'

He let her in, awash with guilt. By now, it was clear - even to him - that there really had been an emergency and, by the look of her, she'd been to hell and back. Meanwhile, he'd been calling her every name under the sun, for standing him up. What a total bastard. Still, he was thankful for small mercies; at least he hadn't called her all those names to her face.

'Tough day?' he asked, settling her into the corner of the sofa, with a glass of wine.

She looked up at him with those soft, grey eyes that made his heart turn over and he swallowed, dryly.

'Want to talk about it?' As he watched, her eyes slowly filled with tears and she shrugged.

'What's there to say? We lost another baby today. That's three, in as many days. Sometimes I hate my job.'

He nodded and topped up her glass. What could he say to that? He couldn't think of anything that wasn't hopelessly trite and facile but, thankfully, she didn't seem to want or expect a reply.

Wiping her eyes on the back of her hand, she said, 'I don't suppose you've got anything to eat, have you, Tom? Only, I'm starving.'

He smiled, suddenly realising he was hungry too.

She talked and he listened, while he fixed them something to eat. They finished the wine and then - when she finally got round to asking just exactly what it was she'd been sitting on all evening - they started on the whisky.

It was a long time since he'd talked and laughed like this with anyone - let alone a woman.

Then, suddenly, she exclaimed, 'God, Tom, look at the time - and I'm on again at eight! I'd better call a cab.'

'Stay the night,' his mouth replied, moments before his brain was engaged. Shit! What did he say that for? He'd blown it now, for sure. 'I can sleep on the sofa,' he added quickly, thinking on his feet.

'You could,' she agreed. 'But I'd much rather you didn't.'

He almost choked.

'I - er - OK. Well, I don't have to,' he stammered. For Christ's sake, he told himself, get a grip! Are you *trying* to make it obvious you haven't had it since Elvis was alive?

'Good,' she said, getting up, as cool as iced tea. 'But I need to shower first. Where's the bathroom?'

He showed her, then went into the bedroom, shut the door and punched the air. He could hardly believe it: he'd actually *scored*! Christ, he hadn't felt this good since…well, it was obviously too long ago to remember.

He kicked off his shoes and began tearing off his clothes, in a frenzy of anticipation. Then, with his shirt half over his head, he suddenly froze, arrested by the most hideous thought imaginable. It was just about the only thing that could have burst his bubble just then - but he could already hear it popping.

'No,' he groaned, agonised. 'Please, God, no!'

Wrestling his way back into his shirt, he wrenched open the bedside cabinet, rifled frantically through its contents - and finally sank down on the bed, in almost suicidal despair.

Typical. Absolutely fucking typical. Just his luck. The story of his sad, pathetic, useless, fucking-shit excuse for a life. He was out of condoms.

Alone (as ever) last New Year's Eve, having no better use for them - and deciding, in a fit of drunken self-pity, he never would have - he'd blown up his last packet as a somewhat unorthodox set of party balloons. They'd still been wafting aimlessly round the flat the following morning, when a neighbour (a little, mousy-looking woman who seemed to have taken an unaccountable liking to him) had called to invite him in for a drink. Come to think of it, she hadn't spoken to him since.

How was it possible, he asked himself, that he'd lasted since New Year's Eve without even noticing his deficiency? And how could he have spent all day anticipating and preparing for the shag that was finally to break his duck, without giving a single thought to the one piece of equipment he was going to need that wasn't located in his shorts? Honestly, it beggared belief. Even for him.

So, what was he going to do now? Tell Susannah he'd changed his mind, didn't fancy her, couldn't get it up or had just remembered he had an incurable venereal disease? Somehow, none of these alternatives seemed like much of an improvement on the truth - and he wasn't going to tell her *that*, at any price. Of course, it was always possible she'd have her own supply but, somehow, it didn't seem likely. And anyway, how could he ask, without making his own want apparent and consequently being confirmed as the most gigantic loser in history?

He glanced at his watch. Ten to. If he ran like hell, he might - just - make it to Ravi Patel's before he closed, at two.

He thrust his feet back into his shoes, grabbed his jacket and crept with exaggerated, Fagin-like stealth past the bathroom door where he could hear the shower still running and, silently, let himself out of the flat. Once outside and safely out of earshot, he clattered down the communal stairs, fought a frantic battle with the street door - which, as ever, stubbornly resisted all merely human efforts to open it - and finally burst out onto the street below.

Five minutes later, he staggered into Ravi Patel's, grey in the face, gasping for breath and bent double with stitch.

'Something up, Tom?' Ravi enquired, anxiously. Tom looked for all the world as if he was about to expire right there on the shop floor - and Ravi'd only just finished mopping it.

'Run out of milk,' Tom gasped, excuse at the ready. He didn't want Ravi to guess the real reason he'd come hurtling into his shop at two in the morning, like a man in the throes of a seizure. He'd much prefer it if Ravi thought he'd just run out of a few essentials and hadn't realised the time. To that end, he'd already decided he needed a couple of decoy purchases.

He grabbed a carton of milk, a loaf of bread and (God knows why, Tom never did) a packet of marzipan and dumped them on the checkout. As Ravi began to ring them into the till, Tom took a packet of condoms from the rack, as a casual, who-knows-when-they-might-come-in-handy   kind   of afterthought.

Ravi stopped and regarded him, for a long moment, over the top of his spectacles. Eventually, still gazing steadily at Tom, he yelled, 'Meera! How much are these condoms?'

Despite being Ravi's only last-minute customer, Tom cringed.

'Ribbed or non-ribbed?' Meera bellowed, from behind the shop.

Tom shifted his weight uneasily from one foot to the other, telling himself embarrassment was an inappropriate, unnecessary emotion, which had no place in the legitimate purchase of contraceptives. He was a mature (not to say middle-aged) man, he reminded himself, not a schoolboy.

Adjusting his spectacles, Ravi studied the packet. 'Sure you don't want ribbed?' he asked. 'For extra sensation?'

'Positive,' Tom assured him, through gritted teeth.

'Non-ribbed,' Ravi bawled, at the top of his lungs - much louder, Tom felt sure, than was strictly necessary. Unless Meera was deaf, which he happened to know, for a fact, she wasn't.

Meera hollered back the price and Ravi rang it into the till.

Slamming his money on the counter and grabbing his goods, Tom bolted for the door.

He was half way there, when Ravi yelled, 'Hey, Tom!'

He stopped and turned.

'Give her one for me, eh?' Ravi said, grabbing his left bicep with his right hand and making an obscene gesture with his forearm.

'Fuck off!' Tom snarled, giving him the finger - just as Ravi's eighty-odd-year-old grandmother hobbled into the shop.

Great. Absolutely, fucking marvellous. Now there was somewhere else he could never show his face again. At this rate, he'd run out of places to shop altogether and would starve to death.

Back at the flat, he was hugely relieved to find Susannah still safely occupied in the bathroom.

He dumped the milk, bread and marzipan (why?) in the kitchen, went into the bedroom and stashed his hard-earned condoms in the bedside cabinet. Throwing off his clothes, he climbed into bed to wait for her. Taken all in all, he thought it was probably better if she didn't see him naked until afterwards (in fact, preferably, not at all) so he'd just have to pray she didn't want the light on.

She came in, her hair still damp from the shower and clad only in a bath towel. She looked at him and frowned. 'You all right, Tom? What have you been up to? You look like you just ran a marathon.'

'I haven't been up to anything,' he lied, thinking if he hadn't spent the last quarter of a century abusing himself, it might have been possible for him to take a woman to his bed, without her being convinced he was about to have a heart attack. 'I'm fine,' he assured her, hoping to God he was right and if he wasn't - well, at least she was a doctor. 'Really. Never better.'

Reassured, she smiled and turned off the light. Thank God.

In the dark, he felt her slide into bed beside him.

'You have got something, Tom, haven't you?' she asked, as he took her in his arms. 'Because, if you haven't, I stopped at the chemist on the way over. You know, just in case.'

Afterwards, he lay awake for some time, while she slept. He hadn't made love like that for a long time. In fact - who was he trying to kid? - he hadn't *ever* made love like that. He turned to face her and lay listening to the soft, regular sound of her breathing, as if he thought it held the answer to something. Did he feel the way he felt about her, because the sex was so good? Or was the sex so good, because of the way he felt about her? Which came first, the chicken or the egg? He'd never been able to decide and, pondering that fundamental but ultimately unanswerable question, he fell deeply and blissfully asleep.

He woke with a smile on his face - and, what's more, he wasn't the only one. Having finally come forth from the dead, it seemed Lazarus was full of an understandable *joie de vivre* and Tom had an erection. It took him a second or two to realise that, for once, he didn't have to resort to his usual (tried and tested) method of dealing with it. With the most delicious sense of anticipation, he rolled over - to discover he had the bed to himself.

She'd gone. Of course. How had he failed to anticipate *that*? She'd woken up, taken one look at him in the cold light of day and bolted. He'd had a good time - the best - but she obviously hadn't. Right now, she was probably heading as fast as possible in the opposite direction, desperately trying to erase the whole hideous experience. And who could blame her?

He sighed and rolled onto his back. Life as usual, then.

He'd just have to be grateful for that one night. But knowing it was going to be just one night sort of took the shine off it. Lazarus had taken his bat and ball home already. But then he'd always been a sulky little fucker.

Tom crawled out of bed and wandered listlessly into the kitchen. If he'd had a cat he'd have kicked it - but life was such a bitch it denied him even that small pleasure.

He reached for the kettle and found a note propped up against it. "Same time tonight?" it said. "Call me." There was a phone number and a scrawled signature that, as he stared at it in disbelief, slowed arranged itself into the word "Susannah".

He yelped with delight, screwed the note up into a ball, tossed it into the air and kicked it across the room. Then - realising he'd need the phone number she'd given him, if he was going to do as she suggested and call her - he spent the next fifteen minutes trying to fish it out from the back of the cooker.

He arrived at work an hour later, feeling like a god. He could have turned wine into water and walked on it, he felt that good.

He was bounding alone the corridor, with the most ludicrous grin of self-congratulation plastered across his face, when he collided with Brunhilde. His *joie de vivre* was now at such a ridiculous pitch, he could have kissed her.

'Feeling better, Mr Lewis?' she snapped, straightening the spectacles he'd very nearly knocked off her face.

Shit! He'd been so preoccupied with Susannah - and the sudden and glorious return of lead to his pencil - he'd quite forgotten he was supposed to be sick.

'Much better, thank you, Miss Frost,' he said, coughing and banging his chest. 'These modern, over-the-counter medicines are truly marvellous, don't you find?'

Before she had chance to reply, he was halfway down the corridor and had shot into the gents, for safety. Even Brunhilde - hard faced though she was - would hesitate to follow him there. He locked himself into a cubicle, sat down on the closed lid of the lavatory and lit his first (illicit) fag of the day.

Practically the first thing Genghis had done on taking over the headship was to outlaw smoking anywhere on the school premises, even (in defiance of all reason and tradition) behind the bike shed. Built-in smoke detectors were sure to be only a matter of time but until then, Tom reasoned, what the headmaster didn't see couldn't hurt him.

How, Tom mused while he smoked, could Brunhilde - or, for that matter *anyone* - possibly lust after that autocratic, uptight, little arsehole? Admittedly, she was probably - almost certainly - desperate, being no oil painting herself. But even so, there were - or, at any rate, there ought to be - limits. He wondered just how long it was since Brunhilde had had a decent shag. Maybe she'd never had one - which, now he came to think about it, would explain a great deal. If not everything.

At the thought that she might be a virgin, he almost felt sorry for her. Not that he was volunteering to do anything about it. Even as an act of charity, he couldn't bring himself to do *that* with someone else's. Like he said, there were limits. No, if it was left to him, Brunhilde would just have to remain sad, lonely and frustrated. Whereas he, on the other hand, was revelling, was glorying - nay, was *triumphant* - in the knowledge that his last, decidedly-more-than-decent shag was a matter of hours ago - and he fully intended to avail himself of another, within a not-dissimilar timeframe.

Appealing though it was (certainly far more appealing than the prospect of teaching 4C, who were just about the biggest set of hapless halfwits it had ever been Tom's misfortune to encounter) he couldn't spend the entire morning smoking in the lavatories, feeling smugly superior to his colleagues. He was compelled to emerge eventually and, when he did, it was (metaphorically speaking - though even that was bad enough) straight into Brunhilde's waiting arms.

'Is that cigarette smoke I can smell, Mr Lewis?' she demanded, twitching her gargantuan olfactory apparatus, like a pig on a truffle hunt.

Genghis didn't need built-in smoke detectors, Tom

realised, watching her. Not with a nose like that in his arsenal.

'It's my aftershave,' he said, thrusting his face into hers - making her recoil in horror, just as he'd intended. 'It's rather distinctive, don't you think? It's called "Woodsmoke" or some such guff. Do you like it?'

'No,' she said, shortly.

'Oh. Shame I bought such a big bottle, then.'

'Mr Lewis, will you please cease this inane chatter. I've been waiting to speak to you. I've a message to convey to you from the headmaster.'

'Message from Geng - from Our Illustrious Leader. Right-o. Fair enough. Say on. I'm all ears. I wait, with bated breath.'

'He asked me to tell you,' Brunhilde said, as soon as she could get a word in, 'that he wants to see you this morning. In his office. Eleven o'clock sharp.'

'Ah,' said Tom, the wind - much to Brunhilde's satisfaction - having visibly gone out of his sails. 'Any - er - *particular* reason?'

The possibilities were endless. His timekeeping? His absenteeism? His drinking? (He'd a secret bottle of whisky in his locker; at least, he *hoped* it was secret.) His smoking? His recent fiasco with the exam papers? The fact was, it could be any or all of these - and more. The only thing he could be sure of was that, whatever Genghis wanted, it wouldn't be pleasant. Nothing pleasant ever associated itself with that lump of excrement in human form. Even by proxy.

'I really couldn't say,' Brunhilde smirked. She obviously knew but wasn't going to put Tom out of his misery by telling him. 'Just don't be late.'

She flounced off and Tom looked after her with loathing. To think he'd just been feeling sorry for her - the dried-up, twisted old hag. What an obscene waste of emotion! He hoped to God she did hook Genghis, in the end. The two of them deserved each other.

Tom spent the interval between receiving the Evil One's summons and the Preordained Hour of Doom, ostensibly teaching but, in reality, desperately trying to decide which of his many sins was most likely to have found him out and (once identified) how the bloody hell he was going to explain it away. His best plea was probably going to be one of insanity. It certainly wouldn't be any use throwing himself on Genghis' mercy or appealing to his better nature, since it went without saying he didn't have one.

No one's road to hell was ever better paved than Tom's. Every time his sins threatened to find him out, he swore he'd reform and, every time the axe failed to fall, he went straight back to his old ways. Even so - even knowing himself as he did and how remarkably little he was to be trusted - by the time he was knocking on Genghis's door, at eleven o'clock sharp that morning, he'd promised himself to reform, had given himself his most solemn and irrevocable undertaking to stop taking the piss and start behaving himself. Forthwith. And, he assured himself, this time he meant it - even if, by some miracle, Genghis *didn't* have him in a vice-like grip by the balls.

His knock was answered by a resounding silence. With considerable trepidation, he opened the door - just a crack - and stuck his head round it. Genghis wasn't the only thing ordinarily to be found in that room that made Tom's flesh crawl; almost as bad as the headmaster himself were the equally malevolent, disease-ridden vermin with which he elected to share it.

Tom didn't like rats - even when they were safely confined to a cage - and, for him, the headmaster's fondness for them set the seal on his character. He kept about half a dozen of the little fuckers (Tom never got close enough to count) in his room, ostensibly as pets. But Tom had his own theory about that. No one was going to convince him it was a mere coincidence Genghis never ate in the refectory, undeniably vile though the food was. Watching the rats now, he had a sudden vision of the headmaster selecting a particularly juicy specimen, momentarily suspending it by the tail above his gaping jaws - then dropping it in and gulping it down, whole.

Just as the tip of the still-squirming tail disappeared between his teeth, the door opened and the headmaster walked in.

'Ah, Mr Lewis. You're on time. For once.'

'I endeavour to please, Headmaster.'

Genghis snorted, as if to say that was the first he'd heard about it. He sat down at his desk and fixed Tom with a long, hard stare.

Now for it, Tom thought. And smiled the smile of perfect innocence.

'What are you smirking about?'

'Nothing, Headmaster.'

'Then stop it and sit.'

Tom stopped it and sat.

'I've been trying to speak to you for days,' Genghis whined. 'It's ridiculous, in a school this size, that I have to make an *appointment* to see you. Why is it that, whenever I catch sight of you, you're always heading as fast as possible in the opposite direction?'

Tom spread his hands. He really couldn't imagine.

Genghis sighed, apparently admitting defeat on that front. 'Anyway, now I've finally caught up with you, there's a pupil I want to discuss.'

'A pupil?' Tom echoed. He couldn't believe his luck. A pupil! Not his drinking, not his time keeping, not his absenteeism, not even his smoking! There was a God, after all. There must be.

'Yes, Mr Lewis. You remember those? I know you don't give them a lot of your attention - but you haven't forgotten them entirely, have you?'

'No, Headmaster,' Tom assured him, through a fake smile and clenched teeth. They're the ones I want to strangle, he added silently to himself, only marginally less than I want to strangle you, you sarcastic little shit.

'Well, we've a new pupil starting tomorrow, an Amy Martin. Her parents are divorced and she's recently moved into the area with her father, who's a High Court Judge.'

Tom struggled to look suitably impressed.

'She's to be entered onto the Gifted Students Programme.'

Tom suppressed a groan. The so-called GSP was another of Genghis's initiatives and was only slightly more popular with Tom than the total smoking ban. Its *declared* aim was to assist "gifted" pupils to learn at their own (accelerated) pace and achieve their potential, without being dragged down by the dead weight of what Genghis euphemistically called their "mainstream" (or stupider) peers. Its *actual* aim was to generate much-needed revenue for the school's much-depleted coffers and, from that point of view, it had been an undeniable success. There was never any shortage of parents able and willing to pay through the nose to have their decidedly average offspring officially labelled as "gifted" and, in practice, Tom had no doubt parental income and ambition had far more influence than IQ - or anything else - on the question of who was entered into the programme and who was excluded from it.

So far, as a matter of principle, Tom had refused to have anything to do with the GSP - though it was possible his stand had gone unnoticed, since Genghis had made a point of excluding him from those "privileged" (his word) to teach on it.

'It appears she's a truly exceptional student,' the headmaster said now. 'And, of course, we're very excited by the prospect of her joining us here at Claremont.'

'Absolutely,' said Tom, whose own excitement had already reached such a pitch he could scarcely contain himself.

'Naturally, her father expects her to do well - *very* well - and he's made it abundantly clear that if - or, I should say, *when* - she does, he will show his appreciation to the school, in the time-honoured fashion.'

The parental chequebook again. Really, Tom thought, Genghis had missed his vocation. He ought to have been a banker - rather than that other thing that only rhymed with it.

'All this is fascinating stuff, Headmaster. Believe me, I'm absolutely riveted. But why are you telling me? You can't want me to teach her.'

'Of course I don't *want* you to, Mr Lewis. But, unfortunately, you're going to have to. It seems Amy's set on reading philosophy at university. She's aware she doesn't have to take that subject now but she wants to and her father's inclined to indulge her.'

Lucky girl, Tom thought. While other kids had to be content with a PlayStation or an iPod (whatever the hell they were) she got to study philosophy. What in Christ's name was her father trying to do, ruin the girl?

'So, as you're the only member of this school's philosophy department, you'll appreciate I have no choice but to entrust her to you.'

'Can't you persuade her to take something else?' Tom asked, unable to contain his lack of enthusiasm any longer.

Genghis shot him a withering look. 'Do you really suppose I haven't tried?'

'No, Headmaster. Sorry. That was a stupid question.'

'Quite. So can we take it as agreed that, though this isn't what either of us wants, it *is* what you'll be doing? There'll be extra work, of course, for you no less than for the girl herself. But in such a good cause, you can hardly object to that, can you?'

Tom guessed that was what was called a rhetorical question - or, in other words, one to which the headmaster had less than no interest in hearing an (honest) answer. Of course, he bloody objected! He had better things to do, especially *now* (he experienced a fleeting but highly gratifying mental image of himself in bed with Susannah) than waste his time pissing about with "gifted" students. So Amy was "exceptional", was she? Tom knew all about "exceptional", "brilliant" and "gifted" students. He'd met them before. And they were monumental pains in the arse, to a man. Or, in her case, woman.

He longed to tell Genghis to go and fuck himself. But he knew life wasn't like that - well, his wasn't anyway. Such unadulterated pleasure was only to be dreamt of. So, instead, he gritted his teeth and said, 'Of course not, Headmaster.'

'Good. I'm relieved to hear you say so. I'm aware we

don't always see eye to eye, Mr Lewis.'

That was putting it mildly.

'And I know you've had certain - reservations - about the GSP but I'm sure you appreciate how important this is. Not just for the school but for you too. If Amy doesn't do as well as expected, if her father isn't pleased and doesn't show his appreciation in the expected manner, I shall know where to look for the cause.'

Right, Tom thought. Well, that's got that straight, anyway. Anything goes wrong, it's my fault. Fair enough. No change there, then.

'Don't let me down, Mr Lewis. I'm sure I don't need to remind you that you already have two unexpired warnings on your personnel record. If you're successful with Amy Martin, I might well be persuaded to expunge them, to wipe the slate clean, as it were. If you're not...well, I'm sure you don't need me to spell it out for you.'

No, he didn't. And he didn't need a dictionary either.

Still, Tom reflected, as he made his way back to the staff room, all was not yet lost. Genghis might have tried to persuade Amy that philosophy wasn't what this year's smart student was studying but Tom had every confidence he could succeed where that particular dimwit had failed. If he couldn't convince Amy Martin that she preferred psychology, or film studies or (for all he cared) basket weaving to philosophy, he wasn't the man he thought he was. And once she was so convinced, hey presto, he was off the hook. If he wasn't teaching her, even Genghis couldn't blame him, if her results weren't up to snuff. And so, when the judge refused to come across in the time-honoured manner, that would be someone else's look-out, not his. Simple. Problem solved.

'Well?' Van said.

'Well, what?'

'Well, what do you think, numskull? How did it go?'

'Oh, you know, pretty much as standard, really. The sort of experience that makes you wish you were dead. Still, I've got to admit, it could have been a damn sight worse.'

'Oh,' said Van, looking a trifle crestfallen. 'Not an unqualified success, then?'

'Hardly! Christ, that *would* be a first.'

'You don't think maybe you're being a bit too hasty? Maybe you should give it a second chance. Mutual attraction's not everything, I know, but -'

Tom spat the coffee he was drinking halfway across the staff room floor. Was she crazy? He didn't know whether he was more revolted by the suggestion that he was attracted to Genghis or that Genghis was attracted to him. He was appalled that *anyone* (even a psychologist) could imagine anything of such hideous and unspeakable depravity.

'Van,' he croaked, when he'd finally finished choking, 'what *are* you talking about?'

'What do you think I'm talking about?'

'The meeting I've just had with Genghis. Aren't you?'

She sighed. 'You know, Tom, sometimes I think you must be the most cretinous man alive. Isn't it perfectly obvious, even to a halfwit like you, that I'm talking about your date last night with Susannah what's-her-name?'

'Oh, that!' Tom exclaimed. *Now* he saw where the mutual attraction came in.

'Yes, that. *Well?*'

Tom didn't quite know how to put it into words, so he let his face say it for him.

Though she'd never have dreamt of saying so, Van thought he looked almost handsome, when he smiled like that. 'That good?' she said. 'Wow.'

'As you rightly say, wow.'

'So you're seeing her again?'

'Just try stopping me. She's coming round again, tonight. I can't wait.'

'I'll bet,' said Vanessa, grinning. 'You remembered what to do then?'

'Christ, Van, it hasn't been that long!'

'If you say so,' she replied, unconvinced. 'Anyway, leaving aside the sordid subject of your sex life, how did that meeting with Genghis go? Did he persuade you to abandon your principles and teach on the GSP?'

'You knew why he wanted to see me?'

'Of course.'

'Then why, in Christ's name, didn't you tell me?' Didn't she realise he'd been driven half out of his mind with worry? Christ, people with a clear conscience! They had no idea how the other half lived.

'I would have done, if you'd asked.'

Right. Why the hell hadn't he thought of that and saved himself hours of needless sweating and unnecessary buttock clenching? She was right; he was the most cretinous man alive.

'Well? Are you or aren't you teaching on the GSP?'

'Certainly not. I'm standing by my principles.'

'You told Genghis that?'

'Well, no,' he conceded. 'Not exactly.'

'Then how are you going to get out of it?'

'Easy. I'll just get the Martin girl to choose something else. That can't be too difficult, can it? Even for a cretin like me.'

Van grinned.

'What are you grinning about?'

'Nothing. Just wait and see, that's all. I bet you end up teaching her.'

'Bollocks!'

'How much?'

He hesitated. He got the feeling she knew something he didn't. But so what? If he stuck to his plan, how could he lose? 'Fifty quid,' he said, recklessly.

'You're on. But remember, I don't take cheques, Tom. At least, not the rubber kind you write.'

In honour of the occasion, Susannah wasn't just on time for their second date, she was early.

He felt absurdly self-conscious letting her in, as if she could guess what was going on and had been going on in his mind, all day. But of course, she couldn't. He gave her a quick, restrained kiss of welcome. He daren't linger over it -

much as he wanted to - or there was no doubt she would guess.

'Can I get you something to eat?' he asked.

'No, thanks. I ate earlier.'

'Something to drink then?'

'OK. If you like.'

Why did he get the distinct impression she wasn't interested? He felt his heart sink. After all, she'd had a whole day to think about it - to think better of it. 'So,' he said, bracing himself for what he felt certain was coming, 'what can I get you?'

She hesitated. Of course, it was never easy to tell someone, especially to their face. At least she'd had the guts - the decency - to do that.

'To be honest, Tom, I don't really want a drink.'

'Right.'

He waited.

'If I'm honest, all I really want to do is go to bed.'

He frowned, feeling like he'd lost the plot. So, she wasn't dumping him, which was good - which was *fantastic* - but she wanted to go straight to bed, which was undeniably something of a disappointment. It really must have been another hard day at the coalface, he thought, looking at his watch. It wasn't half-past eight yet.

'OK. Of course. If you're tired. I understand.'

This time, it was her turn to frown. Then, laughing, she said, 'No, Tom. I meant I want to go to bed *with you.*'

His jaw dropped, in amazement - which, he realised later, probably wasn't the response she'd been hoping for.

'Sorry. Am I too blunt? It's just I haven't been able to think about anything else all day. It's been driving me crazy and now I'm here…well, I can't wait.'

He gulped.

'Bloody hell!' he breathed, staring down at her, as if he'd never heard anything quite like it before - which, to be fair, he hadn't.

He'd expected to have to endure at least a couple of hours of polite conversation, while every other second his eyes strayed to her cleavage and his hand itched to be up her skirt and all he really wanted to do was fall into bed with her and fuck, till they were both exhausted. But he'd never have dared tell her that, anymore than he'd have dreamed she felt the same way. Discovering she was as impatient for him as he was for her was such a turn-on, it very nearly did it for him then and there.

'Bloody hell!' he breathed again. And fell on her, without wasting another word.

To say he was knackered, the next day, would have been an understatement of historic proportions. He felt (in certain of his parts especially) as if he'd been chewed up, spat out and ground underfoot. Susannah certainly knew how to get her money's worth. Not that he was complaining; she gave every bit as good as she got and the result was he'd never been happier. In fact, he was so happy that even the thought of Genghis, Amy Martin and the GSP couldn't quite burst his bubble.

Genghis had insisted that Tom be there with him that morning - bright and early - to welcome Amy Martin on her first day at Claremont. Tom couldn't think why the headmaster had chosen him to partake in this dubious honour, unless it was because he suspected Tom would hate it. If so, he was right. Tom did hate it. Being asked to teach the girl was bad enough, being required to treat her like some minor celebrity was adding insult to injury. Who the hell did Genghis think she was, for fuck's sake, the Queen of Sheba? But, of course, there was nothing he could do about it. The Evil One was there to be obeyed and, as he knew only too well, resistance was futile.

Nonetheless, as they stood there waiting for her outside the main entrance, Tom had rarely felt a more complete prick - and, given the undeniable proclivity he had for making himself resemble that particular body part, that was saying something.

Eventually, a chauffeur-driven limousine swung into the drive and Genghis, springing to attention, plastered a smile of welcome on his face.

'The red carpet's at the cleaners, is it?' Tom enquired,

as the limousine drew to a halt in front of them.

Genghis glared at him but, as Tom had correctly calculated, daren't do more than that, within earshot of the judge and his daughter.

'I hope they won't think that *too* remiss of us,' Tom persisted, exploiting the headmaster's temporary impotence to the full. 'Are we expected to tug our forelocks? Or have we officially been excused that?'

Then she got out of the limousine and came towards him and, suddenly, she was all he could see. She was blond and blue-eyed and...well, there wasn't a word for it. He supposed *gorgeous* would have to do but it scarcely did her justice. She was a child (fourteen, or so Genghis had told him) but she looked every inch a woman and somehow seemed to move in a halo of sunshine - though Tom could have sworn it had been raining a moment ago.

It wasn't until Genghis had pointedly cleared his throat a couple of times, that Tom realised he'd been staring. Not that the girl appeared to have noticed. No doubt she was used to it. No doubt everywhere she went men stared after her, with their tongues hanging out. Tom checked but, fortunately, his was still in his mouth.

Dragging his eyes away from her, Tom turned to the judge and very nearly recoiled in horror. *She* was beautiful but *he* would have made a gargoyle look handsome. He had a pair of beady, close-set eyes, like two miniature raisins in a bun; a nose like a large, decomposing parsnip and ears so huge and protuberant they could have doubled as satellite dishes. How the hell he'd fathered a daughter like that, Tom couldn't begin to imagine. Frankly, it defied comprehension, if not belief. If he'd been the judge, he'd have demanded a DNA test. Tom had heard of genetic mutation but this was ridiculous.

Genghis performed the necessary introductions. At least, that's what Tom supposed he was doing - though he didn't so much introduce Tom, as apologise for him.

'This is Mr Lewis, head of our philosophy department,' Genghis said, as if he'd already warned them not to expect much - but appreciated they'd still be disappointed.

'You'll find my daughter has a decidedly stubborn streak, Mr Lewis,' the judge said, shaking his hand. 'I've told her I don't see the point of philosophy. I want her to follow me into the law. At least there's money in that. But she refuses to oblige me.'

It occurred to Tom to remark that, if money was the criterion, she'd probably be better off with a career in drug smuggling or prostitution - both of which were possibly more lucrative even than the law - but catching sight of Genghis shooting him a warning look, he thought better of it. He was in for enough of a bollocking already.

'Still,' the judge went on, with a sickening grimace Tom assumed was meant to be a smile, 'we modern fathers have to grin and bear it, don't we? Gone are the days when we could command our offspring's unquestioning obedience. More's the pity!'

He laughed and Genghis joined him, with a heartiness Tom felt the joke (if that was what it was) scarcely justified. Under the headmaster's watchful eye, Tom forced a thin smile. The girl's eyes, he noticed, never left the floor. No doubt she'd heard that one before.

'So, I leave her in your hands, Mr Lewis,' the judge said, having recovered from his burst of hilarity. 'If you can persuade her where I have failed, you won't find me ungrateful.'

'I'll do my best,' Tom assured him, thinking there was no chance of that now. Amy wasn't going to listen to a bloody word he said, now the judge had openly enlisted him to the cause. Christ, were all judges this stupid, or was this one just the cream of the crop?

'Well, I'm due in court,' the judge said. 'On the bench, I hasten to add, not in the dock! So, I'll say farewell.'

As Genghis duly obliged and split his sides laughing, the judge shook hands with them both again and planted a kiss on his daughter's cheek, to which she submitted with what was no doubt typical adolescent sullenness. No doubt she wasn't the only teenage girl who was shy of being kissed by her father. No doubt there were wounds to heal on all sides, after the somewhat bloody custody battle, which Genghis had given him to understand the girl's parents had fought over her. Even so, Tom would have hoped for a little more enthusiasm, had he been in the judge's place.

As soon as he got her alone, Tom's plan was to give Amy what he called his "first class speech". There wasn't anything first-rate about it; he just gave it at the beginning of every year to all his new students, with the intention of getting rid of as many of them as possible. The smaller his classes were, the less work he had to do. So he set out to make his subject sound as forbidding, boring and ultimately pointless as he possibly could - and this was, he felt, one area in which he genuinely excelled.

Philosophy was, he said, the rigorous and logical enquiry into life's really "big" questions - the existence of God; the nature of reality; the ethicality of such matters as abortion, euthanasia, capital punishment, etcetera, etcetera. To none of these questions did logic (or, consequently, philosophical study) provide a definitive answer. Philosophy was he said - and round about now he was really getting into his stride - about the questions (which were endless) not about the answers (which remained elusive).

Over the years, this speech had successfully dislodged the lazy, the weak-minded and the downright perplexed, in their droves. But it seemed Amy Martin was made of sterner stuff. She listened to him, in an apparently respectful silence, but the look on her face informed him that she had no intention of taking the slightest notice of anything he said. No doubt he had her father's scorched-earth policy to thank for that.

Having got to the end of his speech and drawn a blank, he was aware of feeling quietly desperate. He *really* didn't want all the extra work this girl would mean for him. If he put in that extra work, no doubt she'd get the results everyone wanted and expected. But if she didn't, it was his balls that were on the line - and, over the years, Tom had grown strangely attached to them. If he could only persuade her philosophy was not for her, he and his balls could breathe a collective sigh of relief, walk off into the sunset and live happily ever after. Why did she have to be so stubborn? What was so bloody fascinating about philosophy anyway? It beat him.

'I appreciate your interest in the subject,' he said, fully aware he was clutching at straws now, 'but you must realise that philosophy doesn't lead very naturally into a career - of any kind.' Obviously, he didn't count teaching. That was a curse, not a career.

She regarded him with thinly (*very* thinly) veiled contempt. 'Is that what you think education is about - training for a vocation?'

'What do you think it's about?' he asked, trying not to squirm under her withering look.

'I think it's about fulfilling your potential.'

'OK. So what makes you think philosophy will help you to fulfil yours and the law won't?'

'Isn't it obvious?'

Not, Tom had to admit, to him.

'Possibly. But tell me, anyway.'

'Because the law is about learning answers; learning what the law is and how it applies. Philosophy isn't about learning answers; it's about finding them.'

Tom laughed. 'Maybe. Just don't expect to find too many.' She was *fourteen*, he reminded himself. Overlooking a certain understandable naivety, he couldn't deny he was impressed. 'No one else on the GSP is taking philosophy,' he told her, after a pause. 'So you have to understand you'll be in a class of one. If you can't face the thought of being one-on-one with me, for four hours every week, I promise I won't take it personally.'

She shot him a corrosive look. 'If you don't want to teach me, Mr Lewis - if you're afraid you're not up to it - why don't you just say so?'

Tom shifted in his seat, suddenly feeling uncomfortably transparent.

The fact was, if he let himself, he *could* feel intimidated; he sure as hell hadn't been doing his 'A' levels (or whatever they were calling the equivalent this week) when he was fourteen. He hadn't taken his job seriously for years; there had been no one and nothing about it that could challenge him. Now that there was (*if* there was, he corrected himself; he didn't necessarily admit that yet) he wasn't sure he feared failure *only* because his balls were on the line. It was just possible he feared it for its own sake.

'I'm quite happy to teach you,' he lied. 'All I'm saying is that there won't be any lurking on the back row, trying to avoid the awkward questions.'

'I agree that's unfortunate for you,' she replied, with just the hint of a smile. 'But I believe it *is* traditional to take the class from the front.'

Caught off guard, Tom laughed. Who'd have thought she'd have had a sense of humour? Although with a father *that* ugly, it was probably a necessity. Let's face it, Tom thought, it'd be laugh or cry. Still, with or without a sense of humour, he had to admit she was a good deal more intriguing than he'd expected to find her. She might do a good - a *bloody* good - impression of a spoilt brat but it wasn't difficult to see there was more to her than that.

She was looking at him and he looked back, frankly, openly, appraisingly. She bore his scrutiny quite calmly, almost defiantly, at first. Then, all at once, she looked down and away - and, as she did so, quite unaccountably, he felt sorry for her.

'All right,' he said. 'If you're sure, we'll give it a go. You can always let me know, if you change your mind in the next couple of weeks. But after that, it'll be too late. OK?'

'OK.'

'Just don't expect an easy ride.'

'I won't, Mr Lewis,' she replied, lifting her eyes to his. 'And neither should you.'

'Did you off-load her then?'

'What? Who?'

'Amy Martin. Did you manage to persuade her that her true vocation was basket weaving, after all?'

'No,' said Tom, realising for the first time that the decision he'd just made was going to cost him fifty quid. How did Van manage it, time after time? Why did he never, ever learn?

She grinned and held out her hand.

'I'll have to owe it to you.'

'Oh, no you don't,' she said, reaching into his inside pocket and relieving him of his wallet, all in one lightning-swift movement.

'Hey! Give that back!'

'Jesus,' she breathed, opening his wallet and rifling through it. 'Is this it? I almost feel sorry for you. Sometimes, making a bet with you is a bit too much like taking candy from a baby.'

'Give it back, then.'

'OK.' Having extracted all the money from it, she tossed him back his empty wallet.

'Gee, thanks. You don't worry I'll starve or anything?'

'Oh, I reckon you'll get by, Tom. It's only a week till payday. I'll get the rest from you then.'

'I don't doubt it. Bloodsucker. Anyway, how did you know?'

'About Amy? Easy. Genghis introduced us, the other day. The rest was a simple matter of psychology.'

'Oh, no. Not more claptrap. Please, spare me.'

'If you'd only listen, Tom, you might learn. I mean, look at it this way: you're a man - of sorts; she's an attractive - a *very* attractive - female. How likely was it that you'd refuse to teach her, once you'd clapped eyes on her? I'd say the odds were about a thousand to one against.'

'You see, that's just where you're wrong. It had nothing - *absolutely nothing* - to do with how she looks!'

'Of course it didn't,' she said, pocketing his money. 'You'll be telling me next, you didn't even notice.'

Chapter 3

'Don't leave me, Susannah. Please. I can't bear it.'

'For goodness' sake, Tom! It's only three days. And she is my mum.'

'Three days *and* nights,' he corrected her.

In the three months they'd been seeing each other that would be the longest they'd been apart by a considerable margin. And he, for one, wasn't looking forward to it.

'Just let me go, will you? I'm going to miss my train.'

'Kiss me, first,' he said, tightening his hold on her and stifling a groan at the thought of just how much he was going to miss her.

What a completely unreasonable, inconsiderate, selfish bitch her mother must be, he thought, as he watched Susannah's cab pull away from the kerb moments later. Three days *and* nights! Didn't the old cow ever spare a thought for anyone else?

Back at the flat, he found Amy waiting for him.

'You're late,' she said.

'Sorry,' he said, fumbling with the street door, which as ever resolutely resisted his efforts to open it. If he didn't know better, he might have taken it personally.

'Where've you been?' she demanded, pushing him aside and opening the door for him, with an ease that made him want to grind his teeth. 'I've been bloody freezing out here.'

'I've been seeing Susannah off,' he said, following her inside. 'Not that it's any of your business. And don't swear.'

'Why not? You do. All the bloody time.'

Somehow, over the last three months, Tom had found himself spending almost all the time he didn't spend with Susannah, with Amy. It had started with her calling round at his flat, to collect work he'd forgotten to give back to her, or books he'd promised to lend her, and soon her presence had become such a settled feature of his life that he couldn't - and didn't want to - imagine it without her.

From an inauspicious beginning, he'd grown astonishingly fond of her in such a short space of time. He'd started out convinced she was a spoilt brat and been determined not to like her but he couldn't have failed more miserably. Within a few short of weeks, she'd found a place in his heart second only to Susannah. In his own defence, it would, he thought, have been impossible not to like her. She was bright and funny, surprising and shocking, by turns. A moment of quite breathtaking maturity and insight, in one so young, would be followed the next by one of equally staggering childishness and naivety, so that being with her was something of a roller-coaster ride - rather wearing at times but certainly never dull.

Then too, he was (it would be useless to deny it) flattered by her affection for him, which appeared to be every bit as quick and keen as his for her. Of course, he had too much sense to set any great store by it; he knew she was neglected at home (her father had no time for and little real interest in her) and shunned at school, not just for being clever but for adding insult to injury and being beautiful too. So, just for now, he was just about her only friend. He knew it wouldn't last but, while it did, he gloried in it.

The only time he wished her out of the way was when he was expecting Susannah. But she understood that, without apparent resentment, and rarely needed so much as a hint to be gone. He usually packed her off before Susannah arrived but, last week, he'd somehow lost track of the time and she'd still been there, curled up on the sofa, when Susannah walked in. Of course, Amy hadn't needed to be told to make herself scarce and had hightailed it forthwith; she couldn't have cleared off faster if Susannah had been carrying the plague. But, quite unreasonably Tom thought, her fleeting presence had somehow still managed to put Susannah's nose out of joint.

The moment she'd gone, Susannah had said, 'What was *she* doing here?'

'Amy? She came to fetch a book I said I'd lend her.'

'You had trouble finding it, did you?'

'No,' Tom said, picking up the first hint of frost in the air. 'I was expecting her. I had it ready. Why? What's the matter?'

'Nothing. It's just…she'd made herself quite at home, that's all. So I guessed she must have been here a while.'

Tom didn't know what to say to that. He got the feeling he was missing something. So, on the basis he was almost certain to shoot himself in the foot no matter what he said, he kept his mouth firmly shut.

'Does she always call you "Tom"?'

'No,' he replied, warily. 'Not in school. At least, not usually. She usually remembers to call me "Mr Lewis" then.'

'I see.'

'What's the matter, Susannah?' he asked, again. 'Have I done something wrong?'

'No. No, of course not,' she'd said.

But he hadn't been convinced she meant it. He didn't know what her problem was but next time, he promised himself, he'd be more careful and keep a closer eye on the time.

'Logic can't prove the existence or nature of God,' Amy was saying now, in the middle of what, up to this point, had been a fairly routine discussion of that subject.

'Which implies what?' he enquired, finding his interest suddenly piqued.

'Either that such questions are unanswerable or that the answer can only be attained by some means other than logic.'

'Such as?'

She shrugged. 'In the case of the existence - or otherwise - of God, perhaps the answer lies in faith.'

'You mean, superstition.'

'No, I don't think so. I mean not just believing but *knowing* something, without being able to prove the truth of it.'

'That sounds very like a definition of insanity to me.'

'I don't care what you call it. I think some knowledge

can only be attained by a kind of quantum leap, a leap of faith - or imagination, if you like - that it's impossible for logic or reason to make.'

'I don't just believe, I *know* you're talking crap. But I can't prove it. So, where does that leave us?'

'I'm not sure. But do you realise you just swore - *again*?'

'Sorry.'

'Do you believe in God?' she asked, after a pause.

'Yes,' said Tom. 'And no.'

'You mean you're agnostic?'

'Yes. I have no faith.'

'If you have no faith, doesn't that make you *atheistic*?'

'No. If you think about it, atheism is a faith too - of sorts. At any rate, it's a belief without evidence to support it; if the existence of God is impossible to prove, it's equally impossible to disprove. I would be an atheist, if I were arrogant enough to assert the truth of something I can't prove - but I'm not.'

After another pause, he said, 'So, do you? Believe in God, I mean.'

'Don't be bloody stupid, Tom,' she replied, shooting him a look of the utmost contempt. 'Of course I don't.'

By the time Susannah was home again - after three days *and* nights without her - Tom was just about as randy as a sex-starved goat. He'd left a message on her mobile, earlier in the day, treating her to a fairly graphic description of what lay in store for her as soon as she got home. So he shot round to her place, straight from work, confidently and eagerly anticipating a night of unbridled lust. If they didn't manage to break the law in one jurisdiction or another at least *once* before morning, he'd wake up a disappointed man.

She met him at the door; obviously, she was as keen as he was.

'Tom! I've been trying to call you.'

'I thought you might. Sorry. I had to stay late at school.' He nearly said, "with Amy". But at the last minute, for some reason, he didn't. 'Anyway, forget that,' he said, pushing his way inside and closing the door behind him. 'You're looking quite exceptionally tasty. Good enough to eat, in fact. Did I mention I'm starved?'

'I did kind of get that impression, from your message. But listen I -'

'Christ, I missed you.'

'I missed you too, but listen -'

'Don't leave me like that again. The thought of you - of what I could have been doing to you - has been just about driving me crazy. I've had a permanent hard-on ever since you left. And if I don't get you into bed, in the next five minutes, I won't be responsible for the consequences.'

He pushed her back against the wall and, pressing himself hard up against her, groaned aloud in a mixture of pleasure and frustration.

'Tom, *wait*!' she pleaded, struggling to fend him off.

But he couldn't wait and stifled any further protest with a kiss.

He'd got one hand inside her blouse and the other firmly clamped to her buttocks, when someone suddenly exclaimed, '*Susannah!*', in tones of…well, outraged disbelief.

When Tom had climbed down from the ceiling and back into his skin, he found himself confronted by a homicidal-looking, middle-aged woman whom he immediately knew - with the most hideous and appalling certainty imaginable - was Susannah's mother. Of course she was. She just had to be. He couldn't have scripted it better himself. They meet for the first time and, just to make sure they get off to the best possible start, what's he doing? His best to shag her daughter up against a wall. Perfect. No danger of getting off on the wrong foot there then. His guardian angel was obviously working overtime. As usual.

'I've been trying to tell you, Tom,' Susannah said, hurriedly re-buttoning her blouse. 'I brought Mum back with me, for a few days. Mum, this is Tom Lewis. Tom, my mother, Marion Barton.'

If there was a moment that summed up his life, Tom

thought, this would have to be it. But just as it seemed things couldn't possibly get any worse, they did.

Being surprised in *flagrante delicto* would normally have been more than enough to return Lazarus to the dead, in double-quick time. But perverse as ever, today the bloody-minded little fucker had other ideas. He was pumped-up and ready to go and not about to stand down for anyone - even Susannah's mother. (Tom didn't even want to think what Van would have said about the Freudian significance of *that* one.) He tried - really hard - but all to no avail. The harder he tried, the harder the obstinate little fucker became.

Panic-stricken, desperate to cover his embarrassment, he made a despairing grab for his groin with both hands, like a footballer defending a free kick.

He noticed Mrs Barton's eyes bulge at that, as if she couldn't quite believe them.

Then, suddenly realising it would be rude not to shake hands with her, he unclamped his right hand from his crotch and extended it to her.

For some unaccountable reason, she seemed reluctant to take it.

'I wish I was dead,' he groaned, as Susannah was seeing him off a little while later.

He had been a man on a promise - a night of the utmost sexual depravity had been all but guaranteed to him - and now, courtesy of Marion Bloody Barton, the best he could hope for was a quick fumble in the front porch, like some spotty, sex-starved teenager. Great.

He sank his head onto Susannah's shoulder and could have wept.

'Oh, come on, Tom. It's not *that* bad.'

'Yes, it is! Your mother's convinced I'm some kind of pervert *and* I've got to go home on my own. How bad do you to want it to be?'

'OK, you probably didn't get off to the best start. But she'll get over it.'

'No she won't. She hates me now. How long's she staying, anyway?'

'I told you, just a couple of days.'

Tom groaned. The remorseless bitch. Didn't the bloody woman have *any* mercy? He took it back. He didn't wish he was dead, he wished *she* was.

'Come to dinner tomorrow,' Susannah said. 'It'll give you a chance to get to know each other properly.'

What on earth, Tom wondered, made her suppose either of them wanted to do that? After the exhibition he'd just made of himself, if he never saw Susannah's mother again it'd be too soon. And he had every reason to suppose the feeling was mutual.

'All right,' he agreed, sullenly. 'But couldn't you come round to the flat first, straight from work? Then we could...you know. I'll go blind, if you keep me waiting much longer.'

'I'm sorry, Tom. I can't. I'm meeting Mum straight from work.'

Oh, great. Her bloody mother *again*. Tom could seriously get to hate Marion Barton. If he didn't know better, he'd think she was on some kind of personal crusade specifically designed to drive him crazy. Everything had been just fine, until she'd shown up. Now, all of a sudden, there she was, frustrating him at every turn, standing guard over Susannah's virtue, like some kind of demented Mother Superior.

'It's only for a couple of days,' Susannah said, moved to pity by his tortured look. 'And then I'm all yours. I promise. OK?'

'I suppose so,' he replied, grudgingly - though he didn't really see how she could possibly suppose it was. He was in torment and she knew it. Why couldn't her bloody mother just piss off back to hell or wherever it was she came from? Didn't she know when she wasn't wanted? Wasn't it bloody *obvious*?

Pulling Susannah hard against him, he said, 'I don't suppose you'd like to give me something to be going on with?

You know, just a little something to get me through the long, lonely nights. It doesn't have to be much,' he added, as his gaze fell to her lips. 'After all, I do realise beggars can't be choosers.'

His mouth was almost on hers - he could almost feel, almost taste her kiss - when, with the predictability of death and taxation, Marion appeared. How did she manage it? Tom more than half suspected she'd got his dick wired up to some kind of alarm system. At any rate, the moment Lazarus showed the slightest signs of life, she was guaranteed to appear, like the grimmest of all grim reapers.

'Still here, Mr Lewis?' she enquired, icily. 'I thought you'd gone.'

'Just off,' he assured her, through a facial contortion he trusted she'd be short sighted enough to take for a smile.

'Cheerio, then,' she said, seizing Susannah proprietarily by the arm. 'Don't let me keep you.'

As Tom walked off alone into the night - with the taste of that almost-kiss on his lips and with nothing to sustain him but the thought of what he'd gone without - he was certain he knew exactly how Tantalus felt. As a consolation for his sufferings, he promised himself that, if he were ever fortunate enough to find himself alone with Susannah's mother, he wouldn't be responsible for the consequences. There was, after all, such a thing as provocation.

At dinner the following day, Marion's reception of him was about as enthusiastic as Tom had expected. In her case, absence had manifestly failed to make the heart grow fonder and she couldn't, he thought, have made him feel any less welcome, if he'd been a dose of the clap. All in all, he guessed the two of them were destined to get on pretty much like an asbestos house on fire.

He'd taken her a bunch of flowers, by way of an apology for the buttock-clutching incident, but recoiling from them as if she suspected they were radioactive, she'd claimed she was allergic to them. Judging by Susannah's somewhat perplexed response, this was the first she'd heard about it. But at her mother's insistence, she dumped the flowers outside the kitchen door - and Tom had no doubt Marion would have been only too delighted if she'd dumped him along with them.

He *begged* Susannah to let him help her in the kitchen (anything to get away from the bitch from hell) but she wouldn't. Instead, she insisted they leave everything to her and "get to know each other". So, for the next half an hour, he and Marion sat in Susannah's living room in an uncomfortable and largely unbroken silence and stared at the carpet, as if it were the most fascinating thing either of them had seen in a long time. Tom did *try* to engage the old bat in conversation but it seemed that, at least as far as he was concerned, a snarl was by far the most encouraging response in her entire repertoire.

Long before dinner was ready, Tom had utterly lost the will to live and was finding the anaesthetic qualities of the wine entirely insufficient for his needs, despite having sunk the better part of a bottle all to himself. He understood the meaning of the look Susannah gave him, when she was forced to open a second, before dinner was even served. But what did she expect? A man could only stand so much, after all. Everyone had their breaking point. Even him.

Dinner was not a resounding success. More than once it occurred to Tom his knife would have been better employed cutting the atmosphere, rather than the food on his plate. But, for Susannah's sake, he kept trying - notwithstanding that Marion remained as steadfastly impervious to his efforts as a dead horse to a bloody good flogging.

By the time the ordeal of dinner was finally over, he needed a smoke - like he'd never needed one before - and, almost before they'd left the table, he had a cigarette in his mouth. He noticed Marion glare at him but, as there was nothing new in that, the reproach was lost on him.

'I hope, Mr Lewis, you're not thinking of smoking that in here!' she exclaimed as, oblivious to her disapproval, he struck a match.

He looked back at her, in surprise. Susannah never objected to his smoking - at least, if she did, she'd never said anything. 'I won't, if you don't want me to,' he said, feeling his fingers burn and dropping the still-lighted match onto the carpet.

'I don't!'

'Fair enough,' Tom said, getting up. 'Then I'll go outside. But do you think you could do something for me in exchange, Marion? Do you suppose you could stop calling me "Mr Lewis"? Or are you frightened you'd choke, if you said "Tom"?'

By the time he'd got outside, he wished he hadn't risen to the bait and had held his tongue. After all, why give the old bag the satisfaction of knowing she'd got under his skin? And then there was the look that had come over Susannah's face - a sort of despairing expression, like that of someone charged with preventing two enraged bulldogs from ripping each other to shreds, using nothing but the power of reason. He didn't mean to make life difficult for her but what could he do? Her mother was a hellhound. No one could be expected to put up with her - not without the comfort of a fag, at any rate.

He lit his second and, remembering there was a pub on the corner, decided a couple of stiff whiskies wouldn't go amiss. After all, what Marion didn't see, even *she* couldn't criticise.

As soon as he let himself back in, three or four whiskies later (that couple of stiff ones had turned out to be woefully inadequate) he could hear them arguing - and it wasn't difficult to guess the cause. Tom knew better than to expect to hear good of himself but, nonetheless, he paused outside the living-room door to listen.

'I thought you said he was forty something,' Marion was saying.

'He is.'

'Then how come he looks more like sixty? For goodness' sake, Susannah, you must be able to do better than this. He's too decrepit for *me*!'

Too decrepit for *her*! Christ, that was rich! She should try looking in the mirror. Jesus! He'd rather shag next-door's

Alsatian.

'Mum, please!'

'I'm sorry, darling, but it's for your own good. You must be able to see you're wasting yourself with this - *oaf.* He has no conversation, he drinks like a fish and he positively *reeks* of tobacco. What can you possibly see in him?'

Silence. Tom waited. More silence. Either Susannah didn't know, or she wasn't saying. Suddenly, seeing himself through Marion's eyes, he was aware of feeling quite horribly depressed. He had a pretty low opinion of himself but even he was capable of being hurt, if abused roundly enough.

'And I simply couldn't believe his behaviour yesterday,' Marion resumed. 'He was all over you, like some sort of *animal.*'

'He didn't know you were there!' Susannah objected, hotly.

'That's no excuse! If that's how he treats you, just because he thinks no one's watching, I'm ashamed of you for putting up with it. It couldn't be more obvious that he's got one thing - and one thing only - on his mind. Where's your self-respect, Susannah? Don't you think you deserve a man who's capable of wanting you for something other than sex?'

Tom's jaw set. He didn't want Susannah just for sex. She knew that, didn't she? Even if her mother didn't.

Susannah said something in reply but too low for Tom to catch it. He hoped she was telling her mother to go to hell - the bloody old hag - but, somehow, he doubted it.

By now, he'd heard more than enough and he was about to walk in on them, when Marion said, 'I saw Clive the other day.'

And something about her tone pulled Tom up. Short.

'He made a point of asking after you.'

'Did he?'

Was that an eager "did he" or an indifferent "did he"? Tom couldn't decide.

'You know, darling, I'm sure he's still very fond of you. If you'd only -'

Just then (no doubt for a reason Vanessa could have

explained but which eluded him - unless it was to be ascribed to sod's law) Tom dropped his keys, thereby announcing his presence and curtailing the conversation. Just as he really *had* wanted to hear more.

So, who the hell was this Clive character? And what business did he have being fond of Susannah? If he weren't bloody careful, Tom'd punch his face in. Whoever he was.

The next day, Mad Marion (as Tom had secretly taken to calling her, on the basis it was the least offensive of the many names he might have chosen) exhaled the last of her noxious fumes and flew back to her cave - or (to put it more prosaically) took the nine o'clock train home. Tom ought to have been ecstatic to see her go and to get Susannah alone at last but, for some reason, like many another eagerly anticipated pleasure, it somehow fell short of expectations. Twenty-four hours ago, he'd have been turning cartwheels. But not now.

Nonetheless, he'd gone round to Susannah's straight from work. They'd eaten a quiet meal together and were now lying entwined on the sofa.

A while ago, she'd said, 'You're very quiet, Tom. There's nothing wrong, is there?'

'No. No, I'm fine,' he'd said. But he guessed they'd both known he was lying.

Now, thinking he had to come to the point eventually and he might just as well get it over with, he said, 'So, who's Clive?'

He'd been practising the question inside his head for some time and he was quite pleased with the way it came out. It sounded almost casual. You really wouldn't have guessed, from his tone of voice, that he'd spent the last twenty-four hours or so wishing the bastard dead and buried. Nonetheless, he felt Susannah stir uneasily against him.

'Who?'

'Clive. I overheard Mad - I overheard your mother talking about him, yesterday. Apparently, he's still very fond of you.'

Disengaging herself, Susannah sat up.

He watched her, conscious his heart was beating somewhat faster than usual. He didn't like to think how much might - how much almost certainly did - depend on her reply. 'So,' he prompted at last, as she said nothing and his anxiety mounted. 'Tell me. Who is he?'

Taking a deep breath, she said, 'He was - is - the consultant paediatrician at the Middleton Hospital, where I used to work.'

He wished he could leave it at that but he couldn't. 'He was rather more than that though, wasn't he? I mean, to you.'

'Yes. He was.'

'And now?'

'What do you mean, "and now"?'

What, in Christ's name, did she *think* he meant?

'I mean, is he more than that to you now? I mean,' he said, steeling himself to hear the worst, 'do you still love him?'

'Oh, Tom!' she cried and, covering her face with her hands, she burst into tears.

So, that was that, then. He'd asked and now he had his answer. Now he knew.

'It's all right,' he said, even though it wasn't. Even though it was just about as far from all right as it was possible to get. 'Really. I understand.'

'No you don't, Tom,' she said, wiping her eyes. 'You don't understand. How could you?'

'You think I don't know what it's like to love someone and lose them?' If she thought that, she ought to be in his shoes, right now.

'But I don't love him. That's the whole point. If you've been worried about that, Tom - if that's what's been bothering you - you've been worrying for nothing.'

'Really?'

'Really.'

His relief was so great it almost choked him and it was a moment before he could speak again, without betraying the fact.

'Then you're right, I don't understand. If you don't love him anymore, why are you so upset? Why are you crying?'

She heaved a sort of shuddering sigh and said, 'Because something happened between us, Tom. Something I've never told anyone. Something no one knows. Except Clive.'

'You don't have to tell me,' he said, into the pause that followed. 'Don't, if you don't want to.' After all, he thought, he didn't need to know anymore. She'd answered the one - the only - question that really mattered to him.

'I think I do have to tell you, Tom. Sooner or later. You won't like me for it but try not to think too hardly of me.'

He took her hand, pretty confident he could promise her that much, no matter what it was she had to tell him.

And so, in a halting voice, never very far from tears, she told him how her affair with Clive Abingdon had begun.

'The truth is, it didn't really start with Clive. I didn't realise it at the time but I can see now it started with Mike.'

'Mike?' Tom queried, beginning to wonder just how many potential rivals he'd got out there. But then what did he expect? He didn't seriously think she'd lived the life of a nun before they'd met, did he?

'We'd been together for years, almost all the way through medical school. Then, suddenly, Mike decided medicine wasn't right for him and neither was I. So he chucked us both.'

Tom was mightily relieved to hear it. Nonetheless, he gave the hand he was holding a sympathetic squeeze - and received a distant, preoccupied kind of smile in return.

'I think now he was right, on both counts, but it hurt at the time. Anyway, almost as soon as Mike had left me, I started working with Clive. He was the Middleton's senior consultant paediatrician and, somehow, I landed the job as his SHO - the junior member of his team. He was a bit older than me and had never married but he'd quite a reputation. He was - is - brilliant, at the very forefront of his field, and handsome and charming with it.'

Tom felt his heart warming more and more to the guy, with every word.

'I don't know whether I was more flattered or astonished, when he asked me out. I'd no idea he'd noticed me, not in that way. Later, he told me he'd fallen in love with me at first sight. I can't describe how that made me feel. I'd never imagined anything like that happening to me.'

Well, no, Tom thought. What sane person would?

'Of course I see now that, after Mike, I was vulnerable and needy and - whether he meant them or not - Clive said all the right things. We were living together almost before I knew what was happening, it was all so fast. Mum absolutely idolised him. He had her twisted round his little finger, right from the start. She'd never hear a word against him. And she still won't.'

Lucky old Clive, Tom thought, trying (and failing) to imagine what it must be like to be "idolised" by Marion. He supposed it must be something like being the apple of a rattlesnake's eye.

'Then he asked me to marry him. And, of course, I accepted. I'd have been crazy not to.'

Absolutely, Tom thought. Mad as a March hare.

'At least, that's what I thought at first. But the nearer the wedding got, the more doubts began to creep in. He wanted a family and kept nagging me to stop the pill. I tried to tell him I wasn't ready - that I had a career to pursue - but he wouldn't listen and, in the end, like a fool, I gave in. He was delighted; Mum was delighted. Everyone was so sure I was doing the right thing, I somehow stopped listening to myself. But when I got pregnant, suddenly I could see everything quite clearly. I could see I didn't love Clive and he didn't love me; all he really wanted was a mother for his children. Marrying him would have been a terrible mistake, not just for me but for him too. Why is that, Tom? Why do we never see, until it's too late?'

'I don't know, Susannah,' he said, swallowing hard. 'I wish I did.'

'Even though I could see the truth,' she resumed, 'I still tried to make myself go through with it, to convince myself that if I married him and had the baby, it would somehow work out for the best. But in the end, I just couldn't do it. The sacrifice was too great; I was just too selfish. I didn't want a baby. And I especially didn't want *Clive's* baby. Not when I knew, when I properly understood, I didn't love him. So, I called the wedding off. I told him I didn't love him. But, of course, I was too much of a coward to tell him the rest. To tell him about the baby.'

'So you had a termination?'

She nodded, as her tears began to fall. 'Can you imagine that? I'm a doctor, a *paediatrician.* I spend my working life saving the lives of other people's babies. And I killed my own.'

'It's not a crime, Susannah. You had the right to choose.'

She looked back at him then with an expression almost of incredulity, as if she could scarcely believe he'd said something so trite, so meaningless, so utterly beside the point.

'Did I?' she asked. 'I wonder. The law's one thing, after all. Sin is another.'

'Maybe. But I don't think you should assume what you did was a sin.'

'I don't assume it, Tom. I know it.' There was a pause, then she said, 'Do you believe we're made to pay for our sins, not in some afterlife but here and now?'

'I don't know,' he said, taken aback. 'But if we are, one thing's for sure, I'm in for a hell of a time.'

'Me too,' she said, softly.

There was another long pause, then she said, 'I didn't tell him but, somehow, Clive found out about the termination. I've never seen anyone so angry. You wouldn't believe the things he said to me - not that I didn't deserve them. Of course, I knew he'd always been pro-life and I suppose that was another reason I didn't tell him. If he didn't know, he couldn't stop me.'

'He had no right to stop you.'

'Didn't he? He was the father, Tom. If you believe I have the right to choose, why do you believe he doesn't?'

'Because it's not the same thing. He isn't the one

who's pregnant. It isn't his body. It's yours.'

'Even so, I should at least have told him, discussed it with him. But I was too scared - and much, much too selfish. He was right to hate me for what I'd done. I'd betrayed him - not just once but twice. Of course, it had been difficult before but after the termination it became almost impossible for us to work together. He just stopped co-operating with me. He was the consultant, we were part of the same team, but he wouldn't help - not if I asked - even though sometimes that compromised patients' safety. Can you imagine that, Tom? Can you imagine hating someone so much, you'd risk letting someone else die, sooner than help them?'

'No,' he said, flatly. 'I can't.'

'Anyway, that's what happened in the end. A patient died. A six-week-old baby girl. And Clive blamed me.'

'You? How was it your fault?'

'It wasn't. I'd had nothing to do with her care. But somehow she'd been given the wrong drug and Clive swore I was the one who'd written her up for it, even though he must have known I wasn't. Conveniently, the paperwork went missing, so it was his word against mine and I ended up taking the blame. I was the junior, it was easy for him to shift it on to me. And, in a sense, I suppose it belonged there. I can clearly remember him saying, "This is one death you *will* pay for".'

'Jesus, Susannah!' It was a bloody good job the Middleton hospital was a couple of hundred miles away. If it had been any nearer, Tom would have gone straight there and rearranged Clive's face for him. And possibly one or two other parts of his anatomy, as well. 'That's an outrageous thing to say!'

'He thought I deserved it. Maybe he was right. There was a disciplinary investigation but without the paperwork it was inconclusive. Of course, that's not the same - not the same thing at all - as being cleared. So it was made plain to me it would be in my interests to move on. Provided I went quietly, the hospital very kindly offered to omit any mention of the disciplinary investigation from my reference. And I think,' she said, with a sorrowful little smile, 'that's what they call making someone an offer they can't refuse.'

'So that's why you left the Middleton? Why you're here now?'

She nodded. 'In terms of my career, it wasn't the best move. St Luke's isn't in the same league as the Middleton. But then beggars can't be choosers, can they?'

There was a long pause, while Tom's blood, brought to boiling point by what he'd heard, simmered nicely.

'Is your mother completely insane?' he demanded, finally. 'How can she possibly want you to go back to that *arsehole*?'

Susannah sighed. 'I told you, Tom, she doesn't know. Apart from Clive, you're the only one who knows the truth. Mum doesn't know about the baby, or the termination, or anything that came afterwards. She still thinks I just got cold feet about the wedding and left my job because it was too painful for Clive and I to keep working together.'

'Yes, but - bloody hell, can't she see it's over between you?'

'No. Because that's Clive's little joke, that's all part of his revenge.'

'What is? I don't understand.'

'He knows how fond Mum is of him; he knows how much she always wanted our marriage. So he pretends to her that he still loves me. He even calls round when I'm there visiting, just to watch me suffer. He knows I'm terrified he'll say something, terrified he'll tell her the truth. Mum has no idea he hates me. She's convinced that, if I'd only take him back, everything would be all right. Of course, it wouldn't. But because I'm too much of a coward to tell her the truth, she lives in hope.'

'Then why don't you tell her?' he asked, gently. 'Wouldn't that be better - kinder - in the end?'

'How can I, Tom? How can I possibly tell her I killed her grandchild?'

He couldn't answer that. He knew she had to tell her secret to be free. So long as she kept the truth from Marion, Clive kept his power over her. But he also knew he only understood that because he had a secret of his own to keep, something *he'd* never told a living soul. And so long as he kept his secret, why shouldn't she keep hers?

'I suppose you hate me too,' Susannah said at last, misinterpreting his silence. 'Now you know the truth.'

'I don't hate you, Susannah,' Tom said. 'I love you.'

He'd never said that to her before (in point of fact, he'd never said that to anyone before) and she looked almost as surprised as he felt. He'd had no idea what he was going to say, until the words left his mouth. But once he'd got over the shock of having said them, he felt quite pleased.

'Do you mean that?'

'Yes.'

'Good. Because it just so happens I love you too.'

'That's nice.'

There was a pause, then she said, 'Now we've got that sorted, I don't suppose you'd like to take me to bed.'

'I can't think of anything I'd like more,' Tom assured her, permitting himself a little smile on the outside. While on the inside, he was grinning from ear to ear.

Chapter 4

'Tom,' Vanessa said, 'if you don't wipe that stupid smile off your face right now, I'll do it for you. You're enough to put a person off their food.'

'You're just jealous,' Tom informed her, happily.

And, indeed, who wouldn't envy him an all-expenses-paid dirty weekend? Officially, as Susannah kept telling him, it wasn't a dirty weekend. Officially, it was a medical conference. But Tom had absolutely no intention of letting that stand in his the way.

As Susannah wasn't the only delegate from St Luke's, they travelled to the conference venue - the once grand but now rather faded Imperial Hotel - with her colleague, Robin Graham, a consultant obstetrician. Tom had tried, but failed, to imagine what Robin's job must like. He couldn't help thinking that if he were obliged to spend half his working life with his head between a woman's legs, a pair of scissors in one hand and a pair of forceps in the other, he'd never have sex again. But thankfully, Robin - a happily married man, with three kids of his own - was made of somewhat sterner stuff.

Having checked in at the Imperial, Tom was disappointed to find they were expected to spend their first evening at a reception for the conference delegates and their partners. He tried hard to persuade Susannah her time would be infinitely better spent in bed with him but sadly - on this one occasion, at least - he failed to convince her. She just kept on about something called "networking" (whatever that was) and the importance of his being on his best behaviour and not drinking *too* much, just because there was a "free bar". Honestly, what did she take him for?

They hadn't been at the reception ten minutes before she'd fucked off and left him so she could "network" and, before another ten minutes had elapsed, Tom was seriously regretting having agreed to come at all. People kept coming up to him and asking him what his field was and, as soon as they discovered he wasn't a doctor, glaring at him like he was some kind of madman and dropping him like a hot potato. Tom was beginning to see what Susannah meant by "networking". As far as he could make out, the objective was to talk to as many people as you could, provided they were likely to prove useful to you, and to fuck everyone else off in the shortest time possible. After ten minutes, it had become pretty clear *he* wasn't much use to anybody.

He was toying with the idea of going back to their room and getting pissed on his own, when he spotted Robin talking to a Dr Attington who, according to his nametag, was from the Middleton Hospital where Susannah had previously worked. Something about the name was familiar and Tom looked again. "Dr C Attington" the badge said. Then he remembered where he'd heard that name before.

So, this was that bastard, Clive, was it? Tom was surprised; the guy was pretty ancient. Admittedly, Susannah had said Clive was older than her but he hadn't thought she meant *that* much older. Jesus, he was practically old enough to be her father. No wonder she'd had second thoughts about marrying a guy that long in the tooth. And then Mad Marion had the bloody nerve to call *him* decrepit! He might be past his best (that much he wouldn't deny) but compared to this guy he wasn't just in the pink, he was a veritable Adonis.

Remembering what Susannah had said about behaving himself, he waited impatiently for Robin to move away. The moment he did, Tom pounced.

'Good evening, Dr Attington.'

The miserable little shit turned to him with an expectant smile, which slowly turned to an embarrassed, perplexed-looking frown, as he realised he hadn't a clue who the fuck Tom was. 'I'm sorry, have we met?'

'No,' Tom said, muscling in nice and close. 'You don't know me. But I know *all* about you. From Susannah.'

Attington's frown deepened. 'Who?'

'Susannah *Barton*!' Tom exclaimed, incensed. He could scarcely credit the arrogance of the bastard, pretending Susannah's entire existence had somehow slipped his mind! Boy, was he asking for it. And boy, given half a chance, would Tom give it to him. 'Name ringing any bells now, is it?'

'I believe I *have* heard it somewhere before but -'

'Christ, you're full of it, aren't you? Well, you might have forgotten Susannah but she remembers you all right. Let's face it, she'd hardly be likely to forget.'

By now, Attington was beginning to look decidedly jittery - like he'd just wandered into the lions' enclosure by mistake, to discover they hadn't been fed for a week. 'You really must excuse me,' he muttered, backing away. 'My wife's waiting for me.'

'Your *wife!*' Tom snorted. 'Don't you mean your secretary? Or your SHO?' He knew Attington wasn't married, so the randy old bastard had obviously conned some poor, unsuspecting cow into giving him an extra-curricular shag. And, of course, he'd just *had* to book her into the hotel as his wife. Fucking hypocrite. 'Whoever she is, she must be fucking *desperate* if she's prepared to shag *you.*'

By this stage, Attington wasn't just backing away, he was all but running.

'That's right,' Tom sneered, following hard on the doctor's heels as he dodged his way through the crowd. 'Make a run for it. Bullies are always cowards underneath. You know what, arsehole? If you really think abortion's such a fucking crime, you could always try wearing a condom. That is, if they make them in your diminutive size. After all, it takes two, you know.'

What Tom really wanted was the satisfaction of smashing Clive's face in. But given that he'd promised Susannah to be on his best behaviour, he recognised he'd have to be content with just scaring the shit out of him. He was delighted to see - from the speed with which Attington shot through the door - that he'd succeeded in that much at least.

He was still wallowing in his success, when Susannah caught up with him.

'I've just put the shits right up that bastard, Attington,' he announced, visibly preening himself.

'Who?'

'*Attington*,' he repeated. What was she, deaf? 'That bastard's here. Haven't you seen him?'

'I don't know what you're talking about, Tom. Who's Attington?'

Tom suddenly had a horrible, sinking feeling. '*Shit!* Wasn't that the name? You know, that bastard, Clive - the one Mad Marion's so keen on?'

Susannah didn't bother to enquire who "Mad Marion" was; she was pretty sure she could guess. 'No, Tom. It's not Attington; it's *Abingdon*. Why? What have you done?'

'Oh, shit!' Tom wailed. 'Oh, *Jesus*!'

'What is it? Where are you going?' Susannah cried, as Tom suddenly sped off in the direction of the door.

'Back in a minute,' he yelled, over his shoulder. 'I've just got to find what's-his-name and explain.'

On the way to the door, he collided with Robin, causing him to spill a liberal quantity of red wine all down his previously pristine shirtfront. But Tom had no time to waste on irrelevancies.

'Have you seen that Abingdon - I mean, Attington - guy?'

'I saw him just now, in the lobby,' Robin said, scowling and dabbing ineffectually at the mess with his handkerchief. 'Why? What's up?'

'No time to explain,' Tom cried, haring off again. 'Got to catch him, before he leaves.' Or, alternatively, he thought, gives my description to the police.

He skidded into the lobby, in time to see Attington and a middle-aged woman disappearing into the lift.

'Wait!' he yelled, hurling himself at the lift doors, just as they were about to close.

Seeing and recognising him, Attington began jabbing at the lift button as if his life depended on it. But too late. Tom's shoulder was already securely jammed between the doors.

'Stay back, Martha!' Attington ordered, pushing his companion behind him. 'Just keep calm and don't antagonise him.'

He obviously had Tom down as some kind of

dangerous lunatic. But, in the circumstances, Tom supposed he could hardly blame him. 'I'm so glad I caught you,' he gasped, panting for breath.

Oddly, Attington looked less than thrilled. In fact, he looked like he'd rather be flattened by a bus than find himself cornered by Tom, for the second time that evening.

'I just wanted to explain,' Tom blundered on. But now he came to think about it - now it actually came to the point - how *was* he going to explain? 'About earlier,' he began, trying and failing to think on his feet. 'It was all a mistake. You see, I thought you were this guy, Clive, who used to be Susannah's partner. Before we met. But then she said you weren't. I mean, I'd got the name wrong. So, it wasn't you, after all. It was stupid of me really. I should have guessed. I mean, you're way too old for a start. Christ, you must be seventy, if you're a day -'

'As a matter of fact,' Attington cut in, icily, 'I'm fifty eight.'

'Ah,' said Tom. 'I see. Sorry.' Shit! Why did he have to go putting his foot in it again? And just as everything was going so well. He'd had the guy practically eating out of his hand, till he'd gone and told him he made Methuselah look like a spring chicken.

'Now you've explained,' Attington said, through gritted teeth. 'Perhaps you'd release the lift doors.'

'Sorry,' Tom said again, removing his shoulder and stepping back - at which Attington's companion heaved a shuddering great sigh of relief. 'You must think I'm crazy.'

Reaching forward gingerly, Attington hit the lift button and snatched back his hand, as if electrocution was the very least he'd expected. As the lift doors finally slid to a close, he said, 'It may interest you to know, young man, that I happen to be a psychiatrist. And, in my professional opinion, you *are* crazy.'

The following morning, Tom was waiting for Susannah in the hotel lobby when a voice behind him suddenly exclaimed, 'Tom! I don't believe it! Is that *really* you?'

He froze. It couldn't be, could it? Surely, God's undeniably perverse sense of humour wasn't quite that twisted. The Almighty obviously enjoyed a joke at Tom's expense - last night and the debacle with Dr Attington being no exception - but there were limits. Surely. Even for Him.

Tentatively, praying his eyes wouldn't confirm what his ears had seemed to tell him, Tom turned to face the speaker. And, of course, it was her. It just had to be. Very funny, he thought, wishing that - just for once - God would pick on someone else for a change. Preferably, someone His own size.

'Frankie!' he said, twisting his face into the semblance of a smile. It wasn't exactly that he bore a grudge but he had rather hoped to get through the rest of his life, without ever clapping eyes on her again. And then there was Susannah to be considered. He categorically didn't want the two of *them* bumping into each other. The very idea was enough to threaten the security of his breakfast. 'What the fu-? I mean, what on earth are you doing here?'

She laughed, apparently oblivious to the queasiness she inspired. 'I'm here for the medical conference. Rupert's giving a talk about some new drug his company's developing. But what about you? What are *you* doing here? They're not holding a *philosophers'* conference, are they?' She all but bent double with laughter, at the sheer absurdity of the idea.

'That'll be the day,' Tom said, forcing a thin smile.

'But it's so good to see you! You look...' She paused, struggling to find a credible compliment.

'Different? Older? Knackered?' Tom suggested.

'Of course not, silly! You look...great!'

He grunted. 'You were never a good liar, Frankie.'

She blushed and, even though he hadn't meant what she'd thought he meant, he wished the words unsaid. He didn't want her to suppose it still mattered to him.

'So what *are* you doing here?' she said again, into the awkward pause that followed.

'The same as you. I'm here for the medical conference too. At least I'm not, but my partner is.'

'Your partner!' she echoed, in surprise. 'You've gone into business with a *doctor*?'

'No, Frankie. Not that kind of partner.'

'Oh! Oh, of course. I see.'

Naturally, she'd assumed he'd be alone. She looked him up and down then, as if searching for the hidden attraction. He got the distinct impression she didn't find it.

'How odd! I mean, what a coincidence! We must get together.'

Tom could think of few things he'd like less. Shoving his genitals in a blender and switching it on was probably one of them. But even then, it was a close call. He was just about to invent an excuse - a prior engagement, a terminal illness, a terrorist attack - when Susannah appeared. For the first time in his life, he wasn't pleased to see her. In fact, just then, he wished her at the antipodes.

He performed the necessary introductions with some difficulty. It ought to have been simplicity itself but, of course, he had to make a meal of it. Everything went smoothly enough with regard to Susannah but, when he got to Francesca, he suddenly found himself blundering about in a minefield.

'This is, Frankie. She's - er - that is, we - er...'

'We're old friends,' Francesca supplied, with an ease he coveted and hated her for. 'From university.'

Well, it was true, wasn't it? As far as it went. Why was a partial truth never good enough for him? After all, this was an introduction, for Christ's sake - a meaningless, chance encounter - not a catharsis.

Whilst he was busy berating himself for his idiocy, Frankie had suggested they meet that evening for dinner and before he could stop her Susannah had agreed.

'Oh, no! No, we can't!' he cried, in such obvious and extreme alarm that they both turned to him in astonishment.

'Why?' Susannah demanded, in some confusion. 'Why can't we?'

'Because...' Why, in Christ's name, did she have to insist on a reason? Wasn't it bloody obvious he just didn't want to? 'You're forgetting that - that other thing,' he concluded, lamely.

'What "other thing"? I don't know what you're talking about, Tom.'

'Yes, you do!' he said, glaring at her with a significance to which she seemed wilfully blind. 'That other thing, you told me about at breakfast. The thing you said you mustn't miss, on *any* account!'

Frowning, Susannah laughed. 'I still don't know what you're talking about, Tom. But whatever it is, I'm sure it can wait. We'd love to join you,' she confirmed, turning to Francesca. 'Shall we say, eight o'clock?'

'I'm not going,' Tom said.

'You keep saying that,' Susannah replied. 'But I don't know what you expect me to tell them, if you don't. They're your friends, not mine.'

'They're not my friends. They're - *she's* - just someone I used to know. Someone I hoped and prayed I'd never see again, as long as I lived. And now - thanks to you - I've got to have dinner with her. Why couldn't you just back me up about the "other thing"?'

'Because it was such manifest nonsense, Tom. She'd have thought we were being rude.'

Tom groaned. So what? Why did women always get bogged down in such irrelevancies? What did he care if Frankie thought he was rude, especially as he planned - as he was *determined* - never to set eyes on her again? If it hadn't been for Susannah, he'd have happily told Frankie to fuck off to her face, if that was the only way he could have been sure of getting rid of her.

'Well, she'll have to think I'm rude then, because - I don't care what you say - I'm not going.'

'Tom! Susannah! You made it, then.'

'Yes. Here we are,' Tom said, through a smile that bore more than a passing resemblance to the grimace of someone in the throes of being strangled.

He'd spent the entire day assuring Susannah he wasn't

going. But here he was. Women. How did they manage it? Like God, they gave you the illusion of freewill but, somehow, you always ended up doing things their way. Not that Susannah had done anything he could put his finger on; she hadn't even insisted he come with her. She'd just quietly got ready and then said, 'So, are you coming or not?' and, somehow, saying "no" hadn't seemed an option.

So, here he was, in some restaurant where he probably couldn't even afford to hang up his coat, doomed to eat food he didn't want, in the company of people he hated - and if he got to the end of the evening, without slitting his wrists, he'd consider it a success.

With that ease he'd envied in her earlier, Frankie performed the introductions. Tom had heard all about but hadn't met her husband before. As Frankie had already reminded him, Rupert was on the board of some big pharmaceuticals company and, as Tom might have expected, in addition to his obvious material success, he was handsome, self-assured, well groomed - and no doubt everything else Tom wasn't. Frankie had obviously had her fill of failure. And who could blame her? Tom certainly didn't.

As for Frankie herself…well, she was exactly as he remembered her. Before they'd even sat down, she'd begun haranguing them with everything about herself, Rupert, Rupert's highly-important, ludicrously well-paid job, their three, highly-gifted children, their houses (one in town and one in the country) and their villa in Tuscany. Listening to her, Tom couldn't help but wonder how he'd put up with her, even for a moment, let alone for the three years they'd actually spent together. Of course, he knew *why* (Lazarus certainly had a hell of a lot to answer for) but the *how* was truly baffling.

'So, Susannah,' Rupert said, when Frankie finally paused for breath, 'you're a doctor.'

Anticipating a sales pitch for one of Rupert's new drugs, Tom inwardly groaned. But that would have been a breeze - a veritable *joy* - compared with what actually followed.

'Didn't you used to be at the Middleton? In

paediatrics?'

'Why, yes!' Susannah exclaimed. 'But how did you know?'

'Coincidence really. Someone mentioned your name to my stepfather, at last night's reception. He'd been struggling to remember where he'd heard it before, when it finally came to him that you used to be at the Middleton. He was appointed senior consultant psychiatrist there, not long after you'd left. Perhaps you've heard of him? His name's Attington. Charles Attington.'

'I have heard the name,' Susannah admitted, with a half-agonised, half-accusing glance in Tom's direction. 'But we've never actually met.'

'Well, we must put that right. I know the old man would be delighted to put a face to the name at last.'

Somehow, Tom suspected "delighted" wasn't quite the word.

He'd known this evening would be a disaster; why did Susannah never, *ever* listen? His sole consolation was that Attington didn't know his name and so couldn't identify him to Rupert (or, worse still, to Frankie) as the lunatic who'd insulted and shown every sign of wanting to brain him at last night's reception. In order to preserve that sole consolation, he had to avoid the threatened introduction. But that shouldn't be too difficult, provided they didn't get back to the hotel too early and were off with the lark in the morning. So, he concluded, there was no need to panic. He could relax. He had everything under control.

But, naturally, being foolish enough to think *that* was just too big a temptation for fate to resist and it was no more than a heartbeat later that Frankie said, 'Tom very nearly became a doctor himself, didn't you, Tom?'

In the attempt to avoid spitting it halfway across the dinner table and full in Frankie's face, Tom choked on the wine he was drinking.

Reaching over to thump him soundly on the back, Rupert said, 'I didn't know you were a medical man, Tom.'

'I'm not,' Tom croaked. 'Please, Frankie.' He knew it

was hopeless but he had to try. 'Please don't -'

'Not that kind of doctor, silly!' she cut in, ignoring Tom. 'The PhD kind. When we met, all those years ago, Tom had just graduated with the highest first ever awarded by his college.'

'Really? Wow!' Rupert said, clearly trying hard to sound suitably impressed.

Tom didn't need to look to see the expression on Susannah's face slowly turn from puzzlement to hurt surprise. They'd been together long enough for her justifiably to resent learning significant facts about him, from a total stranger. Carefully, he avoided catching her eye.

'It was only the highest first awarded by the philosophy department,' he corrected, tetchily. 'Not by the whole college. It wasn't *that* big a deal, Frankie.'

Was she doing this maliciously, he asked himself, or was she just too stupid to realise how she was hurting him? As he could readily imagine her being both that malicious *and* that stupid, it was impossible to decide.

'Yes, it was! At the time, it was a *very* big deal. But, of course, Tom doesn't want to talk about it. That's been his trouble all along. He's always been far too modest for his own good.'

'I'm not modest, Frankie. I just don't want to lay claim to being something I'm not. And I don't want you to do that for me.'

'Don't be silly, Tom! If you won't blow your own trumpet, I will. After all, what are friends for?'

Tom wanted to say they weren't friends, that they hadn't been friends for close on twenty years and they never would be again. But, of course, he couldn't because people don't say such things to each other. They don't tell each other the truth. So, he just sat there and suffered in silence, while Frankie exposed him for the fraud he was.

She'd never been one to do things by halves. It was ancient history but it seemed she'd forgotten nothing; no achievement he ever made, no prize he ever won, no compliment ever paid him. Perhaps she genuinely believed he'd enjoy reliving those long-gone glory days. But in truth, she should have known, better than anyone, that if there was a part of his life he could have buried and forgotten forever that would have been it.

Having waxed lyrical for some time on the subject of his academic brilliance, she turned next to his physical attractions.

'You'd never guess it to look at him now, of course, but back then he was a real hunk. Girls used to follow him around in their droves, with their tongues hanging out. But Tom being Tom, he just thought there was a heat wave! You wouldn't believe the lengths I had to go to, to get him to notice me.'

Involuntarily, Tom glanced at Susannah; she obviously wasn't enjoying herself, any more than he was. 'Frankie, *please*!' he pleaded, growing desperate.

'I think perhaps you're embarrassing him, darling,' Rupert said, with breathtaking perspicacity.

'Nonsense!' Frankie retorted.

She was all set to continue but, before she could say another word, a voice suddenly exclaimed, 'Rupert? Francesca? I don't believe it!'

Tom had imagined he'd be grateful for *any* interruption, from any source whatsoever. And so he would have been. From any source except this one. Even before he turned to look, he just knew. It just had to be. It was. Dr Attington.

God had certainly got the devil in Him this weekend. Given the state of the world, one would have hoped He'd have had better things to do than torment the defenceless. But seemingly not. Still, Tom supposed he ought to be grateful his life gave pleasure to someone.

'Well,' Tom said, screwing up the address Frankie had insisted on giving them and tossing it into the nearest litterbin, 'that was just about the most excruciating evening of my entire life. And given what my life's like, that's saying something.'

'She's not easy, is she?' Susannah replied, slipping her

arm through his. 'I wish I'd backed you up about the "other thing" now.'

Of course she wished that *now*, now it was too bloody late! Why did no one *ever* listen to a bloody word he said?

'I thought she was never going to stop laughing, when Attington described how you laid into him last night. The way he told it, I didn't think it was remotely funny - and I'm not sure he did, either.'

Tom groaned. In the end, the evening had so far surpassed even *his* expectations - there'd been so many moments of the most agonising embarrassment and humiliation - that, even allowing for Attington's appearance, he was hard pressed to select the cream of the crop.

'You know, if we'd stayed much longer,' Susannah said, 'I think I might have ended up slapping her.'

Glad as he was to get away, part of Tom couldn't help wishing they'd stuck around just long enough for him to witness that.

They were back at the hotel and Tom was just beginning to think the worst might be over, when Susannah finally asked the question he'd been dreading.

'So, tell me. What's the story between you and Frankie?'

He didn't want to talk about it but after everything Frankie had said (and there wasn't much she'd left unsaid) he guessed he owed Susannah some sort of explanation. So he took a deep breath and said, 'It was like Frankie said. More or less.'

Susannah waited. Then she waited a bit longer. Then she said, 'Is that it?'

'Well, what do you want, for Christ's sake?'

She shot him a cold look and he stifled what felt like the fiftieth groan of the evening. Why did she have to insist on knowing what wasn't going to do either of them any good? Why couldn't she just leave well alone? But of course, she couldn't - or at least wouldn't. So, seeing he had no choice, he began at the beginning.

'She was an undergraduate, in business studies or some such nonsense. I'd just started my PhD and she took a shine to me. Christ knows why. I suppose she thought I'd got some sort of brilliant career in front of me, which just goes to show how wrong you can be. Of course, we had absolutely nothing in common and I shouldn't have...but...well, you've seen her.'

Frankie had her faults but her looks weren't one of them. Even now, provided she'd been struck dumb first and was guaranteed to disappear in a puff of smoke immediately afterwards, Tom wouldn't have said "no". Those provisos were, he realised, the mark of his maturity; the difference between him now and twenty-odd years ago. That was how far he'd come; the sum total of his advancement. In all honesty, he didn't know whether to laugh or cry.

'I couldn't help fancying her,' he said, uncomfortably aware this was as true now as it had been then. 'She made it clear she wanted me and I was just too witless, too dick-driven to resist.'

'I see.'

Their eyes met and, after a pause, Tom said, 'It's not true by the way, about the droves of girls with their tongues hanging out. Whatever Frankie thinks, I would have noticed that.'

'Yes. I imagine you would.'

There was a pause, during which Tom struggled not to squirm in his seat.

Then Susannah said, 'So, what then? After you'd succumbed to Frankie's charms?'

'She moved in with me.'

'Just like that?'

Tom shrugged, apologetically.

'Were you in love with her?'

'God, no!' he exclaimed, without thinking.

'Did she know you weren't?'

He looked back at her miserably, the answer written all over his face.

'I see.'

Tom wished he knew how Susannah managed to pack such a weight of disapproval into those two little words. 'I'm sorry,' he said, wishing he'd had the commonsense to lie, or at least to dress the truth to make it appear more palatable. But something in him always compelled him to make the most of his sins.

'There's no need to apologise to *me*, is there?'

'I don't know, I feel like there is. But I was different then. I was so focused on my work, I didn't really notice or care about anything else. I was what Frankie wanted - at least she *thought* I was - and she could give me what I wanted. OK, I didn't love her. But the sex was pretty good and, at the time, that was good enough. At the time, it seemed like a fair enough exchange. I wish,' he said, noting the look on her face, 'you wouldn't make me tell you all this. I can't help feeling you won't like me very much, by the time I'm finished.'

'Go on,' she said - in a way that made him feel she didn't like him very much already.

'After she moved in, things were fine for a while. Then one day I woke up and everything was different.'

'What do you mean, "different"? How?'

'I don't know. It was as if everything had been in colour and, now, it was in black and white. Somehow, the shine had gone off everything - me, especially. At first, I thought it was just a phase, that I'd been working too hard and the feeling would pass. But it didn't.'

'Go on,' she said again - but in a different tone this time.

'I just stopped giving a fuck about anything and everything. I started drinking too much and stopped turning up for classes I was supposed to be teaching. I fell behind with my dissertation and everything just started falling apart around me. Well, you can imagine, can't you?'

'I think so. Did you see a doctor?'

'Oh, yes. Frankie insisted on that. She made sure I had a nice, regular supply of antidepressants.'

'Did they help?'

'Not much. But then you can't really expect them to, if

you flush them down the lavatory.'

'What did you do that for? They might - they almost certainly would - have helped, if you'd taken them!'

'They might have changed my *perception* but they wouldn't have changed *reality*. And I thought - I still think - I was entitled to my perception, even if it was painful, even if a lot of people didn't share it and wanted to call it an illness.'

Susannah sighed. She'd heard that, or something like it, too many times before to argue.

'A spark had gone out in me somewhere and that was that. I knew pills weren't the answer. I knew there was no way back, no matter what I or what anyone did. Maybe the truth is I didn't *want* to go back. Maybe the truth is I didn't want the life I had been living, or to be the person I had been. I suspect that's what Van would say. Anyway, I couldn't - or didn't want to - go back but I couldn't go forward either. So, I just drifted along - hopelessly, aimlessly - for a long time, generally trying everyone's patience and Frankie's most of all. Things hadn't exactly worked turned out like she'd planned. She'd thought I was going to be a spectacular success; instead, I was only a spectacular failure. I couldn't help feeling sorry for her. She ended up wasting some of the best years of her life with me.'

'It wasn't a waste if she loved you, Tom.'

'But I don't think she did, anymore than I loved her. But then again, maybe thinking that just salves my conscience. Anyway, in the end, I found out she was having an affair. She'd graduated by now and was working for an insurance company. One day, I saw her with her boss and - I just knew.'

He paused and Susannah waited.

'It's funny, I didn't love her - I'd never loved her - but it still twisted me up inside. I think it was the lies that hurt most. Of course, they were obvious now I knew. But at the time, I'd fallen for them hook, line and sinker. And then there were the little things she'd done to make up to me, to please me, little kindnesses - quite intimate some of them - to distract me and assuage her guilt. I felt such a prick. And now I knew, of course, every new lie was a fresh insult, salt in an open wound.'

'Didn't you confront her?'

'Not at first. What right did I have, after the mess I'd made of everything? But in the end, I just couldn't stand it any longer. One day, she came home even later than usual, with some excuse that was even more absurd than usual - and I just lost it. I remember I said, "Why do you bother to lie, Frankie? Do you think I don't know you're fucking him, that I can't see it in your face when you finally come home to me, that I can't *smell* it on you?" Not surprisingly, she slapped my face. It was as if all the anger, all the frustration, all the *hatred* she'd felt for me for months was in that slap. It stung like hell. We just stood there for a minute, staring at each other. Then, she said, "I'll get my things." And that was that. She packed and left. And when she'd gone, I suddenly felt so relieved. Being free of her meant I was free to admit I'd failed. I didn't have to pretend anymore, to keep trying for her sake - even though I knew and had always known it was hopeless.'

'So what did you do?'

'I gave up on my doctorate. Even though I'd known for months I'd never finish it, it had been eating away at me like a cancer. I can't describe the relief of finally letting it go.'

And once he'd done that, he said, the rest was comparatively easy. He spoke to his professor, who spoke to Max Wainwright, who'd taken pity on him and given him his post at Claremont. And there he'd been ever since. He'd never had any real interest in his job or his students. But there was something to be said for having a reason to get out of bed in the morning - even if, on most days, he'd rather not have bothered.

'I didn't see Frankie again, for a long time. When I did - purely by accident - she was about to marry Rupert. She was so obviously happy and I so obviously wasn't, it seemed it was easy for her to forgive me for the past. Christ, she even asked me to the wedding. Not that I went, of course.'

'Do you really think she's forgiven you, Tom? I don't.'

'No, perhaps you're right. Perhaps she hasn't forgiven

me - and perhaps she's right not to. Anyway that was that, until today. And after Frankie, there was no one. Until you.'

'No one?' she queried, sceptically.

'No one who mattered or to whom I mattered. Since Frankie, my only lasting love affair has been with alcohol and, before you came along, my only goal in life was to be sober as infrequently as humanly possible. You changed all that. For good, certainly. I hope, forever.'

'I hope so too.'

'You're not too angry with me, then?'

'Why on earth would I be angry with you?'

'You were - at least, I thought you were - when I described how I got involved with Frankie.'

'I wasn't *angry*, Tom. I was jealous.'

'Really?' he asked, grinning. Simpleton that he was, he saw no need to conceal the fact that he was pleased. 'I like that idea. I don't think I've ever made anyone jealous before.'

'Well, I'm over it now, so don't crow. How come you never told me any of this before?'

'Can't you guess?' he asked, his smile quickly fading. 'Because I didn't want you to look at me and compare what I am, with what I might have been. I didn't want to look at you and see the look I used to see in Frankie's eyes, the one that let me know I'd let her down. I didn't want you to be as disappointed in me, as I am in myself.'

'Oh, Tom! How can you think I'd be disappointed? I'm not Frankie. And I hope I'm nowhere near as hard on you, as you are on yourself.'

'You're not. And I'm so grateful.' He moved to kiss her but she held him off.

'One last thing, Tom. What you said, about everything being in black and white, is it still like that now?'

'Not when I'm with you,' he said, as his mouth finally closed on hers.

Chapter 5

'That really is the most disgusting habit!' Amy exclaimed, regarding Tom with the sort of expression normally reserved for the contents of a used litter tray.

His blood ran for cold for a second, as he wondered exactly what it was he'd just been doing while his mind was elsewhere. Then he realised she meant his smoking. He took a final drag on the cigarette he'd all but finished and flicked the butt out through the open window.

'Why don't you quit, for Christ's sake?'

'Ever thought of minding your own business?'

'Suit yourself. *I* don't care if you smoke yourself to death. I just thought Susannah might. Especially when you think about her father.'

'What about him?' Tom asked. As far as he was aware, Susannah didn't have a father. Although now he came to think about it, he supposed she must have done. At least at one stage.

Amy looked back at him, this time as if she just didn't quite believe the contents of the litter tray. 'Duh! Like, he died of cancer. *Lung cancer!*'

'Oh.'

'So don't you think maybe - *just maybe* - she might worry about losing you the same way?'

When Amy'd gone, Tom spent some time asking himself how come *she'd* known about Susannah's father and he hadn't. How come Susannah had confided in Amy (Tom had more than half an idea she didn't even like the girl) but had never said a word to him?

She'd never said anything about his smoking, either. OK, so he'd seen the way her eyes slid away from his, every time he lit up; the way she cringed when he coughed and the rapid calculation she made, every time she emptied one of his ashtrays, as to just how many he'd managed to get through that day. But it wasn't as if she'd actually *said* anything.

So that was what he'd told Amy; something fatuous about Susannah's not minding that he smoked.

Treating him to another of those looks in which she seemed to specialise, she'd said, 'Whatever she says, she wants you to quit.'

'And what are you, telepathic?'

'I don't need to be. It's obvious! I mean, assuming she loves you - God knows why she would but let's just assume, for the sake of argument, that she does - it can't be easy for her to watch you killing yourself little by little, day by day, can it? How would *you* like it, if she did that to you? Wouldn't you want her to stop?'

Even now, Tom recalled the effect of those words with a shiver. Amy was right; it *was* obvious. But somehow he'd never thought to ask himself how he'd feel, if Susannah insisted on doing something right in front of his face - almost rubbing his nose in it - that he, she and everyone knew for a moral certainty was killing her. Once he'd finally asked the question, it hadn't taken more than a second for the answer to freeze the blood in his veins. He couldn't bear to lose her. Still less could he bear to stand by and watch her kill herself. And if she felt like that about his smoking, he couldn't carry on torturing her like that, could he? So what, he asked himself, was he going to do about it? Was giving up really too much to ask?

For a moment, he teetered on the very brink of making the commitment. Then he thought - what the hell? - and lit another fag. After all, there was no point rushing into things.

A few days later, out of the blue, he suddenly said, 'I've decided to quit smoking.'

For some reason, the announcement didn't quite elicit the euphoria he'd expected. Instead of jumping up and throwing her arms around him in an ecstasy of delight, Susannah merely looked back at him, in mild surprise.

'Really?'

Her tone was pitched somewhere between hope and what was (Tom had to admit) a forgivable scepticism.

'I've been meaning to for ages,' he lied. 'And I've decided now's the time.'

'OK,' she said, doubtfully. 'Well, if you're really serious, there are all kinds of aids these days. Patches and so on.'

He let out a snort of contempt. 'I won't need any of that nonsense! Christ, Susannah, it's not as if I'm *addicted*. I only smoke out of habit. I can quit any time I want.'

'Really?' Now there was only scepticism in her voice.

'Sure. What's up? Don't believe me? OK. I'll prove it.' Taking a final drag, he stubbed out the cigarette he was smoking in celebration of his decision to quit. 'That's it. That was my last one. I'm now officially an ex-smoker.'

'Congratulations,' she said, softly. She got up, kissed the top of his head and left the room. Tom had a more-than-sneaking suspicion she was going to cry but he couldn't, for the life of him, imagine why.

Five minutes later, he went to find her. As predicted her face was an unspeakable mess and she had a handkerchief full of snot screwed up in a ball, in her fist. Women. How the bloody hell was anyone supposed to make sense of them?

'I'm off to the chemist's,' he said, preferring not to ask for an explanation he knew he wouldn't understand. 'I've been thinking...maybe those patches aren't such a bad idea, after all.'

It wasn't easy to quit. After all, he'd been a sixty-a-day man, for just about as long as he could remember. At first, he was utterly convinced he'd been sold a duff set of patches - either that, or he had totally impervious skin - the fucking things did nothing to ease the craving he'd been convinced he wouldn't feel. He couldn't sleep; he had a mouth full of ulcers and wanted to kill anything and everything that moved, even (no, *especially*) Susannah - because, after all, this was all *her* fault. If it weren't for her, he'd have happily carried on smoking himself to death, until they'd nailed down the coffin lid.

To add insult to injury, he couldn't breathe and was coughing up stuff the sight of which turned even his stomach.

And then they had the nerve to tell you quitting was good for you. Twats.

For the first couple of months or so (which, while he was enduring them, felt like at least as many years) his life was sheer, unadulterated hell and, if he'd had a cat, it would have been black and blue - no matter what colour it had started out. But eventually - when he'd just about chewed both his arms off up to the elbow and made detailed plans for the murder of everyone he knew and quite a few people he didn't - the craving began to ease. So now, he only felt like he could kill for a fag. Rather than just for the sheer hell of it.

That was that cracked, then. Now all he had to do was lose all the weight he'd gained. Susannah (who, contrary to all reason, was still just about talking to him) promised him moderate exercise and a healthy diet were all he needed. He supposed she meant to be encouraging but he felt like he'd just scaled the north face of the Eiger and, like Sisyphus, suddenly found himself with it all to do again. And the prospect of that was enough to make anyone light up.

But he didn't. Because round about then (just as he was starting to tell himself that a couple of fags, every now and again, couldn't really do *that* much harm) quitting produced its first tangible benefit. And if it had been individually designed and tailor made for Tom, it couldn't have suited him any better.

All of a sudden, he was as randy as a goat *all the time* (as opposed to just most of it). Susannah's libido had always been the equal of his own and, without breaking stride, she smoothly moved up a gear to match him now. Tom loved her for it; he couldn't have been more delighted. But of course, life being what it was, there just had to be a snag.

Everything would have been perfect, if only he'd had the energy to follow where Lazarus was suddenly so eager to lead. Desire was one thing but, it seemed, consummation was another. His flesh might be (it *was*) quite shamelessly willing but, more than once, it threatened to be too weak to finish what it had started and lasting long enough to bring them both to the point of satisfaction (again) taxed Tom's stamina, even more than his self-control. And that was one indignity he wasn't prepared to suffer. At least not without making a fight of it.

So, it seemed there was nothing for it. He didn't say anything to anyone, even Susannah; he was too ashamed. But secretly, surreptitiously, under cover of darkness, he began jogging round the block. At first, it was a frightening and horribly humiliating experience. He liked to think of it as "jogging" but, in reality, staggering would have been a more accurate description. Years of self-abuse had taken their toll and, even as an ex-smoker, he couldn't get a hundred yards without turning blue in the face and gasping for breath like a landed fish. More than once, passers-by enquired if he was sure he was feeling all right and one old dear (apparently assuming he was in the middle of a heart attack) even offered to call him an ambulance. For which act of charity, Tom never forgave her.

But public if (thankfully) anonymous humiliation was a small price to pay, in the quest for more and better sex. And imagining all the things he was going to do to Susannah, just as soon as he'd got the strength, kept Tom motivated like nothing else could have done. Before many weeks had elapsed, he wasn't staggering any longer, he was jogging; not long after that, he wasn't jogging, he was running and, very shortly after that, he began to see the results of his labours not just in the mirror but - all importantly - in the bedroom.

He never forgot the first time he left Susannah breathless and sated and gazing up at him, like he was some kind of rampant sex god.

'Tom!' she gasped. 'What on earth have you doing to yourself? Have you been taking some sort of stimulant, or what?'

He turned away to hide a secret smile of satisfaction. She couldn't have paid him a more gratifying compliment and, suddenly, all those hours spent pounding the tarmac, in the cold and the dark and the rain, didn't seem like such a monumental waste of effort, after all.

And Susannah wasn't the only one to be impressed.

'You know, Tom,' Amy said one day, not long after

he'd assumed the mantle of rampant sex god, 'you used to be a real mess. But now you've quit smoking and sorted yourself out a bit, you're not that bad. For a bloke your age.'

'Gee, thanks,' Tom had said, overwhelmed.

As they were lying together on the sofa one evening - and Tom was feeling that all was right with the world and with his own particular corner of it especially - Susannah suddenly spoiled everything by saying, 'Did I tell you, I asked Mum over for the weekend?'

Of course, she knew she hadn't told him or he wouldn't have been lying there, as if he hadn't a care in the world. He'd have been upstairs, slitting his wrists.

'That's all right, isn't it?'

'Of course,' he said, sitting up. What he really meant was, 'Like hell it is!'. But he knew honesty was rarely the best policy, especially where Susannah's mother was concerned. So, short of murdering the old cow (and he'd more than flirted with *that* idea, he'd just about been through the Karma Sutra with it) he'd no realistic means of achieving his ambition of never clapping eyes on her again.

'It's ten years this weekend since my dad died, so I didn't want her to be on her own.'

'I understand. I don't mind. Really,' he assured her. And this time, given the circumstances - hideous though the old crone was - he almost meant it.

'I told her you quit, by the way. She was delighted.'

Tom smiled, thinly. He secretly doubted he could do anything to "delight" Marion. Unless it was getting himself run over by a bus.

'Ever since Dad died, she's had this real downer on smoking.'

Tom would never have guessed.

'Even after ten years, she still misses him. We both do.'

'I know,' he said, squeezing her hand.

'It's the same for you, of course.'

Tom was just about to remind her he'd never met her

father, and so couldn't really be expected to miss him, when he realised that wasn't what she meant.

'Were you and your father very close?'

'Close enough,' Tom said shortly, intending to slam the door firmly shut on the subject.

There was a pause.

'OK,' Susannah said, at last. 'You don't want to talk about it. Sorry. I shouldn't have asked.'

But, when it came right down to it, Tom didn't want there to be things they couldn't talk about; he didn't want her to feel shut out. Anyway, wasn't it time he told someone? Didn't he always say secrets lost their power, once they'd been told? And if he really believed that, why was he still so determined to keep his?

'We *were* close,' he made himself say, before the moment passed. 'After my mum died - well, I was his whole life.'

Susannah thought, but didn't say, that must have been quite a burden for a small boy.

'I couldn't have wished for a better or a kinder father. He worked hard, was never drunk, never violent. He hardly ever even raised his voice to me. And when I won a scholarship to grammar school and later to university, he was ridiculously proud of me.'

'He was right to be proud.'

'No, he wasn't. Not as things turned out. Not as *I* turned out.'

'You mean because of your breakdown? Because you gave up on your PhD? He'd have understood, Tom.'

'That's not what I mean.'

'What then?'

Even now he wasn't sure he could tell her, that he could actually make himself say the words.

'When I left for university, I left him behind. In every sense. I left home, walked straight into a new life and left him with nothing. I went home once or twice in the first year but hardly at all after that. There was always somewhere more exciting to go, somewhere else I'd rather be than stuck at home with my old man. Christ, I hardly even remembered to phone him.'

'Lots of us were like that, Tom! I know *I* was. We were young and selfish but I'm sure our parents understood.'

'You think so? Well, when it comes to selfishness, I wrote the manual. My dad had no one. Except me. And the first chance I got, I left and never looked back. He never said a word to me about it. He never complained. But it must have hurt. It must have hurt like hell to discover what a selfish, ungrateful little bastard he'd got for a son.'

'Oh, Tom! You're -'

'Don't, Susannah. Please don't tell me I'm too hard on myself. You don't know. You weren't there.'

He tried to convince himself he'd said enough, that there was no need to tell her the rest. But the floodgates were open now and he found he couldn't stop, until he'd told it all.

'I hadn't been home for - Christ knows how long. Then, one day the police turned up and told me he was dead. Just like that. Out of the blue. At least I thought it was. But it seemed he'd been ill for months. He hadn't told me but - well, how could he? I never gave him the chance.'

Susannah would have taken his hand but he withdrew it. He couldn't bear to be comforted just then, knowing he didn't deserve it.

'He'd suffered for months and died alone. But the worst thing was, he'd been dead nearly three weeks before anyone found him. You can't imagine the shame of it. He was my father. He'd devoted his whole life to me. Yet he'd lain there for weeks, undiscovered. And the truth is, he'd have lain there longer still, if finding him had been left to me.'

He stopped, finding a lump in his throat. It was ancient history but he'd never spoken about it before to anyone and telling his secret now, after all these years, suddenly made the past alive again. He could almost see his father's face, his smile; could almost smell him, almost touch him. But it was only an almost and almost too painful to bear.

'He was the only person in my whole life who'd ever loved me. Until you. And look how I repaid him. I was almost too ashamed to go to the funeral, to show my face, to have people point at me and say, "That's him. That's the son. The one who -"' He stopped, just too late to prevent the break in his voice from giving him away.

'I'm sorry, Tom. I wish there were something I could say.'

'There's nothing to say. I just have to live with it - and with myself.'

'Your breakdown...' she ventured, softly.

And he smiled sadly because, of course, he'd known that she would guess. 'You're right. It had nothing to do with burnout. And everything to do with guilt. For a long time, I was as angry as hell with my dad for dying - for making me discover what I couldn't bear to know about myself. And because he wasn't there anymore, I couldn't atone. I'd never realised the value of forgiveness, until I found myself beyond its pale.'

'But you must know, Tom, if he were here now, he would forgive you.'

'Oh, yes. *He* would. But I don't forgive myself.'

'But don't you think perhaps you should? For his sake, if not your own.'

He looked up at her then, as if she'd suddenly turned on the light in a darkened room. Of course, he saw immediately what she meant (though in the twenty or so years he'd spent brooding on the subject, the thought had never once occurred to him) but it took him some while longer to see that she was right.

A few days later, Tom was waiting for Susannah to come home, when the phone rang.

He answered it and sensed the caller hesitate, torn between asking for Susannah and hanging up. Whoever it was obviously didn't want to talk to him. If he'd been of a more suspicious turn of mind, he might have imagined Susannah was having an affair. But as it was, he said, 'Hello, Marion. How are you?'

'Is Susannah there?' she asked, ignoring his question.

'She's not home yet. Shall I ask her to call you, when she gets in?'

'OK.'

There was a pause. Then, as he sensed she was about to hang up, something in Tom made him say, 'You can still make it this weekend, can't you?'

'You'll be there, will you?'

'I'm afraid so. But don't let that stop you. Susannah's looking forward to it. She misses you, you know.'

'I miss her too,' Marion replied. 'I hardly see her these days. I wish -' She broke off, apparently remembering just in time that she was speaking to Tom.

'I understand,' he said. And, quite suddenly, he did. 'I'll get her to call you. I promise.'

As he put the phone down, the realisation finally dawned upon him that - just like his own father, all those years ago - Marion was all alone in the world. Susannah was all she'd got. Except, of course, that she didn't really have Susannah - because Susannah was his and he didn't want to share her. From the very beginning, he'd resented every moment she took from him to give to Marion. He'd told Susannah he'd written the manual on selfishness. But, until this moment, he hadn't realised he was still following it.

When Susannah got in, it seemed she'd already spoken to Marion.

'I've been thinking, Tom. Rather than having Mum here this weekend, maybe I should visit her. On my own.'

Half an hour ago, such an unlooked-for reprieve would have had Tom turning cartwheels. But since speaking to Marion, he'd somehow lost all interest in acrobatics.

He didn't need to be told what had precipitated this change of plan. Marion didn't want to spend the weekend with him. He didn't blame her; she was grieving and vulnerable and the last thing she needed was to go another fifteen rounds, toe-to-toe, slugging it out with him. She needed that about as much as Susannah needed to stand by and watch. He knew - he'd *always* known - how much Susannah hated their rows.

Why hadn't that been enough to stop him? How could he claim to love her and not even *try* to get along with her mother? He deserved to be beaten within an inch of his miserable life. And if he'd had the least taste for self-flagellation, he'd have set about it then and there.

As it was, he said, 'No, Susannah. Let Marion come here. It'll be all right, I promise. I'll be on my very best behaviour. You'll see.'

He could tell from her smile, she had no faith in him. He could only hope he wasn't going to prove her right.

When Marion arrived, Susannah was still at the hospital.

Tom was cooking dinner and she sat at the kitchen table and watched him work.

'I didn't know you could cook,' she said, with a look on her face that announced her perfect confidence he couldn't.

He bit his tongue and smiled. 'You know what, Marion? I'm full of surprises.'

Yes, her expression said, and all of them nasty. But at least she didn't say it out loud. 'What's all this about?' she asked, instead.

'All what?'

'This,' she said, with an expansive, all-encompassing gesture. 'You. Quitting smoking. Cooking. Trying to pretend you're pleased to see me. What's it all about? Is something the matter with Susannah? She's not pregnant, is she?'

'No,' Tom said, overlooking the horror in Marion's voice as she'd asked that last question. 'It's nothing like that.'

'Then what?'

He lifted a pan off the stove and turned to face her. He'd been rehearsing this speech all day - in fact, if he was honest, all week. He hoped he could get it out now, without making a complete balls-up of it. He was going to feel like one gigantic arsehole, if he couldn't. In fact, to be fair, he was probably going to feel like that, anyway.

'Look, Marion, the thing is...I wanted to say, I'm sorry. OK?'

'For what?' she enquired with another gesture, implying the list of possibilities was endless.

'For everything - just about - from the moment we met. I haven't been very kind or very fair to you.'

She stared at him, as if she'd always known he was crazy but now he was just taking the piss.

'I could see you didn't like me, which made me determined not to like you. But it didn't dawn on me, until the other day, quite how selfish I was being. I love Susannah and, the truth is, I'm so greedy for her I didn't want to share her with anyone. Even you. That was wrong of me. I'm sorry, Marion. I mean to do better in future, so I hope you can forgive me for the past.'

There was a pause.

'Is that it?'

Tom sighed. He'd been right, when he thought this wasn't going to be easy. 'Not quite, Marion. Whether you forgive me or not, I want us to bury the hatchet. And not in each other,' he went on quickly, as she opened her mouth to suggest it. 'I know I'm not what you would have chosen for Susannah -'

'No. You're right. You're not!'

'I know. And if the truth were told, Marion, I'm not what *I* would have chosen for her, either. But the point is, the choice wasn't mine and it wasn't yours; it was Susannah's. And she chose me. Believe me, I don't understand - anymore than you do - what she sees in me. I know I don't deserve her and, however hard I try, I never will. But I love her. And - incredible though you and I may both find it - she loves me too.'

'Perhaps she *thinks* she does.'

'Do you really believe Susannah doesn't know her own mind?' Tom asked, thinking anyone who believed that didn't know her very well.

'I don't know!' Marion exclaimed, beginning to sound rattled. 'I just don't want her to get hurt.'

'And you don't trust me not to hurt her?'

'Damn right, I don't!'

'No. Well, why should you?' She was right not to trust him, if his past was anything to go by, but he was determined it shouldn't be. 'But I won't hurt her, Marion. Not if I can help it. Her happiness is more important to me than anything, even than my own. That's why I'm standing here now, making a complete prick of myself. Because, between us, we *are* hurting her. We're making her miserable, right now.'

'*We* are? I don't know what you mean. What have *I* done?'

If Tom didn't know better, he'd have sworn Marion was blushing; the consequence, no doubt, of a pricked and guilty conscience - not unlike his own.

'It's not you, Marion. It's both of us. Susannah doesn't just love me, she doesn't just love you; she loves us both. And it hurts her to have us bickering and sniping at each other, the whole time. If we're honest, we both know that. But we've been so busy taking pot shots at each other, we've forgotten all about Susannah and her feelings. And I think - I *know* - she deserves better than that, from both of us. That's why I'm asking if we can't just start over and at least *try* to be friends. For her sake.'

At last, he paused for breath. He was puce in the face and his insides were one cringing mass of embarrassment - he couldn't have felt more exposed, if he'd been standing there with his pants around his ankles - but at least he'd said it. At least he'd tried. It was up to Mad - that is, it was up to Marion now.

He glanced up at her - it had been much too tall an order to say all that *and* look her in the face - and was astonished to find she had tears in her eyes.

Luckily, the pan that was still left on the stove chose that moment to boil over, giving Marion a chance to dry her eyes and Tom an opportunity to pretend he hadn't noticed.

When Susannah walked into the kitchen an hour later, she found the two of them bent double with laughter.

'What's the joke?' she asked, not quite believing her

eyes or her ears. But as her question was greeted only by renewed howls of laughter, she never got to share it.

She spent an extremely perplexing evening, watching them falling over themselves in the effort to be polite to one another. It was, "After you, Marion," and, "No, after you, Tom," and, "I quite agree, Tom," and, "I couldn't agree more, Marion," until she began to think she'd gone mad.

When Tom finally announced his intention of going home, she really didn't believe her ears, when Marion told him - with something very like a twinkle in her eye - that she was a woman of the world and there was certainly no need to go on *her* account.

So, when Tom slid into bed beside her, not surprisingly Susannah demanded an explanation.

'What have you done to her, Tom? Have you been spiking her drinks, or something?'

'Of course not!' How could she think such a thing? 'We just had a bit of a chat, that's all. Before you came in.'

'A chat? About what?'

'Oh, you know, this and that. Anyhow, we decided to have a go at burying the hatchet. It was all Marion's idea. She had this whole speech prepared, about how we weren't being fair to you. You know, behaving like a couple of pricks -'

'That was her word, was it?'

'Maybe she didn't put it quite like that. But that was what she meant. Anyway, I have to admit, I was pretty impressed. I thought she behaved with remarkable maturity. So, I agreed to give it a go. And the funny thing is, she's not that bad. Once you get to know her.'

Susannah had the distinct impression Tom wasn't being straight with her. She wasn't quite sure what he was hiding - but she thought she could guess.

'I don't know what you've done, Tom. But whatever it is, I love you for it. And now,' she said, climbing astride him, 'I'm going to show you just how much.'

'What about Marion?' he said, tensing and holding her off.

'What about her?' Susannah replied, with a startled

look - as if she thought Tom might be suggesting Marion should join them.

'Well, you know...do you think we should? I mean, what if she hears us?'

'Oh, really, Tom!' Susannah exclaimed - and this time it was her turn to double up with laughter. 'Honestly, you're priceless!'

'What?' he demanded, scowling. '*What*? I wish you'd tell me. I don't see what's so bloody funny.'

The occasion being what it was, in many respects the weekend was a painful one for all of them - if Marion was unhappy, so was Susannah and if Susannah was unhappy, so was Tom - but in hatchet-burying terms, it was an unqualified success. In fact, if it had been any more successful, Susannah thought, she may well have been driven to scream. But she supposed she ought to regard the weekend as a bizarre sort of honeymoon - and forgive the besotted pair their excesses.

Since Susannah was on duty, it was left to Tom to see Marion to the station.

As her train was announced, she suddenly took hold of him and hugged him tight. He was surprised and somewhat embarrassed by the embrace but not at all displeased.

'Thank you,' she said, as she released him. 'I mean for the kick in the pants, where you and Susannah were concerned. I needed it.'

'Anytime, Marion,' he assured her. 'It'll be my pleasure.'

'Hedonism verses eudaemonism,' Tom said.

'Easy. Pleasures pall, happiness never does. No one ever tired of being happy.'

Sometimes, Tom wondered quite what he had on hand in Amy.

'All right. Suppose I asked you to refute the argument there's no objective reality.'

'I couldn't do better than emulate Dr Johnson. So, I'd kick you on the shin and say, "I refute it *thus*".'

'Yep,' Tom agreed. 'That'd do it every time. At least for me.'

'Thought so. But we could always try it, if you like. Just to be sure.'

'No thanks, I'll pass. Anyway, if you're so clever, try this one. If a green cube suddenly materialised in the corner of this room, how would you know it wasn't human?'

There was a pause. Then she said, 'Have you been drinking?'

'No! And don't be impertinent. It's a serious question. Think about it.'

She did. 'I suppose,' she said, having thought, 'that what you're really asking is what, if anything, is the essential characteristic of - or qualification for - being human.'

'Exactly. Just so. Well spotted. So?'

She laughed. 'What? Just like that, you think I've got the answer?'

'Of course not, idiot. No one has. My question was merely an invitation for you to say something intelligent. In your own time. No pressure. But any time,' he said, glancing at his watch, 'round about now would be good.'

'OK. Well, I've thought about this before and it seems to me that what separates us from other animals - I can't comment on green cubes - is more a question of degree than of kind. Except - possibly - for two things.'

'That "possibly" is good; I like that. When about to stick your neck out, always hedge your bets.'

'Isn't that a mixed metaphor?'

'Do I look like a man who cares? Go on, please, with what you were saying. I'm intrigued to know what comes after "possibly".'

'Well, logic - our ability to reason - is one thing.'

'As you say, *possibly*. But mightn't that, in the case of some animals - say, primates or dolphins - fall into your first category and prove to be a matter only of degree and not of kind?'

'Possibly.'

'So what's the second thing?'

'God.'

After a pause, he said, 'Was that an expression of exasperation, an appeal for divine intervention - or a reply?'

'It was my attempt to say something intelligent.'

'I see. I take it that what you mean is human beings are, so far as we know, the only species to have invented God?'

'Yes.'

'But that won't do as our defining characteristic, will it?'

'Why not?'

'Because - although you wouldn't be the first person to try to mount that argument - it isn't really on to claim that someone who doesn't believe in God fails to qualify as a human being.'

'But *believing* in God isn't the point. The point is being able to conceive of the *idea* of God, irrespective of belief in His actual existence.'

'Then ideas are what make us human? And that idea in particular? You're arguing for a sort of variation on the "I think, therefore I am" theme; something like, "I can conceive of the idea of God, therefore I'm human"?'

She grinned. 'Possibly.'

It was, Tom knew, one of life's little ironies - further evidence of God's malevolence, if any were needed - that anticipated pleasures rarely bring the pleasure anticipated. Between anticipation and realisation, as he had long since discovered, falls the inevitable shadow. But, just for once, that tired old joke had backfired. When Genghis had pressed him into tutoring Amy, neither of them had supposed he would derive the smallest pleasure from it. Genghis had confidently expected Tom to cock the whole thing up and (scarcely any more ambitious himself) the best Tom had hoped for was to get Amy the required results - by dint of a lot of extra, unpaid, thankless and frustrating work on his part - and so hang on to his job. But just for once, anticipation had fallen short of the reality.

He didn't quite know how she'd done it but, somehow, Amy had lit up his working life, just as Susannah had lit up everything else. He spent hours (voluntary, unpaid hours, at that) talking with her; most of it was arrant nonsense but it was quite astonishing how much pleasure there was to be had from it. And, somehow, the pleasure she gave him made teaching even the dullest of her peers more tolerable - and seeing the look *that* had put on the headmaster's face had really made Tom feel life was worth living. If he'd known he could piss Genghis off to that extent, just by doing his job properly, he'd have become the model of competence and efficiency long ago.

But even disregarding the joy of thwarting the headmaster, witnessing Amy's almost breathtaking progress made Tom feel not just pleased but unconscionably proud. These days, she could actually make him think, which was something he hadn't wanted (or needed) to do for a long time. Once or twice, she even came close to tripping him up - and this was ground he'd been over a thousand times before. Of course, he knew he could take little, if any, credit for her success. She didn't need him; she was the sort of kid who, abandoned at the bottom of a black hole, would still somehow find a way to thrive. The reality was he needed her far more than she needed him.

At least, so he thought. Until one day he discovered that, just like everyone else, she had a secret.

He was sitting on the floor at her feet and she was teasing him, holding a book he wanted out of his reach. As he leaned across her, in an attempt to snatch it from her, she let out a sudden, involuntary yelp of pain.

'What's the matter?' he demanded, horrified. 'Have I hurt you?'

Clutching her side, she shook her head in mute denial.

'Yes, I have!'

'No, *you* haven't,' she retorted, with unconscious emphasis. 'It's nothing. Don't fuss.'

'Let me see,' he said, suddenly suspicious.

'I've told you, it's nothing. Leave me alone.'

Their eyes met and then she didn't need to tell him. He just knew.

'Please,' he urged, softly. 'Let me look.'

Seeing he'd already guessed and so she had nothing left to hide, she lifted her blouse to reveal a bruise - the perfect imprint of a large, angry hand. Blushing, she covered it again, as if it were something of which *she* should be ashamed.

'I told you, it's nothing.'

'Jesus, Amy!' Tom breathed. 'Has he done this before?'

She shrugged. 'When things aren't going well. When he's under pressure. When he's been drinking too much. He used to have Mum to take it out on. Now he's got me.'

There was a pause. Tom was at a loss to know what to say or what to do. He knew what he *wanted* to do. But regretfully, he was forced to acknowledge that, even if he hadn't been a judge, beating Amy's father to a bloody pulp probably wouldn't have been his smartest move. Or, in the long run, have done much to help her.

He couldn't look at her but, hard as it was to say the words, he had to know. 'I'm sorry, Amy. I have to ask. Does he -?'

'No,' she said quickly, without waiting for him to finish. She didn't want to hear the question, any more than he wanted to ask it. 'I promise you. He doesn't.'

Tom sighed with relief. But later, he wondered if perhaps he hadn't allowed himself to be too easily convinced; if he hadn't just taken the easy way out, for both of them.

'Have you told anyone? I mean that he hurts you?'

'Like who? He's a High Court judge, Tom. Who's going to stop him?'

'I will,' he said, rashly.

She looked back at him then, as if she didn't know whether to laugh or cry. 'Oh, Tom! I wish -'

'What?' he asked, eagerly. 'What do you wish?'

'That the world was the place you think it is. *You* can't stop him. Don't try. He'll make you pay, if you do - and he'll make me pay, too. Mum tried and she lost everything, including me. You don't know what he's like, what power he's got. No one questions him, whatever he says is believed. You can't win against him. He's unimpeachable and he knows it.'

'But you've got evidence!'

'Of what? It's a bruise. Anyone could have done it. Anyway, he's usually careful not to leave a mark. You'd be amazed how much pain can be inflicted, without leaving any visible trace.'

In point of fact, Tom was very far from amazed, though it's possible they were thinking about different kinds of pain.

'But -'

'Trust me, Tom. I know what I'm talking about. Besides,' she said, forcing a smile, 'before too much longer, I'll be sixteen. He can't touch me, then. I can leave him and there won't be anything even *he* can do about it.'

'But -' he said again.

'Promise you won't tell anyone. I mean it,' she insisted. 'Promise me, Tom!'

And when she begged him like that, what could he do but promise?

Of course, he told Susannah. So he broke his promise, almost straightaway. But, he told himself, it didn't count. It must be permissible to break a promise, mustn't it, if doing so will procure a greater good than keeping it?

'I have to do something to help her,' he said.

'I thought she made you promise not to tell.'

'She did. But I can't just stand by, knowing what he's doing to her, knowing what she's going through. I can't just do nothing.'

'But what can you do, Tom? As she said herself, there's no real evidence. You only have her word for what happened.'

Tom looked back at her, in disbelief. 'You don't believe her!'

Though he'd no idea why, Tom knew Susannah didn't like Amy very much. But surely doubting the girl's word was taking that dislike a step *too* far. Maybe he was biased - no doubt he *was* - but it seemed to him Susannah had a bias of her own, whether she chose to acknowledge it or not.

'I'm not saying I *don't* believe her, Tom. But just suppose, for a second, that it isn't true. What if she made it up to get back at him for some reason?'

'Such as?'

'I don't know…maybe because of the divorce. I mean, she wanted to stay with her mother, didn't she? She might feel resentful because of that.'

'Don't be ridiculous, Susannah. She's not like that!'

'Like what? Human? Look, Tom, all I'm saying is be careful. I mean, after all, he is a *judge*.'

'Which means what? That he's necessarily innocent?'

'Of course not. Not necessarily. But they do vet such people, don't they? If there was any reason to suspect him - any *hint* of the sort of thing Amy's accusing him of - he'd never have been appointed, would he?'

'Well someone's mistreating her. She couldn't have inflicted that bruise on herself. So who do you suppose it is, if it's not the oh-so-perfect, butter-wouldn't-melt-in-his-mouth judge?'

'I don't know. Maybe a boyfriend?'

'She hasn't got one.'

Susannah raised an eyebrow at that.

'She hasn't!'

'How do you know?'

'Because…she'd have told me.'

'Oh, really, Tom!'

'What do you mean, "Oh, really, Tom!"? What the bloody hell's that supposed to mean?'

Tom didn't care what Susannah said, he was convinced Amy was telling the truth. After all, he reasoned, Susannah hadn't heard Amy's account firsthand. If she had, he didn't doubt she'd have been just as convinced as he was. But believing Amy and finding a way to help her were two different things. He wanted desperately to help and - notwithstanding

Susannah's scepticism - only the fear of doing more harm than good held him back.

'Does it matter, if a villain is convicted by a lie?'

'You mean like when the cops fix the evidence?'

'I think you've probably been watching too much trashy TV. But yes, that is kind of what I meant.'

Amy shrugged. 'Well, it's the lesser of two evils, which ought to count as a kind of good.'

'Even so…' Tom began, doubtfully.

She laughed. 'You worry too much. Look, the convicted man was a villain. He's been made to pay. Isn't that all that matters? Who cares about the details?'

'You mean the end justifies the means?'

'Machiavelli thought so.'

'But Aristotle said that, without truth, there can be no reality.'

'I don't care about Aristotle. I'm with Machiavelli. Because, when you really think about it, if good has to win by fair means and only evil may use foul, it's no great wonder evil's winning, is it?'

'But are results the only thing that matters? What if someone does something with the best of intentions - intending only good - and evil results?'

'Well, that's just unfortunate, isn't it? We can't always control the consequences of our actions; if we only acted in situations where we could, we'd never do anything. And didn't someone or other - Edmund Burke, I think - say that for evil to triumph all that's needed is for good men and women to do nothing?'

For once, Tom conceded the argument. She'd answered his question; he had to do something. He had to try to do good, even if evil resulted. If he didn't, wasn't evil bound to win? At least, if he tried, there was a *chance* good would triumph.

'Miss Frost, may I have the contact telephone number for Judge Martin?'

Brunhilde scowled at him. 'What for?'

'It's a pastoral matter and therefore confidential,' Tom replied, drawing himself up to his full height. Admittedly, that didn't give him much of an advantage over her - she was a woman of truly gigantic proportions - but as it was all he'd got, it had to do. 'May I have the number, please?'

He had come prepared for a point blank refusal but, having hesitated a moment longer, to his utter amazement, she actually gave it to him. No doubt the shock of seeing him standing on his dignity had temporarily unhinged her. After all, that wasn't a sight many people had witnessed.

Having obtained the number, and praying he was doing the right thing, he rang it. He had a bit of a struggle to get past the judge's clerk (who probably did a better job than St Peter in restricting access to his boss and certainly appeared entirely convinced his was the more important of the two) but, eventually, he got to speak to the great man in person.

His next task was to persuade the judge of the urgent necessity of a face-to-face meeting, without divulging the reason for it.

'What's it about?' the judge demanded, sounding (to Tom's ears, at least) not so much concerned or even suspicious - as just plain guilty.

'I can't discuss it over the telephone, Judge.'

'This is a secure line.'

'Even so.'

There was a pause. Then the judge said, 'Four o'clock tomorrow afternoon. Don't be late,' and the line went dead.

Tom had expected the judge to come to him. But he supposed he should have realised the mountain never went to Mahomet.

By requiring Tom to attend his chambers, the judge had obtained a clear territorial advantage and Tom felt its full effect as he sat nervously waiting to be admitted into The Presence. The judge might not be shitting himself but Tom certainly was. He couldn't quite believe what he was doing. He hoped to God it was the right thing but the closer the confrontation got the more unlikely that seemed.

Just after five o'clock - presumably concluding he'd let Tom sweat long enough - the judge finally condescended to see him.

Sitting behind a desk that must have been at least an acre square, the judge didn't just look calm and composed - he looked *amused*. Suddenly, Tom was quite sure Amy's father knew precisely why he was there and, moreover, was entirely confident he hadn't a thing to fear. Tom had forgotten quite what a nauseating specimen he was but it wasn't only his uncanny resemblance to a rotting vegetable that turned the stomach.

He motioned Tom to sit and then he waited. He had no intention of making it easy for Tom to open the conversation, by asking what he wanted.

Somehow, Tom managed to get out that he'd discovered Amy had a large, painful bruise on her ribcage.

The judge raised an eyebrow, with the appearance of mild surprise. 'And how precisely, Mr Lewis, did you come to see my daughter without her shirt?'

Very clever, Tom thought. But he wasn't going to let the judge turn the tables on him quite that easily. Ignoring the question, he said, 'She claims it was an accident.'

'So, no doubt, it was. If she says so.'

'No,' Tom insisted, looking the judge hard in the eye. 'It wasn't an accident. The bruise is the perfect replica of a hand. A man's hand, judging by the size of it. I've tried but I can't imagine how a girl gets a mark like that by accident. Can you?'

The judge gazed back at him, unflinching. 'So it's your belief that someone has assaulted my daughter?'

'That much is obvious.'

'And you have a theory as to - or perhaps even *evidence* of - the culprit's identity? Perhaps Amy has confided that to you?'

Tom couldn't help feeling insulted by the ease with which the judge expected to trip him up. He might, Tom thought, have done him the courtesy of crediting him with *some* intelligence. 'According to her, there isn't a culprit. I told you, Judge, she claims it was an accident.'

'So you did,' the judge replied, with a smile. He clearly enjoyed a game of cat and mouse, so long as he believed he was playing the cat. 'So what are you expecting me to do, Mr Lewis? If Amy denies an assault took place, what *can* I do?'

'You can be vigilant. You can be on the lookout for any repetition. As I shall be.'

'Of course. Naturally, I'm grateful for your concern...'

But mind your own business, Tom silently finished for him. Not a chance, mate.

'Gratitude isn't necessary, Judge. I'm Amy's teacher. It's my *duty* to be vigilant and to report anything suspicious to social services or the police, as appropriate. And I assure you I won't hesitate to do so, should Amy be unfortunate enough to suffer another - accident.'

He gazed back at the judge and smiled, sweetly. It was a threat beneath the thinnest of veils and any genuine parent would, Tom thought, have asked him what the bloody hell he was driving at - or, more probably, have punched him on the nose. But the judge only smiled back, still more sweetly.

As he shook the judge's hand - which had all the warmth and appeal of a dead halibut - Tom didn't doubt he'd been understood. So all he could do now was hope that knowing he'd been found out - knowing that Tom knew the truth - would be enough to induce the bastard to keep his fists in his pockets. If it wasn't, if his interference had only made matters worse, Tom would simply never forgive himself. Why he wondered, not for the first time, was doing good - or at least trying to - never straightforward? Why, despite the best intentions, was it never as easy to do good as it invariably was to do evil? He wished to Christ he knew.

The judge had acceded to Tom's request to say nothing to Amy about their little chat. But watching Tom's back as he walked away, he wasn't entirely sure he meant to keep that promise. His was a confrontational nature and his instinct was to require his daughter to explain herself. Forthwith. However, on more mature reflection, he concluded it was just possible discretion would prove to be the better part of valour. In which case it might, after all, be to his decided advantage to do as Tom requested and keep his daughter in the dark.

Chapter 6

'Tom,' said Susannah. 'I'm pregnant.'

'Oh,' said Tom. 'I see.'

He wasn't entirely surprised. They'd known there was a chance she might be, Tom having withdrawn to find the mangled tatters of a condom attached to his testicles - but not to anything else.

Not surprisingly, a fair amount of consternation had followed that discovery. Getting pregnant now wasn't any part of Susannah's career plan. No doubt her plans could be changed but did they actually want children? It wasn't something they'd discussed and now the question was suddenly too loaded to be debated freely. And then there was the question of commitment. Once they had a baby - *if* they had a baby - there was no going back, no deciding they weren't right for each other after all, or fancied someone else more, or were just plain bored with each other.

So deciding what to do hadn't been easy. But Susannah had checked her dates (or whatever it was women did on these occasions) and said she was confident it would be all right. The dates were all wrong (or all right - Tom supposed it depended on your point of view) and there was very little chance and really nothing to worry about.

'Fine,' Tom had said.

'I'd rather not take the morning-after pill; it hardly seems worth it, when the risk is so slight.'

'Right,' Tom had said.

'So, that's all right with you, is it?'

'Fine,' Tom had said.

If she didn't want to take the morning-after pill, he certainly wasn't going to insist. But he'd have been lying if he'd said it didn't prey on his mind over the next couple of weeks or so. He wanted to ask her about it - he wanted to know *exactly* where she'd been in her cycle and *precisely* what the chances were - but he didn't ask, because he didn't want her to know it was bothering him.

He remembered having once seen a poster, which informed the world at large that keeping its fingers crossed wasn't a reliable method of birth control. He'd thought that was rather stating the bleeding obvious. Nonetheless, ever since the tattered-condom incident, he'd had his fingers very firmly crossed. Just in case.

And now, the suspense was over.

'So?' Susannah prompted. 'How do you feel about it?'

Inwardly, Tom groaned. Put on the spot like that, what was he supposed to say? Was he meant to apologise? Or commiserate with her? Or start turning cartwheels? He needed a clue but - as ever - he hadn't got one.

'Maybe I should have taken the morning-after pill, after all. But I checked my dates and...I really thought it would be all right.'

'Well,' he said, with a sensation rather like jumping out of an aeroplane at thirty thousand feet, with only half an idea he'd remembered his parachute, 'it *is* all right, isn't it?'

There was a pause, while she scrutinised his face - and he held his breath.

'Do you *really* think so?'

'Well, I mean...I don't know,' he said, changing his mind at the last minute and deciding it was better to fall between two stools than sit on the wrong one. He'd have given anything to say the right thing. But as he had no idea what it was, he was acutely aware the odds weren't in his favour. 'Does it really matter what I think?'

'For goodness' sake, Tom! What's that supposed to mean? You think I don't care what you think, how you feel about it?'

This time, he groaned out loud. 'Bloody hell, Susannah!' How much more of this was she going to put him through? Didn't she have any idea what this was like for him? 'For Christ's sake, what do you *want* me to say?'

'It's not a question of what I *want* you to say! I want to know how you feel! Is that *really* too much to ask?'

To be honest, Tom thought it was bordering on it.

'You want to know how I feel?'

'*Yes!*' Susannah exclaimed, looking and sounding as if it wouldn't take too much more provocation to make her wring his neck.

'Right. OK. If you really want to know, I'll tell you. Ever since you - *we* - decided to leave it to chance, I've had my fingers crossed. So bloody tight, they're just about knotted. You, me - and our baby. You want to know if that's what I want? The answer's yes. I want it more than I've ever wanted anything. But, if you don't,' he concluded, in a rush, 'well, OK. That's your right.'

There was a long pause.

He couldn't see her face - she was staring down into her lap - so he couldn't tell how she'd taken it. But did he really need to see her face? Didn't her silence say it all? She didn't want the baby but now - because she'd insisted, because she'd made him commit himself - she'd feel under pressure to keep it, because she knew he did. So now, no matter what she decided, she was always going to resent him; part of her was always going to hate him, for saying the wrong thing.

'Well, you did ask,' he said, at last.

Then, finally, she looked up at him with huge eyes and trembling lips - and he suddenly had an awful feeling he knew what was coming next.

'Oh, Tom!' she cried, throwing her arms around him and burying her face in his neck. 'I can't tell you how happy you've made me!'

Then she burst into tears. Just like he'd known she would.

Women. You make them happy, they cry. You make them sad, they cry. They were a great mystery. Tom wasn't complaining - but he would have appreciated the *occasional* clue.

Some while later, she said, 'So how come you didn't say, if that was what you wanted, all along?'

'How come you didn't?' he countered.

And, just for once, *she* was the one stuck for a reply.

They had the weekend to accustom themselves to the idea but before Tom went back to work the following Monday, knowing he'd otherwise be bound to tell Vanessa, Susannah asked him not to say anything to anyone just yet. There were, she said, so many things that could go wrong, especially in the early stages of a pregnancy.

'I know it sounds silly but I just feel it's tempting fate.'

Tom didn't believe in fate but he supposed you had to forgive a certain amount of irrationality in a woman in Susannah's condition. So, instead of scoffing at her, he grimaced and said, 'Sorry, Susannah. I've already told someone.'

'Who?'

'Amy.'

'Oh, honestly, Tom! I haven't even told Mum yet! Can't you deny that girl anything, even the intimate details of your private life? She's got you twisted round her little finger!'

Rubbish, Tom thought. 'Sorry,' he said, again.

Whilst it was the grossest of exaggerations to suggest that there was the remotest degree of intimacy between Tom and Amy's little finger, he couldn't help being concerned for her, knowing her secret as he did.

Ever since his interview with the judge (which he'd kept from Susannah, as sedulously as he'd kept it from Amy herself) he'd been watching anxiously, endeavouring to assess its results. Had he forced the judge to mend his ways? Or only goaded him on to still further excesses? Though he watched Amy's every move and weighed her every word, it was impossible to decide. So, in the end, he just had to ask.

'Things all right at home?'

Of course, she knew immediately what he meant - and was immediately suspicious. 'Why?'

'Why do you think? I'm worried about you, for Christ's sake!'

'You haven't said anything?'

'No!' he lied. 'I promised, didn't I? You can trust me.

You know that.'

'I hope I can, Tom.'

He refused to feel guilty on the basis that, if he didn't feel it, it couldn't show on his face. 'So? Are you going to tell me, or not?'

She shrugged. 'Home's fine.'

'Is that it? Don't you think I might need a bit more than that?'

She heaved an exasperated sigh. 'Why do you always need everything spelling out?'

'Because I've a very simple mind. So take pity on me and spell it out.'

'Everything's fine,' she said, again. 'He hasn't...not since the time I showed you.'

'Really?' Tom said, careful not to betray quite how relieved he felt. Even if he hadn't done any good, at least it seemed he hadn't done any harm. 'God, Amy, I'm - I'm so pleased.'

She pulled a face. 'I'm not *displeased* myself. Anyway, everything's fine. And he often goes for months without...so, there's no need to worry. OK? And I'd much rather not talk about it, if you don't mind.'

'Sure. I understand. Thanks for putting my simple mind at rest. I know I'm a pain.'

She grunted. 'You've worked that much out for yourself, then.'

A couple of days later, as if to prove the point, Amy turned up at Tom's flat wearing so little he could see for himself there wasn't a mark on her - almost anywhere.

Tom had seen bigger handkerchiefs than the skirt she was wearing. She had something which, if he hadn't known any better, he would have assumed was a *scarf* wrapped around her breasts and, to complete the effect, she was naked from that point to some distance (Tom daren't look) below her navel.

'Bloody hell, Amy!' he exclaimed. 'What have you got on?'

'Do you like it?' she asked, twirling around to give him the benefit of an eyeful from every angle.

Tom spluttered, in an attempt to say several things all at once.

She laughed. 'I'll take that as a "yes".'

'You can't -! Bloody hell!' he exclaimed, again. 'Have you been *out*, dressed like that?'

'Jesus, Tom! You sound just like my dad.'

Tom didn't need to be told there was nothing worse in Amy's book, unless, possibly, it was *being* her dad. For which, in all honesty, he couldn't blame her.

'I don't care. I'm not teaching you dressed like that.'

'I wouldn't dream of asking you to. You'd look ridiculous.'

'Very funny. I'm serious, Amy. You can't walk round dressed like that.'

'Why not?'

Put on the spot, he found it hard to say. 'Well, because…it's immodest.'

'You think modesty's a virtue?'

'How should I know? But I *do* know what every red-blooded male who claps eyes on you is thinking.'

She grinned. 'So what? What's wrong with being noticed?'

He didn't find that such an easy question to answer, either. 'Nothing,' he conceded, reluctantly. 'But you're young, you're clever and you're beautiful. Believe me, Amy, you don't need to walk round, wearing a sign saying, "Fuck me," to get yourself noticed.'

'Did you just say, "Fuck me"?'

'Yes. Sorry. It just sort of slipped out.'

She shook her head at him. 'Honestly, Tom, you're hopeless! But, all right. If you really find me that distracting, you'd better give me something to put on.'

When Susannah walked in, an hour later, she was more than a little taken aback to find Amy wearing one of Tom's shirts and, apparently, nothing else.

All in all, it was quite a cosy little scene. The two of them were sitting side by side on the sofa. Amy had one leg curled under her; she was leaning eagerly towards Tom and he was smiling back at her, with all the appearance of thoroughly enjoying himself. They were so engrossed in each other that, for a minute, they didn't even notice her.

'Sorry to interrupt,' she said, with just the slightest edge to her voice.

Tom almost started. 'Hello! You're early.'

Unruffled, Amy got to her feet with an easy, feline grace. 'I'd better be off,' she said.

Susannah, for one, wasn't arguing.

As soon as he'd seen Amy out, Tom came up behind Susannah - who, for some reason, had turned her back on him - and kissed her on the neck. 'You smell wonderful,' he told her, turning her to face him. 'And you taste even better.'

She pushed him off - not angrily, but with more determination than Tom would have liked. Just then, he had only one thing on his mind and he was feeling particularly keen to share it.

'Why was Amy wearing one of your shirts?'

'I'll tell you later.'

'No, Tom. Tell me now.'

He sighed. He was in urgent need of something - and it certainly wasn't a discussion about Amy's wardrobe - but he could see he wasn't going to get it, until he'd told her.

When he had, she said, 'I see.'

Knowing that expression of old, Tom suppressed a groan. 'What's the matter? What have I done?'

'Nothing. It's just a shame that girl hasn't got a mother to keep an eye on her, that's all.'

'Of course it is! But I don't see -'

'No, Tom. You don't see a lot of things.'

'Such as what?' he asked, surprised by the sharpness of her tone.

'For instance, that she always leaves the moment I arrive.'

'Well she would, wouldn't she? She thinks she's in the

way, when you're around. And she's right.'

'Unless, of course, she thinks *I'm* in the way.'

'What on earth are you talking about, Susannah?'

She sighed, as if he was the stupidest person she'd met in a long time, then said, 'Tom, didn't it *ever* occur to you she might be getting fond of you? In the wrong way.'

He followed a blank stare with a sudden snort of incredulity. 'You think she *fancies* me?'

'Why not? Young girls often get crushes on older men.'

'Yeah, right! Not in real life, Susannah. Not on me, at any rate. For Christ's sake, I'm very nearly old enough to be her grandfather.' Maths had never been Tom's forte but, even so, he thought he'd made his point.

'So what? That doesn't mean -'

'Look,' he interrupted, thinking he'd known pregnancy made some women irrational but not *delusional*, 'if you're really worried - if you're convinced I won't be safe otherwise - I'll wear a chastity belt. They make them for men, don't they?'

'Don't be ridiculous!'

'It's not ridiculous,' he insisted, braving her stony expression and slipping his arms around her waist. 'I rather like the idea of your keeping the key to the lion's den. In fact,' he said, guiding her hand down to his groin, just to prove the point, 'it gives me a hard-on just thinking about it.'

'I'm serious, Tom,' she said, pulling her hand away. 'I want you to stop seeing her. Outside school, I mean.'

'Fine.'

'I mean it, Tom. I want you to promise me.'

'OK, OK. Whatever you say, Susannah. Now, for Christ's sake, stop tormenting me and come to bed.'

Tom meant to keep his promise. But as he obviously couldn't just march up to Amy and tell her never to darken his door again, he guessed what Susannah had really meant was she wanted him to cool it, to keep his distance a bit more. And he could do that. No problem. At least, so he thought. Until he saw Amy with Brad.

Brad wasn't Tom's favourite person. In fact - much to Van's amusement - Tom hated just about everything about him. *She* thought (but then she would, it being well known that all psychologists are mad) that he was jealous. But jealous of what, Tom wanted to know? Of the fact that Brad was a first-rate, five-star, gold-plated plonker, the sort of total, unmitigated arsehole that ought to have been enough to give every man on the planet a bad name? Except that, apparently, there wasn't a woman alive (even a *gay* one) who was capable of seeing it. All right, so he was good looking (gorgeous wasn't a word Tom could bring himself to apply to another man, no matter how many times everyone else lauded Brad with that epithet); admired by his own sex (Tom excepted) and lusted after by the other; academically gifted; good at football, rugby, cricket and every other sport the school had to offer and quite a few it didn't. So what? Tom still had not the slightest urge to throw himself, in homage, at Brad's feet. Kicking the little shit's feet from under him would have been a different matter. But regrettably, teachers weren't allowed to do that to pupils. Not any more. Not since the good old days, when Tom might have relieved his feelings - and done the boy no end of good - by the repeated application of a nice, sturdy cane to little bastard's backside. And thoroughly deserved it would have been, too.

So, anyone who supposed that Tom took a dislike to Brad merely because he discovered that Amy had failed to break with tradition - and, like countless others before her, had succumbed to the boy's decidedly dubious charms - would have been very wide of the mark. His dislike had been quite healthy enough already and hadn't needed that additional (or, indeed, *any*) boost to keep it in the pink.

When he first saw them together, it was little short of a shock. They were standing together outside the school gates. Snogging.

Tom didn't properly realise, until afterwards, that the sight had stopped him dead in his tracks. He should have played it cool, of course. He should have pretended he hadn't noticed or didn't care. But, instead, he'd stood there glaring at the two of them - and at *Brad*, in particular - as if he'd never been confronted with a more offensive object, in his whole life before.

When Brad finally came up for air, his eyes met Tom's and Tom could have sworn the cocky little bastard actually *smiled*. Then, as he'd stood there transfixed, Brad had placed his hand possessively and provocatively on Amy's backside and, all the while, he'd been gazing into Tom's eyes with a leering, *triumphant* look - as if he thought he'd got something Tom wanted.

At the time, Brad's look had fairly made Tom seethe and it haunted him for a long while afterwards, though he was never quite sure why. The sight of a couple of randy teenagers getting it on, to one degree or another, wasn't exactly uncommon in a school that was stuffed to the rafters with them. But for some reason, he couldn't get that particular image - that picture of Amy and Brad - out of his mind.

What did it matter to him what Amy did? He wasn't her father; it was none of his business. He told himself so, over and over again, but what he'd seen still hurt. Maybe it was because Amy hadn't told him and he'd thought she told him everything - he remembered Susannah had laughed at him for that. Then again, maybe it was simpler than that; maybe it was just that Brad was such a fucking pillock.

Usually when something was bothering him, he'd tell Susannah. But this time he didn't. He was too certain of being laughed at, or scolded for being unreasonable - or both. But even though he couldn't tell Susannah, there was one consolation; he was right and she wrong. Amy didn't have the hots for him; she had them for Brad. At least, he supposed that *ought* to be considered a consolation. Of sorts.

Having failed to get the better of his feelings and reason himself into indifference, he made a point of tackling Amy, the next time they were alone together at his flat.

'I saw you outside the school gates, the other day,' he said. 'With Brad. He had his hand on your -' He stopped, suddenly realising he couldn't (or, at least, shouldn't) say "arse". At least, not to Amy. So he gestured towards the body part in question.

As he might have predicted, she laughed. 'So? What's the matter? Not jealous, are you?'

'No! Don't be stupid! I'm just...concerned, that's all.'

'About what?'

She'd always had the knack of asking awkward questions, which was all the more irritating since that was supposed to be *his* job. 'The way you've begun dressing, for a start,' he said, averting his eyes from the expanse of naked flesh, which she was currently displaying. 'I suppose that's his idea, is it?'

She shrugged. 'He doesn't exactly object. But I make my own decisions, Tom. I'm not his puppet. Or yours.'

For some reason that really stung, maybe because he didn't like - because he hotly resented - being compared to Brad, or maybe because what she said was true and a part of him did see her like that. His to mould.

'What's up, now?' she asked, watching his face. 'You look - what's the word? Peeved.'

'Of course I'm not peeved! What have I got to be peeved about? It's just...'

'Just what?'

'Well,' he said, struggling to do what he'd been unable to do all week and put his concerns into words. 'I suppose what I really want to know is - is he responsible.'

'What do you mean "responsible"? I'm not thinking of *marrying* him.'

'God damn it, Amy, give me a break! You know perfectly well what I mean. Do you think this is easy for me?'

'I'm sure it's not,' she replied, laughing.

'Then don't be such a - tease,' he said, only at the last moment finding an acceptable substitute for the word that had been begging to complete that sentence. 'I'm worried about you.'

'All right. Look, I don't know if Brad's responsible, OK? But you don't have to worry, because I am. I've been on the pill for *ages*.'

He stared back at her and felt his jaw drop - about six inches. She was *fifteen* and she'd been on the pill for *ages*! What did that mean, for Christ's sake? How long was "ages", when you were fifteen? Was it weeks, or months, or years? He'd heard about ten year olds being on the pill but he'd never believed it. Until now. Now, all of a sudden, it seemed entirely possible - and he felt inordinately old, as if the world had passed him by, leaving him a country mile in its wake, and somehow he'd only just noticed.

'You know,' she said, spelling it out for him. 'The *contraceptive* pill.'

'Yes, I do know what it is, Amy. I have heard of it. I'm not completely -' He was going to say "past it" but thought better of it. She'd only give herself a fit, laughing. 'But that's only part of it, isn't it? I mean, what about...' What did they call it these days? Somehow, "the clap" didn't seem to strike the right note. 'What about STIs?' Christ only knew where Brad had been; Tom didn't even want to think about it. 'You should be using a -'

'I'm not using a *rubber*!' she broke in, with a grimace of disgust. 'They're *gross*!'

'Not as gross as a dose of the clap!' Tom exclaimed, forgetting all about the need to strike the right note.

She blushed and he cursed himself for losing his cool. What was the matter with him? He wasn't going to achieve anything by shouting at her; she got enough of that at home. She didn't need him to bully her, as well as her father.

'Sorry,' he said. 'I didn't mean to shout.'

There was an awkward pause.

Then, sounding close to tears, she said, 'I wish I hadn't told you. I wouldn't have, if I'd known you'd be like this.'

She looked and sounded so childlike - so utterly vulnerable - it seemed nothing short of surreal to Tom that they were in the middle of a row about her sex life.

'Promise you won't tell the judge,' she said, fixing him with a petulant, resentful stare.

'Of course I won't,' he replied softly, coaxingly,

wanting to show her he was contrite. 'You can trust me. You know that, don't you?'

'I suppose so,' she admitted, sullenly. 'Anyway, I've got to go.'

She got up and began throwing her books into her bag. They still had work to do and there was more Tom wanted to say but he didn't dare try and stop her. He just stood there and watched her, wishing to God he didn't feel quite so hopelessly out of his depth. What did he know about girls her age? What did he know about *anything* come to that? It was none of his business. He should just keep out of it. But he couldn't.

'Wait a minute,' he said, as she was almost out of the door.

She stopped and turned back to him. She was still sulking but she wouldn't openly defy him. If he said wait, she waited.

He went into the bedroom and came back, with a packet of condoms. 'Please,' he said, holding them out to her. 'I know it's not cool. I know you think it's *gross*. But...please. For me.'

She hesitated, reluctant to forgive him, to give in and give him what he wanted.

'Please,' he said again, wondering quite how he'd ended up begging a fifteen-year-old girl to take a supply of condoms from him.

With a sigh, meant to let him know he was one monumental pain in the arse, she half-took, half-snatched the packet from him and stuffed it into her bag.

He couldn't do any more.

'And tell Brad, if he hurts you, I'll string him up by the balls.'

Looking up at him then, she was suddenly all smiles again. 'Sure, I'll tell him. But you'll have to beat me to it.'

Now Susannah's pregnancy had been announced and they were going to be a proper family, Tom had finally moved in with her. For months, he'd been spending almost all his time at her place but, nominally at least, he'd still been living at his flat. It would probably have made better sense to sell it but, for some reason, he didn't. Maybe a part of him still didn't believe his luck. Or maybe it was just that he needed somewhere to meet Amy - though, true to his word, he'd been seeing much less of her lately. If he was honest, Tom knew that was more Amy's doing than his own; she had a lot less time for him, now Brad was on the scene. But he didn't suppose it mattered too much how (or why) a promise was kept. So long as it was.

It felt strange, officially abandoning his life as a single man, but he couldn't have been happier and - which was even better and infinitely rarer - he knew it. He thanked his lucky stars, blessed his great and totally-undeserved good fortune. A year ago, he would never have believed that anything so wonderful - so very nearly *miraculous* - could have happened to him. His life had been transformed - almost beyond recognition - and now, as if both to confirm and complete that transformation, the woman he loved was going to have their child. Presented with such a gift from the gods, how could he fail to be over the moon? How could he fail to be the happiest man alive?

When he received Susannah's message asking him to come to the hospital straight from work, he was surprised but not in the least alarmed.

When he arrived, the sister asked him if he'd just step into Robin Graham's office for a moment, as he wanted a word. And somehow, Tom still managed to suspect nothing.

Robin was at his desk when Tom walked in and he looked exactly like Tom felt, after a really punishing night out.

'What's up?' he asked, grinning. 'You look like the cat just died.'

'Sit down, Tom,' Robin said, without so much as the hint of a smile. 'I've got something to tell you.'

Tom sat, abruptly. All of a sudden, he didn't feel like grinning any more. All of a sudden, he put two and two together. And he didn't like what it amounted to, one bit.

'It's Susannah, isn't it?'

Robin nodded. 'I'm afraid so. We did a scan earlier today. It was - should have been - routine. But, unfortunately, we found certain...abnormalities.'

'Abnormalities? You mean the baby's deformed, in some way?'

'No. It's not the baby. It's Susannah. I'm afraid we've found a tumour.'

For one awful moment, Tom really thought he was going to wet himself.

'You mean, *cancer*?'

Robin nodded again. He was so calm, not unfeeling, or uncaring but - *detached*. How did he manage that? Tom couldn't have done it, even if they hadn't been discussing Susannah.

'The lump looked very suspicious on the scan and the biopsy confirmed it's malignant.'

'You've done a biopsy? Already?'

'We thought it best to get on with it. I wanted to let you know but Susannah wouldn't let me. She said there was no point in worrying you. Unless we had to.'

There was a long pause. Tom's mind was blank. He couldn't think what to say or do. He sensed there was more Robin had to tell him. He didn't know what it was but he knew for certain he didn't want to hear it.

'I'm sorry,' Robin said.

'So -?' Tom asked, finally galvanised into speech, but not quite certain what it was he was asking.

It didn't matter. Robin knew his cue. He'd had this conversation, or something very like it, too many times before. So he told Tom some technical stuff - about the type of tumour, its location and predicted growth rate - and some other stuff, about the various treatment options and the impact of each of these on Susannah and the baby.

Tom listened. He heard and he understood. But somehow, he couldn't take it in - couldn't quite believe that any of this was really happening.

'So,' Robin concluded, 'the bottom line is, if we treat the cancer now, Susannah's likely to survive but the baby almost certainly won't. The treatment will be too much for it. On the other hand, if we delay, the baby will almost certainly survive but Susannah won't. By the time the baby's delivered, the cancer will have progressed too far.'

There was another long pause.

'Do you understand, Tom?' Robin asked, at last.

Tom nodded, cleared his throat and said, 'Yes, I understand. You're telling me we're going to lose the baby.'

Robin grimaced and shifted uncomfortably in his chair.

Tom frowned. 'What? There's something else? Something you haven't told me?'

'It isn't for me to say, Tom. You need to discuss it with Susannah.'

'Don't fob me off! Tell me! What? What is it?'

Robin sighed. He wasn't sure Tom was ready for this but he sensed a refusal to tell him would only agitate him further. And anyway, he had to find out sooner or later. 'Like I said, you need to talk to Susannah - and, of course, she might change her mind - but, at the moment, she's refusing treatment.'

'*Refusing -?*'

'We've had quite a long talk about it, as you might imagine. But she's adamant she doesn't want any intervention, until after the baby's born.'

'But she can't. That's crazy! You just said, she'll die if -'

'Yes. Quite. But Susannah understands that, Tom. And she's adamant. And at the end of the day - no matter what you and I might think - it has to be her decision, doesn't it?'

Tom went to her, on the ward. Robin had told him she'd be kept in overnight, following the biopsy, just to be "on the safe side". Safe, Tom had thought. As if there was any such thing.

He had no idea what he was going to say. He felt so sorry for her, not because she was going to die - she wasn't, he wasn't going to let that happen - but because, when she came to her senses and accepted the treatment she needed, she *was* going to lose the baby. And he knew how that was going to make her feel, because he felt like that already.

'I'm so sorry,' he said, taking her hand. It was such a lame thing to say but what else was there?

'I know. But don't worry, Tom. I know this is scary - for both of us - but I've got a feeling it's going to be all right, in the end.'

Even as she spoke, Tom could hear Vanessa saying psychologists have a word for that irrationally-optimistic outlook. The word was denial, or perhaps it was insanity - Tom wasn't sure. He'd never really been able to see the difference, no matter how many times Van had explained it.

'I hope you're right,' he said, 'because, I don't know about you, but I'm scared witless. If anything happens to you -'

'It won't,' she interrupted firmly, squeezing his hand. 'I know it's hard, Tom, but we just have to keep our nerve. Have faith. It'll work out. You'll see.'

Tom did his best to force a smile but it wasn't a success. It seemed his face was on strike - although, admittedly, he could have burst into tears easily enough.

When he left her, Tom went straight to Vanessa's. It was Ellen's birthday and they were just finishing a romantic dinner for two. Somehow, Tom failed to spot the candles, the soft music or the remains of an elaborate meal. The fact was, he was so preoccupied with his own feelings, if they'd been making out on the living-room carpet, he wouldn't have noticed.

When he told Vanessa, he was almost relieved to see her turn white. At least she wasn't going to tell him everything would be all right, when he knew - with the certainty traditionally reserved for death and taxation - that it wouldn't.

'How long does it last?'

'How long does what last?' Vanessa asked, nonplussed.

'This insane phase. Denial, or whatever you people call it. How long till she sees sense and agrees to the treatment?'

Van grimaced. 'I'm not sure you're right to

characterise Susannah's decision as *denial*, Tom. She is a doctor, after all. I'm sure she understands the - potential - consequences of her decision.'

'Of course she doesn't understand! If she did, she'd be making a different choice, wouldn't she?'

'I suppose so,' Vanessa conceded, sensing now wasn't the right time to debate that point.

There was a pause. Then, suddenly sinking his head in his hands, Tom said, 'You know, I don't fucking believe it. I mean, I - really - just - don't - believe it. For a quarter of a century, I drink too much, I smoke, I treat my body like a sewer. And *she* gets cancer. I mean, for fuck's sake, Vanessa, where's the sense in that?'

As Robin had anticipated, Susannah was sufficiently recovered to be allowed home, the next day. For the rest of that day and the two or three that followed, Tom waited - with an impatience he could scarcely contain - for her to come to her senses. But she didn't. When she told her mother everything (because, as she said, there was no point in hiding it) and despite all Marion's tears and protestations *still* held firm, Tom could bear it and keep silent no longer. He wanted their baby but he wanted Susannah more and he begged her - as he'd never begged anyone for anything in his life before - to have the termination that would save her.

'You can't want this baby more than I do, Susannah. You can't. I'd give anything for it. Except you.'

She looked back at him then, as if she was disappointed in him, as if she'd expected better than that. 'You forget, I've already had one termination. I can't go through that again, Tom.'

'I haven't forgotten,' he assured her, gently. 'But this is different. You *have* to do it, this time.'

'No. I can't. And I won't.'

He knew that tone and that look and he felt sick with desperation. But he wouldn't give in to it. Not yet.

'Even if it means you'll die, otherwise?'

'Even so.'

'This is because you think you'll be killing our child - and you believe that's a sin. But if you don't kill it, it - or at any rate the untreated disease - will kill you. This is self-defence, Susannah. It's you - or it. And you're more important.'

Under pressure from both Tom and Robin, Susannah had reluctantly agreed to have her labour induced at 34 weeks - if the baby hadn't come earlier - and to undergo treatment for her cancer at that stage. But as Robin had been at pains to point out, all the indications were that would be too late. Delay was a death sentence for Susannah; action was a death sentence for their baby. If they couldn't both live, whose right to life was greater?

If that had been put to him as a hypothetical question, Tom might have hemmed and hawed and doubted. Faced with it as a practical, real-life question, he hadn't the smallest doubt he knew the answer. So, why couldn't Susannah see it?

'*You're* more important,' he told her, again.

'How can you say that? Who are you to decide?'

'So you want to leave the decision to chance, or fate - or *God*?'

He expected her to scoff at that but, instead, she looked down and away and was silent.

'For fuck's sake, Susannah!' he exclaimed, incredulous. 'You can't mean that! You can't mean to abdicate responsibility for yourself and your actions, just like that. If you're going to let God decide this, why not everything else as well? And where would freewill, where would self-determination be, then? Think about it; if you're going to let God decide everything, *you're* out of a job for a start. There'll be no more CPR, no more transplants, no more *aspirin*, if God-All-Fucking-Mighty's the only one allowed a say.'

'Don't be so fatuous, Tom! CPR - even a transplant - doesn't involve deliberately taking the life of another human being. This does.'

'But even if I admit the argument that there are two lives - which, incidentally, I don't - there's a huge difference *between* those lives, Susannah. You must see that. On the one hand, there's you. On the other, there's a clump of cells, without sentience, without consciousness, without personality. Right now, the life you're allowing to outweigh your own is about as complex - and about as *meaningful* - as a gnat's!'

She opened her mouth to argue but he knew what was coming and hadn't the patience to listen.

'Oh, don't try the "potential" argument - don't tell me the embryo has the *potential* to be a human being, so that killing it is no different to murder - or I'm going to puke. A single one of my ejaculations has the *potential* to repopulate the entire globe. If we're going to allow that argument, I hate to think how many millions of *potential* human lives I've mopped up with a tissue and flushed down the lavatory. Trust me, you couldn't even hope to come close to me, in the all-time league of mass murderers, if you started now and made a career of it!'

Because he'd rehearsed them any number of times over the years, Tom knew the arguments to be made for and against most issues of any importance; that was what philosophy was all about, after all. But as Susannah had frequently told him before today, just because he knew all there was to be said - just because he could invariably win the argument - that didn't necessarily make him right.

'You still don't understand, Tom. Whatever you say, there'll always be one objection you can't overcome. The treatment will make me infertile. This is my - our - one and only chance to have a child. Ever.'

He knew that - Robin had made that abundantly clear to both of them - and, of course, it hurt. But for Tom there was no price too high - nothing he wouldn't give - to save Susannah.

'OK. That's tough. I agree, that's tough. But what's the good of a child you'll never know, Susannah? One you'll never see grow up?'

'The child will have its own life. And it'll have you. You'll have each other.'

'But I don't want *it*,' he told her, desperately. 'I want

you.'

'Don't you see that's what we're really arguing about, Tom? We're both making a choice, aren't we? But a different one. I choose our child. You choose me. But we can't both have what we want. One of us has to be strong enough to sacrifice their own choice, for the sake of the other.'

'You mean *I* do. *I* have to make the sacrifice - even though you'll be the one who dies.'

'Yes, I suppose that is what I mean, Tom. Logically, it has to be you because I might do what you want - I might sacrifice our child - and die anyway. And I don't want to leave you with nothing.'

'You might die. But you might live. I'm asking you to take that chance.'

'No.'

'Because you care more about this unborn child - this anonymous, unconscious, unfeeling clump of cells - than you do about me.'

'That's not true, Tom!' she exclaimed and - overwrought, pushed too far - at last, she began to cry.

'Oh, that's right, cry!' he told her, goaded beyond the point of endurance himself. 'After all, why use logic, when you can use emotion to get what you want? To hell with you, Susannah! I don't care what you do. If you want to commit suicide, for the sake of some crazy, half-arsed principle, go right ahead. Be my guest. Who the hell am I to stop you?'

And with that, he stormed out, slamming the door behind him.

About 2.30 the following morning, Vanessa was woken by an almighty banging at the front door. She opened it to find Tom standing in the porch and staggering like a giraffe on a jelly.

'Tom! Where the hell have you been?'

'Drunk,' he announced, somehow imagining it possible she might not have realised that already. 'Left Susannah. Doesn't care about me. Doesn't give a fuck about anything. Except the bloody *baby*.' He paused, gesticulating wildly with his left arm, as if suddenly possessed by an overwhelming desire to demonstrate the operation of a windmill. 'Bastard!' he exclaimed.

'Quite,' Vanessa agreed, taking this to be a comment on the world at large - life, the universe and everything. 'You'd better come in and sit down, Tom. Before you fall down.'

She grabbed him by the lapels and hauled him inside. He lurched past her and - forgetting her existence entirely, the moment she was behind him and therefore out of sight - reeled off, in the direction of the living room.

'Ellen!' Van yelled up the stairs. 'It's that idiot, Tom. Can you phone Susannah and tell her we've found him? Apart from being unspeakably paralytic, there doesn't appear to be too much wrong with -'

She broke off, interrupted by a hideous, deafening crash - something like the sound of a giant redwood being felled. It was followed by a really quite unnerving silence.

'What the bloody hell,' Ellen demanded, appearing, white-faced, at the top of the stairs, 'was that?'

With no little trepidation, Vanessa went to investigate.

'It's all right,' she called back, from the sitting room. 'It's only Tom. He's just demolished the coffee table and passed out on the floor. Can you give me a hand to get him onto the sofa? And fetch a couple of blankets down, will you?'

When he eventually came to, much later that morning, Tom's first coherent thought was that he wished he was dead. He wasn't waking out of a nightmare, but into one.

Gingerly, he opened one eye, just a fraction. The room was in semi-darkness; the curtains were still drawn - thank God. He opened the other eye, cautiously, and discovered Vanessa sitting opposite, watching him, her ankles crossed on what was left of the coffee table.

He closed his eyes again. Slowly and carefully moistening his mouth with his tongue, so as to be able to speak, he said, 'What time is it?'

'Ten-ish.'

There was a pause. Then he said, 'What day is it?'

'Thursday.'

Another pause. Then, 'Aren't we usually at work on Thursdays. At ten-ish?'

'Usually. But not today.'

'How come?'

'We've got food poisoning.'

Recklessly, he opened both eyes at once and frowned. 'Both of us?' he queried, thinking Genghis was never going to buy that one.

'We were at the same barbeque. A mutual friend's.'

'Wrong time of year for a barbeque,' Tom observed.

'So? We have unconventional friends.'

Tom grunted.

Very slowly and carefully, he eased himself into a sitting position. An industrial hammer was at work inside his head and, if he didn't employ all his powers of concentration, he had the distinct feeling he was going to lose the breakfast he hadn't eaten.

Vanessa rose with a sigh and brought him water and painkillers. And then, after a decent interval, dry toast and coffee. And after a while, he stopped feeling like he'd died and was just left wishing he had.

'I suppose I did that,' he said, having spent some time studying the remains of the coffee table - and having finally come down against its being a work of modern art.

'Who else?'

'Sorry.'

Vanessa shrugged. 'It's all right. I never liked it anyway.'

'I ought to go,' he said, not moving.

'Not yet. Susannah's got more than enough to put up with at the moment, without you. I told her I'd hang on to you, until you were fit to be seen.'

'And I told you,' he replied, with the oddly-selective memory of the spectacularly drunk, 'I've left her.'

'Don't be bloody stupid, Tom. You can't.'

'Why?'

'You know why. Because she's - because she might be dying. And she needs you.'

'What about what I need?'

'And what's that, apart from a bloody good kick up the arse?'

'Very funny.'

'I'm serious, Tom. *This* is serious. You've got to stop behaving like such a selfish prick and start thinking about Susannah.'

'Selfish! How am I selfish? All I want is for Susannah to live. If that's selfish then, OK - you've got me bang to rights - I'm the most selfish man alive.'

There was a pause. Then Vanessa said, 'Have you asked yourself why you want her to live?'

Tom stared at her, not quite believing his ears. 'Have you *completely* lost your mind? Why do you think?'

'Maybe because that way, there's less pain for you. But what if, your way, there's more pain for Susannah?'

'Don't be stupid! Her way's crazy,' Tom objected, fiercely. 'If she gets her way, she'll *die*.'

'In your terms, maybe that *is* crazy - but not in Susannah's. She wants the baby to live, more than she wants to live herself. That's her choice. You're two different people, Tom, with different ways of looking at things. It's tyranny for you to decide that you're right and she's wrong, about a question that has no "right" answer. You would say - God knows, I've heard you on the subject often enough - it's in the choices we make in the grey area, between what's clearly right and what's clearly wrong, that we define who we are. Well, you have to let Susannah do that now. Don't you?'

When Tom finally got home, he found Marion there. He'd known she was expected but somehow, in amongst everything else, that fact had got lost. He guessed she'd be pretty pissed off with him - for storming out and getting so paralytic it had taken him more than half a day to sober up again - but he ought to have realised she had other things on her mind.

As soon as she saw him, her eyes filled with tears - not

that, judging by her face, she'd done anything other than cry for some time. Days, probably. At the sight of her grief, which seemed so exactly to mirror his own, Tom felt a lump appear in his own throat.

'Marion...' he began, without much idea what he was going to say next. But if he could have seen his face through her eyes, he'd have realised he didn't need to say anything.

'Oh, Tom!' she wailed, rushing towards him.

A moment later, Tom found they were hugging each other for all they were worth. And of course, by now, he was crying too.

'Can't you make her change her mind? Surely, she'll listen to you. Surely, you can make her see what she's doing just isn't *fair*.'

Tom sighed. 'Believe me, Marion, I've tried. But it's hopeless. Her mind's made up.'

'I don't understand it. I'd never have believed my own daughter could be so *selfish*.'

'It's hardly that,' Tom said gently, though he'd thought much the same thing himself many times. 'She has her reasons, Marion.'

'You mean she won't have a termination now because she's had one already - and she can't bring herself to have another?'

'She told you?' Tom asked, surprised. But in the same moment, he realised that, of course, she would have done. How else could she explain her - inexplicable - decision to Marion? Not that, even then, Marion was alone in failing to understand it.

'Why didn't she tell me, before?' Marion asked, her eyes filling with tears all over again. 'Am I really such a terrible mother? How could she think I wouldn't understand, that I wouldn't forgive her?'

'At least she knows now,' Tom said, as he put his arms around her. 'And that's worth something, isn't it?'

'I suppose so,' she conceded, sniffing and wiping her eyes. 'But I wish she'd told me before. When I think of all the time and emotion I've wasted on that worthless bastard, Clive, I want to scream!'

And when she said that, despite everything, Tom very nearly laughed.

Of course, he couldn't persuade Marion that Susannah was doing the right thing, any more than he could persuade himself of it. But he did make her see - as Vanessa had made him see - that, heartbreakingly painful though it was, they had to let Susannah decide. Marion didn't like it, any more than Tom did. But in the end, she had to agree, because (just like Tom) she loved Susannah and so (just like Tom) she had no choice.

So, when Susannah came home - Tom could hardly believe she'd gone back to work but he supposed he oughtn't to have been surprised, given the stubbornness of the beast - he followed her into the bedroom. He had something he needed to say to her.

'You look lousy,' she told him, as he sat down next to her on the bed. 'And I thought I was the one who's supposed to be dying.'

'Don't joke,' he pleaded, pained. 'It's not funny.'

'Sorry,' she said, taking hold of his hand. 'This is awfully rough on you, I know.'

'And it isn't on you? Like you just said, you're the one who's dying.'

'Yes, but I didn't mean that. I mean, of course dying's rough - it's not exactly top of my wish list right now - but I meant my refusing treatment. I know it isn't what you want.'

'No,' Tom agreed. 'It isn't what I want. But if it's what you want - if you're *really* sure - I won't argue any more.'

She looked back at him, incredulous. 'Really?'

He nodded. 'If that's your choice, I'll just have to accept it. And learn to - live - with it.'

'Oh, Tom,' she said, her eyes filling with tears in an odd mixture of gratitude, relief and compassion for his pain. 'I know how hard this is for you. Th -'

He put a finger on her lips to silence her.

'Don't thank me,' he said. 'Please don't. I don't think I could stand it. It's your decision and I respect it, because I don't have any other choice. But let's just leave it at that. OK?'

'OK,' she agreed softly, taking his beloved face in her hands and tenderly kissing it. 'Whatever you say, Tom.'

Chapter 7

Though Tom would never have believed it, somehow, it was possible to carry on *almost* as if nothing was wrong.

The routine of their lives continued, just as before. They worked, they ate, they slept, just like everyone else - and though their situation was always on Tom's mind, it wasn't always at the forefront of it. Sometimes, for whole, indescribably-precious moments together, he was *almost* able to forget.

Then, suddenly, without warning, he would look at Susannah and think: soon she'll be gone, I must remember this moment - that look, that smile, that laugh, that touch; I want to remember her *always*, just as she is now. And he would strive to print that moment on his memory, indelibly. But it would inevitably slip away from him, just as he had known it would, like mist through his fingers.

Then he would ask himself again, for the thousandth time, how this nightmare was possible. How could such a thing happen to *her*? If he'd believed in God, he might have taken comfort, some solace at least, from blaming Him. But Tom knew Susannah's illness wasn't an act of God; it wasn't divine retribution for some sin, some unspecified wrongdoing; it was just a random, meaningless consequence of the chaos by which we're engulfed in a godless universe. And knowing that - knowing that our lives are devoid of purpose or meaning - inevitably left Tom wondering quite how we can bear to live them.

Of course, he put a falsely brave face on things for Susannah (as he had no doubt she did for him) and because of that there were certain things they couldn't discuss, certain things that were simply never mentioned between them. They never spoke of the time that would come after the birth, of the remoteness of Susannah's chances of survival, or of the time when Tom would find himself alone - or, at best, alone with their child.

He thought of those things, as he was sure she did, but

they belonged to an unimaginable, an unthinkable future and by mutual (if unspoken) consent they strove to confine themselves to the moment, to live in the finite, ever-decreasing interval between the present and what was to come.

Perhaps for that reason - because here and now had to be enough, because there simply *was* no more - Susannah had refused to allow the progression of her disease to be monitored. What was the point, she asked, when there was nothing to be done about it?

No doubt (only a fool would have doubted it, for only fools believe in miracles) the cancer was progressing, unseen. Tom knew that. But looking at her, it was sometimes difficult - if not quite impossible - to believe it. She looked so well, never better in fact; she was never sick and hardly ever even tired. It was a cliché but she was simply - blooming. She was almost embarrassed by the apparent rudeness of her health, so much so that she joked (though not a second time, in Tom's hearing) that dying obviously suited her.

So the days passed and the days turned into weeks and the weeks into months and Tom watched as Susannah's belly grew and felt - quite absurdly proud. It stirred him indescribably to feel their baby kicking inside her. For some reason, too, it made him unexpectedly and quite astonishingly randy. He couldn't leave her alone and, thankfully, she didn't seem to want him to. Something about the fullness of her belly - its flagrant, shameless fecundity - drove him to distraction. The bigger she got, the more urgently he wanted her. It was almost, he thought, as if he were trying to devour her, to sate himself with her. Now. Before it was too late.

'Tom!' Susannah said, gently prodding him.

It was the middle of the night and, still half asleep, he turned over and put an arm around her, thinking there was insatiable - and then there was Susannah. God bless her.

'No, Tom, not *that*! It's the baby.'

Suddenly, he was wide awake. 'Are you sure?'

'Positive.'

'Jesus!' he said, thinking - Christ, what do I do now? It

was a whole week before her labour was to have been induced. Even so, he was supposed to be organised, prepared, have all this rehearsed, planned down to the finest detail - and, right now, he couldn't even think of his own name.

'Don't do that whole panic thing, Tom,' she said, just as he was about to launch into it.

'Right,' he said, pulling himself up so sharply he gave himself a whiplash. 'What should I do, then?'

'There's no rush to get to the hospital, just yet. So, I'm going to take a shower. Would you make me some tea?'

'Of course,' he said, leaping out of bed as if the house was on fire. Tea. That was easy. He could do that.

He paced up and down the kitchen like a caged animal, waiting for the kettle to boil. What the fuck was the matter with it? It wasn't normally *this* slow, surely. He switched it off and on again and shook it and unplugged and plugged it in again. But all to no avail. It continued to perform with all the urgency of a geriatric snail. And all the while, his mind was a kind of maelstrom, in which thoughts came and went with such rapidity they could scarcely be grasped before they were swept away again.

Her labour had come early. Was that good? Or bad? It meant the treatment for her cancer could be started sooner, which was good. But would a week make any appreciable difference to its outcome? And mightn't a week be enough to make all the difference - mightn't it even be *crucial* - to the baby? So, should he be glad, or not? Was it for the best or the worst thing that could possibly have happened?

Long before he'd even begun to get a handle on these and a hundred other questions, the kettle (slow though it was) had boiled and the tea was made.

When he took it upstairs, she was sitting on the edge of the bed with her back to him, so he didn't realise anything was wrong, at first. Not until he saw her face.

'Jesus, Susannah! What is it?'

'Don't know,' she gasped, clutching her belly as if she were trying to stop herself being torn in two. 'Better get an ambulance.'

Without even noticing it, he dropped the tea he was carrying and shot to the phone.

It seemed to take an age for the ambulance to arrive - though, in reality, it wasn't ten minutes - and there was nothing Tom could do but wait and watch her trying not to show just how much pain she was in. He stood over her, fists clenched into iron balls, feeling so utterly helpless - so monumentally useless - he suffered almost as much as she did.

All he wanted was to get her to the hospital; everything would be all right then, wouldn't it? But, somehow, he didn't feel any better when they finally arrived.

Susannah was whisked straight into a cubicle in the assessment area. For a while, he hovered uselessly in the background but he couldn't get anywhere near her. She was surrounded by people asking questions, shouting instructions, hooking her up to every conceivable kind of monitor and sticking needles into just about every available inch of flesh.

'What's happening?' Tom asked, over and over again. 'What's the matter with her?'

But no one took any notice of him until, finally, a nurse told him bluntly that he was in the way and should "take a seat outside".

He didn't want to leave Susannah but she was in such pain and distress he doubted if, right now, she really cared whether he was in the cubicle with her, on the corridor outside - or the dark side of the moon. So he did as he was told and went and paced restlessly up and down outside. How they imagined he could sit down at a time like this was beyond him. They'd be telling him to take a nap next.

While he prowled, a seemingly endless stream of people in white coats came and went from her cubicle but no one told him anything. He watched their faces, trying to gauge from their expressions just how serious it was. Every time he asked what was happening, they told him, 'Wait for the doctor. He'll be out to speak to you, in a minute.' Tom would have been interested in having that minute calibrated; he'd have been more than happy to stake his life on its being the longest one in history.

Eventually, though Tom hadn't seen him go in, Robin emerged from the assessment area.

'What's happening?' Tom demanded, for what felt like at least the fiftieth time.

'The baby's in a breech position,' Robin replied, as if that explained everything. 'The heart monitor indicates it's in some distress, so we need to do a c-section as soon as possible. Susannah's signed the consent form and she's being prep'd at the moment. You can see her before she goes into theatre, if you like.'

If he *liked*. Jesus! What planet did they get these people from?

'Is she going to be OK?'

'Well, we don't know, Tom, do we? You know her problems as well as I do. But in terms of the operation - the caesarean section itself - I think we can be reasonably confident of getting them both through that.'

Well, that was a comfort. Susannah might die. The baby might die. If not now, then sometime soon. But since no one knew for certain, he'd just have to wait and see, wouldn't he?

He wished they'd let him see Susannah, before she was "prep'd" (whatever that meant) because, by the time he got to her, she was out of it already. She just about knew who he was but she wasn't making much sense. If this *was* goodbye, he wished they'd let him say it, while she could still make sense of it.

'You know I love you, don't you?' he said, unconsciously squeezing her hand so hard that, drugged to the gills though she was, she withdrew it with a wince. 'I mean, I know you do. But I wish I could find the words to tell you how much.'

'That's quite all right. It's lucky for both of us I found it. But you really shouldn't be so careless.'

He looked back at her, utterly lost.

'It's the pre-med,' the nurse explained. 'Makes them

wander a bit sometimes. It's best to just humour them, you know?'

So, he humoured her. He talked nonsense to her, all the way down to theatre. Right until they closed the doors to the sterile area, in his face. And told him to wait.

And so he waited.

Robin had said the operation should take about an hour - unless there were complications. Somehow, Tom wasn't surprised when the first hour came and went and there was no news. He paced up and down, to and fro, back and forth - until in the end, he was just so exhausted he *had* to sit down. Even then, his heart was racing, his palms were sweating and his mouth was so dry his lips stuck to his teeth. If this was an adrenalin rush, he concluded, you could keep it.

Coherent thoughts were few and far between - his mind was more of a maelstrom than ever - but there was one constant, like the eye at the centre of the storm, something he couldn't help silently repeating over and over like a mantra. Let it be all right. Let it be all right. *Please*, let it be all right. He repeated the words, knowing they couldn't do any good; no one on earth had the power to give him what he wanted, so he surely knew he was wasting his breath.

Sometime - well into the second hour - his mind slowed too, from sheer exhaustion. There descended on him then an odd feeling, a sensation almost like being at peace, a perfect, irrational confidence - not that everything would be all right but that, somehow, he would cope when it wasn't. He told himself this feeling must be something akin to madness but it refused to go away and, in the end, he stopped fighting it and just gave in to the relief it brought - temporary though he knew it to be.

Sitting there then - still and with a quiet mind - it suddenly occurred to him how lucky, how blessed he had been to know her, to have shared with her the time they'd had together. It passed in front of his mind's eye, in a kind of flash - the moment they'd met, him with his head in his briefcase, her looking on, bemused; that kiss he'd *never* forget outside St

Luke's; their first night together; the moment she'd told him she was having their baby; the way she'd held his face in her hands and kissed him, when he'd finally accepted she would keep it. She had changed his life - both for good and forever - and he was profoundly grateful. Even if he lost her now, even when she was taken from him, that legacy would remain. He wished he'd realised that sooner; he wished he'd had the sense to be grateful for what he'd been given and not to waste time pining for what he couldn't have. If she was going to die, he had to accept it; that wasn't going to make it one atom easier to lose her but it might mean he'd make better use of the time (if any) that yet remained to them. No doubt this feeling wouldn't last - no doubt its promptings were the counsel of perfection - but if she was spared a while longer, he meant at least to try.

Towards the end of the second hour, a nurse came to take him to Robin's office where, she said, he was "waiting to have a word". She told Tom the operation was over but that was all she could - or would - tell him.

When Tom walked into his office, Robin came out from behind his desk and anxiously ushered him into a seat. He looked exhausted, utterly drained. Tom didn't need to be told things hadn't gone well. He knew the news was bad - the only question was how bad.

Robin started to talk and Tom listened but, somehow, he couldn't take in what was said. Not that it mattered. He could guess, all too easily.

'I'm sorry to have kept you waiting,' Robin was saying, 'but we had to try everything. To leave no stone unturned. To be sure we'd done everything we possibly could.'

So, that was it then. They'd done everything they could but she hadn't survived. There was no more time. No second chance. In his heart, Tom felt he'd always known this was how it would end and yet, somehow, he still couldn't believe, couldn't *feel* the terrible, irrevocable truth of it. She was gone but his mind wasn't ready to adjust - to accept not just the possibility but the *fact* of a world, without her.

While these thoughts were passing half-formed through his brain, Robin was still talking. Tom heard the words, "safely delivered" and "little girl". So he gathered, he had a daughter. A daughter who had survived.

'She's - you're both - really very, very lucky,' Robin said.

Lucky, Tom thought, bitterly. He didn't feel lucky. He knew he ought to be thankful but he wasn't. Without Susannah, their child wasn't a joy. She was a burden. It was a shameful thought and thinking it brought tears to his eyes, for the first time.

'I want to see her,' he said, wiping his eyes on the back of his hand.

'OK,' Robin said, watching him carefully, as if he couldn't quite make sense of what he was seeing. 'But she's sleeping, at the moment.'

'Not the baby. Susannah.'

'I meant Susannah.'

Tom looked up at him and froze - with a feeling as if what tenuous link there had been between his mind and reality had finally been severed. 'Susannah's *sleeping*? But you said - I thought you said - you'd lost her.'

Now it was Robin's turn to stare and, for a moment, he was simply too stunned by the gap between reality and Tom's understanding to contemplate speech.

Then, getting up, taking Tom firmly by the shoulders and looking him squarely in the face, he said, 'Tom, old man, I think you must be a bit overwrought. Don't you understand what I've been telling you? Susannah's fine. Better than fine. The cancer's gone. We've checked and double-checked. There's absolutely no trace of it. Anywhere. She's *cured*, Tom.'

No doubt because he had been prepared for the worst, had been anticipating disaster ever since the first moment of Susannah's diagnosis, it seemed it was even more difficult for Tom to accept that she was cured than that she was dead and gone. Robin had to reiterate that fact many times - had to insist upon it, with real and repeated conviction - before Tom could even begin to allow for the possibility of its being true.

'Cured? But how? How can she be? You said, *everyone* said -'

'I know, Tom,' Robin said, for the umpteenth time. 'There's no explanation for it. Not really. But spontaneous remission *does* happen - it's not *entirely* unheard of - although, admittedly, it's not what anyone expected.'

Tom wondered if the understatement was unconscious - or if Robin actually intended it as some kind of joke. To say Susannah's cure was *unexpected* was rather like saying no one really anticipated that time would start running backwards - at least, not any time soon.

'It is just possible,' Robin went on, ruminating aloud, 'that her cure and her pregnancy are one and the same thing. It is just possible that - in a sense - we've your daughter to thank, for saving her life.'

'I don't get it,' Tom said, thinking that was an understatement to rival Robin's. 'How could the *baby* save her?'

'I'm not saying she did, Tom. As I said, there is no explanation, not really. But it could be - it is theoretically possible - that something connected with the pregnancy, perhaps the alteration in hormone levels, was responsible for killing the cancer. I'm not saying it was that. I'm just saying it's possible.'

Acknowledging that possibility, Tom felt his blood run cold. If Robin was right, if what he said *was* true, Tom had spent days literally pleading with Susannah to kill herself. If she'd had the termination he'd begged her to have, there would have been no reprieve. If she'd done as he'd begged her to do, she wouldn't have been cured; she'd have been living - if at all - under certain sentence of death.

One of the very few memories Tom had of his mother was of her telling him, enigmatically, to be careful what he wished for. Now, forty years later, for the first time, he thought he understood what she'd meant.

He wasn't prepared for the way he felt, when he saw her. She was lying there asleep, a bit wan perhaps but just like her old self. He said her name - and then he burst into tears.

Sinking down into the bedside chair, he buried his face in the bedclothes and sobbed. He hadn't meant to wake her but, almost immediately, he felt her hand in his hair. He looked up and, as their eyes met, she frowned.

'Tom,' she murmured, in a hoarse, frail-sounding whisper. 'I'm disappointed to see you *cry*.'

'Sorry,' he said, choking hard on his emotion. 'It's not very manly, I know.'

'It's not that. It's just...well, I rather hoped you'd be *pleased*.'

He stared back at her, in disbelief.

'Oh, Susannah!' he wailed, bursting into tears all over again. 'How *can* you?'

It was a long time, before he forgave her for that one.

A little while later, he went to introduce himself to his daughter. She was on the special care baby unit, because she was premature and a bit on the small side - but, they assured him, she was going to be just fine.

'Hello, Miranda,' he said, when the nurse had pointed her out to him and left them alone together. He knew her name simply because no other name was possible, in this brave new world into which she'd been born.

If he was honest, Tom had always thought all newborn babies uniformly ugly, like a puce and horribly constipated Winston Churchill. But somehow, Miranda was different. She was beautiful. In fact, she was the most beautiful thing Tom had ever seen.

He looked down at her and thought, with a pleased smile, that he wasn't going to stand a chance between the two of them. He could already hear her saying, 'Oh, *Daddy*!' in just that same tone of affectionate reproach, in which Susannah invariably said, 'Oh, *Tom*!'

He put his finger into her tiny hand and, as her fingers curled around it, his heart felt so full he thought it would burst.

When Robin finally persuaded him to go home, Tom was amazed to find it was still night - still the same night on which Susannah had woken him, with the news that the baby was coming. Somehow, Tom felt he'd lived a lifetime between then and now; certainly his world - the world as he'd known it - had been turned on its head, so that he felt he barely recognised it anymore.

Well aware that good news is no less capable than bad of inducing a state of shock, Robin had wanted to send Tom home in a cab, but he preferred to walk. The air would do him good, he said - and as he was more than sufficiently agitated already, Robin hadn't argued.

The truth was Tom didn't want to go home. What was he going to do, when he got there? He knew he was tired - *exhausted* - he could feel it, but he was far too restless and excited to sleep. He couldn't keep still and the long walk home seemed to promise him far more relief than trying to force himself to do the impossible and rest. Nonetheless, as he walked across the park, which lay behind St Luke's, he felt suddenly compelled to sit down on one of the benches - to pause for a moment, if not quite to rest.

As he sat down, his mind was running on the call he'd make to Marion, when he finally got home. He pictured her astonishment, her delight, her joy - and felt oddly humbled to be the one privileged to give her such wonderful news. He could still, even now, scarcely believe it himself.

It was a fine, starlit night and all around him the city was as near to sleeping as it ever got. He drew the cold, clear night air deep inside him and felt his heart swell with an inexpressible gratitude. He had a daughter *and* Susannah - both were alive, both were safe, both were well - and that fact was so miraculous that, just for a moment, it seemed impossible not to believe in a universe that was both purposive and benign.

Throwing back his head and gazing up at the infinite panoply of stars swirling above him, he softly murmured, 'Thank you, God.' Not because he believed but because he simply *had* to thank someone, even if there was no one to thank.

The words had scarcely left his mouth - in fact, he wasn't entirely convinced he *had* spoken them out loud - when a voice next to him, said, 'Come again?'

Tom leapt several feet into the air. When he landed, it was to discover the most enormous individual he'd ever seen, sitting right next to him and grinning from ear to ear. The guy was huge - in every direction - like some sort of cross between Santa Claus and a containership. How the hell had he got there, without Tom so much as feeling the ground shake?

'Did you say something?' the newcomer asked again.

'I - er - no. I was just talking to myself.'

'Ah, I see. That explains it.'

There was a pause.

Tom was just about to make a run for it, on the basis that even he could outdistance that much bulk, when the man-mountain let out a comfortable, satisfied sigh and said, 'Beautiful night, wouldn't you say, Tom?'

Tom stared. How did this guy know his name? He was beyond certain they'd never met. He couldn't have forgotten someone *that* reminiscent of a brick shithouse.

Watching his face, the man laughed. 'Don't mind me, Tom. You might not know me but I know you. I know everyone. Just about. You can't help it, in my business.'

'What business is that?' Tom asked, thinking it best to feign a polite interest, on the grounds he wanted to live.

'I suppose you might call it God's business,' the man replied, with a chuckle at his own joke, if that's what it was. 'I've just been helping out at St Luke's.'

'You mean - as the chaplain?'

'Something like that.'

'I see,' said Tom, even though he didn't. Not really.

Tom hadn't been anywhere near any kind of religious establishment, let alone the hospital chapel, in more than twenty years. But even *he* knew the chaplain at St Luke's was a tiny, decrepit wisp of a chap, named Wilf, whom he might have blown over with a sneeze. No matter how extreme the makeover, there simply wasn't enough of Wilf to make someone even a quarter of the man-mountain's size. And that was leaving aside the fact that Wilf was white and the man-mountain was black. So, if this guy wasn't the hospital chaplain, who was he? And more to the point, what did he want with Tom? Tom couldn't begin to guess. He could only pray the guy had taken a vow of celibacy - or, at the very least, preferred girls.

'So how are things with Susannah?'

Tom's jaw dropped, still further. He had no objection to this man's minding *God's* business but he'd have preferred him to have left it at that and kept his nose out of his and Susannah's. Not that Tom was about to take issue with him; he'd sooner have picked an argument with a combine harvester, on the grounds it would have been a hell of a lot easier to win. So, instead of telling the Incredible Bulk to mind his own business, he said, 'She's OK. In fact, she's better than OK. She's going to be just fine.'

'And Miranda?'

Was there *anything* this guy didn't know?

'Wonderful. Absolutely perfect. I'm so lucky.'

'Yes,' his companion agreed, folding his hands contentedly across the huge expanse of his stomach. 'Yes, you are. But I like a happy ending. It kind of restores your faith, don't you think?'

'I guess so,' Tom said doubtfully - though faith in what, he wasn't quite sure. 'I'm not a believer,' he added, just to get that much clear.

'You know what, Tom?' the man-mountain replied, with a wink and a grin like a piano keyboard. 'I'm not always certain I am.'

Chapter 8

Naturally, it didn't last. Nothing so perfect could possibly endure. So in little more than a moment, it was gone.

Tom felt he should have known, should have anticipated that. Nonetheless, looking back on it, he could still scarcely credit even he'd managed to fuck up something so perfect, so completely. Three days, that's all it took him to ruin everything and drive his fortunes from their zenith into the dust.

As soon as it happened, he'd known it spelt trouble. Real trouble. So he hadn't been surprised to find a grimfaced Brunhilde waiting for him, the moment he'd arrived at school the following morning, or to hear her announce that Genghis wanted to see him. Immediately.

Even so, as he walked out of the main gates an hour later, clutching his few, meagre personal belongings - which Brunhilde had ready-prepared for him, in a cardboard box - he was fairly stunned.

He was suspended. A bollocking - a major bollocking - he'd expected; that, he had to admit, he deserved. But *suspension*, he hadn't foreseen. Genghis had given him ten minutes to get off the school premises - so he hadn't even had chance to say goodbye to Vanessa - and he was forbidden to return, pending a full investigation and disciplinary hearing.

Still, Tom had to acknowledge the truth of the old saying that it's an ill wind that blows nobody any good. Genghis had been and had looked *delighted*. It had been a long time coming but the headmaster had got him bang to rights at last. And the worst of it was, Tom had no one to blame but himself.

He went straight from school to the hospital, to see Susannah. He didn't know what else to do. He just had to be with her. Nothing and no one could comfort him like she could, even when she didn't even know he was in pain.

Right up to the last moment, right up to actually seeing

her, he meant to tell her everything. But when it came right down to it, he just couldn't. She'd been through so much - too much - already. And what if she didn't believe him? He knew he should trust her (in his heart of hearts, he knew he *could*) but there was still a part of him that balked at the prospect of putting that faith to the test. She'd believe him, he knew she would. But she was still going to be angry, she was still going to be hurt and disappointed and he couldn't bear to witness that. Not yet. He needed to get the better of his own feelings first.

So in the end, he fixed a smile on his face. And lied to her.

'Tom!' she exclaimed, her face lighting up at the sight of his like no one else's ever had or ever would. 'What on earth are you doing here? Shouldn't you be at work?'

He pulled a face. 'Didn't feel like it today, so I phoned in sick. I told Brunhilde I've got the pox. You know, chicken pox. So they're not expecting me back anytime soon.'

Chicken pox? Where the hell had that come from? Sometimes, the ease with which he could lie - could dismiss and reinvent reality - almost took his breath away.

'*Chicken pox?* What did you say that for? Why didn't you just tell them you wanted paternity leave? You are entitled to it, you know.'

He hadn't thought of that.

'Honestly, Tom, you're hopeless!' She was trying to sound disapproving but failing miserably. She wanted him with her almost as badly as he wanted to be there and, in all honesty, she didn't much care how he made that possible.

'I know. But don't scold,' he said, even though he knew she didn't mean it. 'I'm not in the mood. Kiss me, instead. I'm always in the mood for that.' He bent down to her but, at the last moment, she held him off, with a frown.

'What happened to your face?' she asked, just as he'd known she would. Sooner or later.

He had his answer ready. 'It's nothing. I walked into the bedroom door in the dark, that's all. I must need glasses.'

Of course, it was another lie. But she believed him,

without question. Just like the first time. And he hated himself just a little bit more, in consequence.

By the time he got home, they were waiting for him - a Detective Inspector Monroe and a Detective Constable Lumley. They were from vice, they said, and would like a word.

'You'd better come in, then,' Tom said. After his interview with Genghis, their visit wasn't entirely unexpected. But he could still barely believe it.

'Not here,' the inspector said. 'At the station, if you don't mind.'

'Am I under arrest?' Tom asked, wishing he knew his rights - assuming he had any.

'Not yet, Mr Lewis. Just get in the car, would you?'

It was an unmarked car. Even so, Tom felt as if every eye in the street was on him as, flanked by the inspector on one side and Lumley on the other, he climbed into the back seat. Maybe the car wasn't marked - but he sure as hell felt like he was.

'So,' Monroe said, when he'd got Tom in the interview room, when what rights he'd got had been explained and the tape recorder was running, 'in your own words, let me have *your* version of what happened last night.'

Tom told him, just like he'd already told Genghis. He told the truth, more or less exactly as he saw it. But he didn't need to be told the police didn't believe him, any more than Genghis had.

When he'd finished, the inspector said, 'And that's it, is it? There's nothing else you want to tell me? Nothing you want to add to that statement?'

'No,' Tom said, with the distinct feeling that was a trick question.

'OK. Well, let's start again, at the beginning, shall we? What time did she call?'

'I don't know. About eleven, I think. Maybe later.'

'And what were you doing?'

'I told you, I was in bed.'

'And you were alone?'

'Yes! For Christ's sake what do you think, I'm running a harem?'

'I meant you were in the *house*, on your own.'

'Oh, I see. Sorry. Yes, I was alone in the house.'

'So, she rang the doorbell and what did you do?'

'I answered the door. I ignored it for a bit - I mean, I was half asleep already. But when whoever it was didn't go away, I thought it might be important. So I answered it.'

'What were you wearing?'

For a minute, Tom thought he'd misheard. 'You want to know what I was wearing, what *clothes* I had on?'

'Yes, please, Mr Lewis.'

'Well, I - I wasn't wearing anything.'

'You answered the door naked?'

'No, for Christ's sake!' Were all policemen this stupid? Or did this guy just think he was funny? 'I wasn't wearing anything in bed. I put my pants on before I answered the door. I think you'll find most people do. It avoids giving offence.'

'If that's supposed to be a joke, Mr Lewis, I have to tell you I think it in very poor taste. Given the circumstances.'

Well, fuck you, Tom thought. But he kept his mouth shut.

After a pause, the inspector said, 'When you say "pants", do you mean trousers, like the pair you're wearing now?'

'Yes,' Tom said, wondering what other kind the inspector thought he meant.

'But you weren't wearing anything else? Underwear, for example?'

'You want to know about my *underwear*? What, in Christ's name, has that got to do with it?'

'Just answer the question please, Mr Lewis.'

Tom heaved a long-suffering sigh. 'No, I wasn't wearing anything else. Including underwear.'

'I see.'

Apparently that condemned him, though Tom was damned if he could see how.

'Were you wearing a belt?'

Oh, good, they'd moved on to accessories now. 'Yes,' Tom said, shortly. 'I was. Do you want to know what colour?'

'No. Not particularly. Did you fasten it?'

'What? Well there's not much point in wearing it otherwise, is there?'

'Is that a "yes"?'

'Yes. I fastened my belt. OK?'

'OK,' Monroe confirmed. 'Let's move on, shall we?'

'Yes, let's,' Tom said, thinking if he had to answer just one more question about his clothes, his underclothes or the accessories he'd been wearing, he'd end up punching someone. And Monroe would have to be favourite.

'The doorbell is ringing; you put your trousers on; you fasten your belt; you go downstairs and open the door and find Miss Martin there. What then?'

'I asked her in.'

'I see. You open the door to a vulnerable young girl; she's distressed; you're alone in the house; it's late; you're half naked - so you invite her in. Didn't *anything* about that decision strike you as just the tiniest bit unwise?'

'Well, of course it does *now*. But I didn't know what was going to happen, did I?'

'What did happen?'

'I've told you already.'

'Tell me again.'

'I opened the door and she just sort of threw herself into my arms. She was crying - sobbing - and I thought something was really wrong.'

'So what did you do?'

'I told her I was sorry but I couldn't help her. I was alone in the house; it was late and I was half naked - so she'd have to go and whatever it was would have to wait till morning. Then I threw her out.'

There was a pause.

'Is that another joke, Mr Lewis?'

'No, it's not a joke. That's what you think I should have done, isn't it? So I thought I'd tell you what you want to hear, since you obviously don't like the truth.'

'You're not helping yourself, Mr Lewis,' Monroe replied, coldly. 'We're investigating very serious allegations against you and such - flippancy - is extremely ill-advised. Believe me, it won't earn you any sympathy from the judge or the jury.'

Tom passed an overwrought hand through his hair. He didn't mean to be flippant. He didn't mean to feel angry, or defensive, or guilty, or scared. He just couldn't help it.

'Do you want to tell me what *really* happened next?'

Tom sighed. 'I took her into the living room and sat down next to her on the sofa. I asked her what was wrong and she told me.'

'What did she say?'

'That she'd had a row, that she'd broken up with Brad - this boy she'd been seeing. And I wanted to laugh because I'd thought there was something really wrong. You know, something serious. And then I remembered this *was* serious. For her. So I didn't laugh. I asked her what the row was about and she said it was - because she wouldn't have sex with him. He'd said a lot of nasty stuff to her, calling her a baby and making fun of her because she was a virgin. But then he would, because he's a total -' Tom stopped, just in time.

'You don't like Brad?'

'No.'

'Why?'

'Does it matter why?'

'It might.'

'Because you think I'm jealous of him?'

'Are you?'

Tom's jaw set and very deliberately - reminding himself about Susannah, reminding himself he was a father - he sat on his hands. 'There's no point in my answering that, is there? If I say "no", if I deny it, you won't believe me. You've got your mind made up already.'

Ignoring the accusation, Monroe said, 'What then? When she'd told you what was wrong and what Brad had said?'

'Well, obviously, I tried to comfort her. I told her she'd done the right thing, the *mature* thing. I told her she should wait for the right person to come along - someone who wouldn't bully her or laugh at her - and that, when they did come along, she'd know and it would feel right then.'

'It must have been quite a speech.'

'Fuck off,' Tom said, because he was still sitting on his hands.

Ignoring him, Monroe said, 'And were you touching her, during this speech you were making?'

Tom was reluctant to admit it, because he knew what would be made of it. But he'd have been lying, if he'd denied it. 'I had my arm around her shoulders and she was sort of - resting her head on my chest.'

'I see. And?'

'What do you mean, "And?"?'

'She's upset. You're comforting her. You have her in your arms. What next?'

Tom swallowed, dryly. This was the bit he wished he'd handled differently. He blamed himself - there was no one else he could blame - for what had happened next. At the time, it had felt perfectly natural. Now, somehow, he could clearly see it was on the wrong side of a line he hadn't even known was there.

'Well?'

'I touched her face. It was wet, because she'd been crying - and I sort of brushed the tears off her cheeks, with my fingers.'

'I see.'

'Look, I know it was stupid, OK? I mean, of course I see that *now*. I shouldn't have touched her like that. I was only trying to comfort her but she obviously got the wrong impression. I know I have to take responsibility for that. It's my fault, she's only a kid. I should have been more careful.'

'Yes, Mr Lewis, I believe you should. So, what

happened then?'

'She looked up at me and...'

'And what?'

'She kissed me.'

'*She* kissed *you?*'

'Yes.'

'You're quite certain about that?'

'Yes,' Tom said. He wasn't. He wasn't certain at all. But he knew admitting doubt on that point was suicide.

'What kind of a kiss was it?'

'An inappropriate kind.'

'I see. Did she put her tongue in your mouth?'

'*What?* No! For Christ's sake, what's the matter with you? Do you get off on this stuff or something?'

'I'm attempting to establish the facts, Mr Lewis,' Monroe replied, icily. 'That's all.' After a pause, he said, 'Did you put your tongue in her mouth?'

Tom stared at him, in disbelief. 'Does she say I did that?'

'Just answer the question.'

'No, I didn't. She kissed me, OK? On the mouth. I was shocked - I mean, I hadn't expected it - and I kind of froze, just for a second. Then I pushed her off. And that's it.'

'What did she do then, when - as you say - you pushed her off?'

'She just stared at me. I don't think either of us could believe what had just happened. I should have laughed it off, made light of it - I mean, it was nothing, it was just a kiss - but I didn't. I said something really stupid like, "What the bloody hell do you think you're doing, Amy?". And the way it came out, it sounded really hard and angry. I didn't mean it to sound like that but, before I could say or do anything else, she burst into tears - and ran.'

'And you followed her?'

'Yes.'

'Why?'

'Why do you think? Because she was upset. Because I'd obviously hurt her feelings. Because I wanted to say "sorry" and make things right between us.'

'So what happened?'

'She was half out of the front door before I caught up with her. I was yelling at her to stop but she wasn't taking any notice. I didn't want her to run out onto the street, alone and upset. I mean, anything could have happened to her. So I made a grab for her. I caught hold of her arm but she wrenched it from me and her sleeve tore. She ran and I tried to follow but I stumbled and hit my head.'

'Which is how you acquired that graze and the bruising, above your left eye?'

'Yes. Anyway, by the time I'd got myself together, she was out on the street. I ran after her but she'd got too much of a head start on me. At the bottom of the road, she jumped onto a bus that was just pulling away from its stop. And I lost her.'

'That's it? You're sure? You have one last chance here, Mr Lewis, to come clean. Are you quite sure there's *nothing* you want to add?'

'Yes. I mean, no. I've nothing to add.'

Monroe sighed, as if that disappointed him. 'OK, then let's go back a bit. Up to the point at which you say Miss Martin kissed you - and she says you kissed her - your accounts are remarkably similar. It's from that point onwards our problems start. Let me tell you what she says. She says, you kissed her. Like you, she was shocked and froze for a moment. Then you put your tongue in her mouth.'

'No! That's a lie! No way -'

'Let me finish, Mr Lewis. You'll be given ample opportunity to comment on Miss Martin's story then. As I was saying, you put your tongue in her mouth and it was at that point she started to get frightened. You put your hand on her breast, she tried to push you off but you were too strong for her. You forced her down onto her back and got on top of her. You told her - just like you said - that she'd been right to say "no" to Brad. You told her you were the right man for her and that she'd been right to wait for you.'

'No!' Tom said again. 'No, I swear. That's just not true!'

'She pleaded with you to stop but you took no notice. You put your hand underneath her skirt and, forcing it between her legs, you thrust one - or more - of the fingers of your right hand inside her.'

There was a long pause. Tom was simply too stunned, too utterly appalled to speak. He could feel his face burning, with a scalding-hot mixture of emotions - embarrassment, shame, disbelief. But no doubt it just looked like guilt.

Watching him, Monroe went on, 'She attempted to scream but you put your other hand over her mouth. Eventually, you withdrew your right hand to unbuckle your belt. As you lifted your weight off her, she managed to struggle free. In attempting to prevent her, you grabbed at her arm - her blouse tore and she ran. You pursued her. At the front door, you stumbled. You were momentarily off balance and she pushed you, causing you to strike your head against the doorjamb. She ran out onto the street. You followed but she leapt aboard a passing bus and so made good her escape.'

In the silence that followed, all Tom could hear was the sound of his own heart beating wildly. He wasn't scared now. He was bloody terrified.

'Well, Mr Lewis? You were keen to comment a moment ago. So what's the matter now? Cat got your tongue?'

'So, everything Miss Martin says is a lie?'

'Yes,' Tom said, wearily. They'd been over it and over it, till he couldn't think straight anymore. He was almost beyond caring what happened now, all he wanted was to go home.

'Tell me again what happened when you kissed her.'

'I didn't kiss her. She kissed me.'

'And it was then you put your hand on her breast?'

'No, not then.'

Just too late, Tom realised what he'd said. He felt himself flush, as he watched an unmistakable gleam of triumph appear in Monroe's eyes.

'Not then? But you admit *now* that you did touch her

breast?'

'No,' Tom said, knowing he was wasting his breath, knowing he wasn't going to be believed. Not now, anyway. 'It wasn't like that. It was an accident. I was trying to stop her from leaving. Like I told you, I caught up with her at the front door and made a grab for her. She sort of twisted away from me and my hand...'

The feel of her breast, at once soft and firm beneath his hand, had acutely embarrassed him at the time and did so again in recollection. He knew he should have mentioned it before; he saw only too clearly how that omission would be made to tell against him. It was embarrassment, not guilt, that had kept him silent. But how could he expect Monroe to believe that?

'It was an accident,' he said again.

'I thought you said it was when you made a grab for her at the front door that you tore her sleeve.'

'It was.'

'Then did you have your hand on her arm or her breast?'

'I don't know. Both, I suppose.'

'Both?' Monroe echoed, incredulously.

'Well, I must have done. Look, I don't know, all right? I can't remember. It all happened so fast.'

'Your recollection was clear enough when we started, Mr Lewis. You were adamant then that you hadn't touched Miss Martin inappropriately, even by accident. And you were quite clear how her sleeve got torn. So, what's happened to change that? Why are you struggling to remember now what you could remember quite clearly a couple of hours ago?'

'I don't know. I'm tired. I can't think straight.'

'Well, I'm sorry if we're keeping you up, Mr Lewis. But there are still one or two points I'd like to clarify. If that's all right with you.'

Tom wondered if anyone had ever told Monroe that sarcasm is the lowest form of wit. On balance, he thought probably not.

'When the chief medical officer examined Miss Martin, he found bruising consistent with the struggle that she alleges took place between you. How do you explain that?'

'I don't know. I did grab her arm - I told you that - but not hard enough to leave a bruise.'

'I think you said earlier that you grabbed her upper arm.'

'Yes. Where her sleeve tore. We've been through all this.'

'So we have. But humour me, Mr Lewis. So you grabbed her upper arm, not her wrist?'

'Yes.'

'Then how do you explain her having bruising on both wrists, consistent with having been pinned - having been forcibly held down - by her arms?'

'I don't. I can't explain it. Whoever did that to her, it wasn't me.'

'So she was unfortunate enough to be attacked twice, on the same evening?'

'I don't know. You'd have to ask her.'

'We already did, Mr Lewis. She reports just the one attack.'

There was a pause but Tom was getting used to them.

'So, do you want to tell me the truth now?'

'I've told you already. I can't help it, if you don't believe me.'

The inspector sighed. No doubt he was tired of going over the same ground too. 'I told you earlier,' he said, 'that there are independent witnesses, who corroborate Miss Martin's story in certain, important particulars.'

'Yes,' Tom said, dully. 'I know.' He did know - and he'd known at the time that they spelt trouble.

Just like he'd told the inspector, he'd chased Amy out onto the street. He hadn't stopped to think how that might look. It wasn't until he'd lost her and had turned back to the house that he'd noticed a middle-aged couple and an older man out with his dog. They were standing there, stock-still, in the middle of the street, staring at him - and he suddenly saw what he'd just been doing, through their eyes. It was near midnight; he was half naked and had just been chasing a young girl with torn clothes down the street. If they glared at him with open suspicion and hostility, could he blame them? Afterwards, he wished he'd tried to explain. But what could he possibly have said that wouldn't have sounded mad - or worse?

'All three witnesses are agreed about one thing,' Monroe continued. 'And I'd like to check that with you again, just to be sure I've understood what you said. When I asked you earlier, you said you were wearing trousers, like those you're wearing now, when you answered the door to Miss Martin. You were wearing trousers but you weren't wearing anything else. Even underwear. Is that correct?'

'Yes.'

'Do you usually wear underwear? Are you doing so now?'

'Yes.'

'Then why not last night?'

'Because I was in bed, like I told you. And when the doorbell rang, I dressed in a hurry. I was just concerned to make myself decent, that's all.'

'I see. You dressed in a hurry but you fastened your belt before you answered the door?'

'Yes.'

'You're quite sure?'

'For Christ's sake, how many more times? Yes, I'm sure!'

'Then how come all three witnesses who saw you later describe your belt as being undone?'

Tom stared at the inspector in disbelief. After a minute, he remembered to close his mouth. 'They said it was *undone*?' he queried, in a voice so unlike his own it took him a second to realise he was the one who'd spoken.

'Yes. Why do you suppose that is?'

'I - I don't know.'

'Because you see, Mr Lewis, that presents us with a bit of a problem, doesn't it? You say you fastened your belt before you answered the door and you're quite adamant about that. Yet, when you emerge from the house in pursuit of Miss Martin, your belt is undone and our three, independent witnesses are all equally adamant about that. Now, if what Miss Martin says is true, there's an obvious explanation for that apparent discrepancy, isn't there? You unbuckled your belt when you had her pinned down underneath you, on the sofa. Indeed, she describes you lifting your weight off her to do just that. But I've heard your account a number of times now, Mr Lewis, and I can't find any explanation in it for what our witnesses saw. If what *you* say is true, precisely how - and why - did your belt come to be undone?'

They left him in a cell for a bit, while they discussed his interview with the superintendent.

So, he had plenty of time to think.

Everything had been perfect, as perfect as possible. He had Susannah; he had Miranda; against all the odds, they had both been spared. How, given such a miraculous, such an underserved gift, was it possible that he had fucked up *again*, just like every other time something good had threatened to happen to him? There were no words adequate to express his disgust, his *outrage* with himself. He deserved everything that was coming to him, though the mere thought of it was enough to make him quail.

Why had he ever got involved with Amy? He'd got too close to her; he'd let her get too close to him. Susannah had been telling him that for months; why hadn't he listened? And why, in Christ's name, had he touched her like that, making it so easy for her - almost *begging* her - to get the wrong idea? Sitting here now, locked in a police cell, it seemed incredible that he could have been so stupid, that he could have done anything so wilfully and culpably reckless.

But, severely though he censured himself, he knew the fault wasn't entirely his own. Maybe she really believed he'd kissed her - even he wasn't entirely certain she hadn't been kissing him back; maybe she really believed he was trying to hurt her, to *molest* her, when he'd chased after her - even if he didn't understand how she could think that of him. But he could make no excuse for the rest of it; hard as he tried, *that* refused to be explained away.

Amy knew he hadn't touched her in the way she claimed. In his whole life, he'd touched fewer than half a dozen women in that way and she certainly wasn't one of them. The mere thought of touching her like that, let alone of *forcing* himself on her, racked him indescribably. How could she have made such an outrageous claim? There was no possibility of a mistake; her story didn't - couldn't - arise out of a simple misunderstanding, a difference of perception or recollection. She hadn't told the truth, as she'd perceived it. She'd just lied. Her claims were deliberate, calculated, malicious *lies*. There was no other word for them, no way to make them seem otherwise, no way to hide from the truth. She had lied and he could think of nothing she could have done, no other lie she could have told, that would have hurt him half as much. He'd been hurt and let down many times - but he'd never before felt quite so betrayed.

Eventually, Monroe reappeared.

'So, can I go now?' Tom knew the answer before he asked but he just couldn't stop himself. He'd never wanted to be somewhere - *anywhere* - else so much in all his life. Even though he knew it wouldn't do any good, it was all he could do to stop himself *begging* Monroe to release him.

'No, Mr Lewis. Not yet. We need to search your flat first. And the house you share with Dr Barton.'

'Search? For what?'

'It's fairly standard procedure in these cases. Of course, we *can* get a warrant but it will be easier - better for you, in the long run - if you just co-operate.'

They started with the flat.

He stood there watching, while they ransacked it, while they emptied cupboards and drawers, turned his furniture upside down and even pulled up the carpets.

'I wish to God you'd tell me what you're looking for,' he said, at last.

'What do you suppose we're looking for, Mr Lewis?' Monroe replied. 'Videos, photographs, the usual sort of stuff.'

For a minute, Tom didn't get it. He seemed to be particularly slow witted at the moment - it was probably something to do with feeling like he'd been run over by a bus. Then he realised.

'Bloody hell!' he exclaimed.

All of a sudden, he knew exactly what sort of stuff they were looking for - stuff with kids in it - and his outrage was so great, it was all he could do to keep his hands off Monroe's neck. He almost ground his teeth in the struggle to quell his emotion and it was a full minute before he was master of himself again.

When he was, he went into the spare bedroom, which had still to be searched, and returned clutching a magazine. He thrust it into the inspector's hands. Despite himself, he was blushing.

Monroe flicked through it and handed it to Lumley. 'Put that in an evidence bag, will you, Darren?'

'That's it,' Tom said, hoping to put an end to this ordeal. 'Really. You won't find anything else. You can keep looking but -'

'Oh, we will, Mr Lewis,' Monroe assured him. 'We not finished with you, yet. Not by a long chalk.'

So they went through his private papers, his books, his photographs, his clothes - every inch of the space he'd once considered private and his own. He had nothing (else) to hide but the intrusion was no less painful for that. He'd never felt so humiliated - so *violated* - but there was absolutely nothing he could do, except stand there, impotent and fuming, and watch.

In his bedroom, Lumley found a card Susannah had sent him. The message she'd written inside was no more than six words long but it was so loving - so touchingly tender - that, though half ashamed of his sentimentality, he'd kept it. Now, he'd never be able to look at it again, without seeing the smirk on Lumley's face when he read it, or the nudge he gave Monroe when he passed it to him, so the inspector could share the joke. Tom's fists fairly ached with the desire to wipe that smirk off "Darren's" face - and shove it down his smug, self-satisfied throat.

From the flat, they went straight to Susannah's house. Tom felt he really ought to ask her. Was his permission enough, when the police would be pawing all over her stuff too? But how could he ask, without admitting what was going on? And the longer it went on, the worse it got and the more impossible that admission became.

If possible, watching them pick through her things - her private correspondence, which Tom had never read and never would read; her underwear drawer; the place where she kept her little store of tampons and panty liners - was even more painful than watching them rifle through his own. He was half afraid they'd find something he wouldn't want to know about but he needn't have feared. There was nothing. Nonetheless, they took her computer away for analysis, just in case; even though Tom assured them - quite truthfully - that he couldn't even switch the bloody thing on.

Eventually, when it seemed there was no intimate corner of Tom's life into which the searchlight hadn't been shone, no conceivable way left in which he could be humiliated, it was time to return to the police station.

Back in the interview room, Monroe threw Tom's magazine, still sealed in its evidence bag, onto the table in front of him.

'Would you care to explain that?'

'Explain it?' Tom echoed, feeling as if he'd gone mad - or, at the very least, joined Alice through the looking glass. 'What do you mean, "explain"?'

'What was it doing at your flat?'

'What the bloody hell do you think?'

'You admit it's yours?'

'Of course it's mine. What do you think, I'm keeping it safe for a friend?'

'You're not helping yourself, Mr Lewis,' Monroe told him, not for the first time.

Tom groaned. No doubt he wasn't helping himself. But what was he supposed to do? Wasn't he bound to get angry - bound to lose his composure - when, all of a sudden, everything seemed to be conspiring to incriminate, embarrass and humiliate him?

Taking a deep, steadying breath, he said, 'OK. Look, not that long ago, I was a single man. I was on my own and I hadn't had a - that is, I hadn't been in a sexual relationship for some time. So…well, come on…I mean, you can understand why I had the odd magazine, can't you?'

Ignoring the question, Monroe said, 'But you're in a relationship now - a *sexual* relationship - with Dr Barton?'

'Yes,' Tom said. Between them, he and Susannah had produced Miranda, from which the police had correctly managed to deduce that they'd had sex. You really had to admire such perspicacity. After all, Tom thought, credit where credit's due.

'So is there some other - some *special* - reason why you kept this magazine?'

Tom toyed with the idea of saying he preferred masturbation to sex, that compared to the former the latter was always a disappointment, that his right hand was the most intuitive lover he'd ever had. But he suspected Monroe would only tell him he wasn't helping himself. Again.

'I didn't keep it. I mean, not deliberately. I just didn't - I just forgot to throw it out.'

'You forgot?'

'Yes,' Tom said, thinking he knew exactly what Van would say - some half-arsed crap about there being no such thing as *forgetting* - and that something very like it was written all over the inspector's face.

Looking him hard in the eye, Monroe removed the magazine from its evidence bag. He flicked through it, appearing to know what he was looking for and, when he'd found it, he pushed it across the table to Tom.

'For the benefit of the tape,' he said, 'I'm now showing the suspect the magazine, marked exhibit "A". Would you look at the picture I'm showing you, Mr Lewis?'

Tom looked.

A girl lay sprawling on her back in front of the camera, her eyes half closed, her mouth half open. Her blouse was undone, exposing her naked breasts and beneath her tiny scrap of a skirt, she wore stockings and suspenders - and nothing else. Her legs were flung wide open and she was reaching between them, to ensure that nothing there was left only to the imagination.

He looked away. Staring down at his hands, he felt the flush that had spread across his cheeks, the moment Monroe had thrust the magazine in front of him, suddenly deepen.

'Do you notice anything in particular about that picture, Mr Lewis? Take another look.'

Tom swallowed. He'd never really understood before, what was meant by "breaking out in a cold sweat". He knew now. His shirt was sticking to him already.

He knew he'd seen that picture before but the feelings it had aroused in him then were very different to ones he was experiencing now. Somehow it had - it *must have* - looked different then. Now, despite Monroe's prompting, he was so horrified he almost *couldn't* look. How had he ever looked at that photograph and felt only lustful pleasure? How had he ever looked at it and not seen what he was seeing now?

'Would you answer the question, please, Mr Lewis?'

'She's -' He stopped, cleared his throat and tried again. 'She's wearing - I mean, she's...'

'She's a schoolgirl, isn't she, Mr Lewis?' Monroe said, for him. 'Just like Miss Martin.'

Of course, she wasn't a schoolgirl; she'd only been made to look like one. And she didn't look anything like Amy, at least not to Tom. But - no doubt as Monroe had intended - the suggestion that she did increased his already intense discomfort, no end.

'She's not - I mean, it's just what she's wearing. She's obviously older than that - *much* older than Amy. Look, if you could arrest people for having stuff like that, half the population'd be banged up. Not to mention half the police force.'

'Maybe,' the inspector conceded. 'But *you're* a teacher, Mr Lewis. Such material's hardly suitable for someone like you, with the guardianship of young people - of young *girls*. What do you suppose the parents of the girls you teach would think, if they knew you liked to look at pictures like these, pictures that might almost be of their own daughters?'

Tom was silent. There was nothing he could say to that. After all, Monroe was right, wasn't he? When Tom had first looked at that picture, what the model was wearing hadn't seemed to matter. He'd never connected it with his students; it was just a harmless fantasy - at least, it had *seemed* harmless. But as he sat there now - under suspicion, under interrogation, his every weakness under the spotlight - that picture seemed enough in itself to condemn him. OK, so the model wasn't a schoolgirl; she wasn't a girl at all, she was a woman - but how could he ever have thought it right to fantasise about - to lust after - a woman who, even if she wasn't a child, was being held out as one?

'Van, it's me.'

'Tom! Where the hell are you? I've been looking everywhere for you!'

'I'm at the police station.'

'Oh.' For some reason, she didn't sound too surprised. 'Are you under arrest?'

What did she think, he'd been overcome by a sudden desire to take a guided tour of the inside of his local nick and the old bill had been sporting enough to oblige?

'I've been charged with - with assaulting Amy. I'm not getting out of here tonight, not until some kind of court hearing in the morning. And, according to the police, maybe not even then.'

'Oh, Tom!'

'So, I need you to cover for me. With Susannah.'

'*Cover* for you! Are you crazy? You can't keep this from her.'

'What do you want me to do, Van? I only get one phone call and I'm making that now. Look, if I get out tomorrow, I can explain everything to her myself, in person. If I don't...well, I suppose I must get another phone call or something. Anyway, just cover for me for tonight. OK? She's going to be wondering where the hell I am.'

'And what am I supposed to say to her?'

'Christ, Van, I don't know! Use your imagination. Make something up. Trust me, I've got other things to worry about.'

There was a pause.

'OK?'

Vanessa sighed. 'I must be mad but, yes, I suppose so. OK.'

This time it was Tom's turn to sigh, with relief.

'Thanks, Van. Listen, I've got to go -'

'Wait! Have you seen a solicitor, yet?'

'No. What's the point? I told you, I've already been charged.'

'For God's sake, Tom! Look, stop being such an imbecile and tell those fascist bastards you demand to see the duty solicitor. Right now. Have you got that?'

'The duty solicitor? Well, if you really think so.'

'Yes, I do, Tom. Just tell them, all right? And don't take no for an answer.'

When Mr Gibson, the duty solicitor, was finally shown into his cell, Tom didn't find him a very inspiring specimen. He didn't like to judge by appearances but, if the guy had shaved and washed his hair and taken his suit to the drycleaners now and then, he might have looked a little less like *he* was the one spending the night behind bars.

'Smoke?' he offered.

'No, thanks,' Tom said. 'I don't. Not any more.'

'Mind if I do?'

Yes, Tom thought. 'No,' he said.

Mr Gibson lit up and inhaled deeply, as if he hadn't smoked in days - though his breath and the nicotine stains on his hands and teeth suggested otherwise.

'So, you're Mr...?'

'Lewis,' Tom supplied.

'Yes. Yes, of course. And the charge is...' His voice

trailed off again as - lighted cigarette dangling from his lips, squinting against the smoke - he rifled hopelessly through his papers, in a seemingly directionless search for the answer.

Tom didn't want to tell him. He didn't want to say the words out loud. But in the end, if they weren't going to be there all night, it seemed he had no choice.

'Assault,' he said, sidestepping the nature of it; he couldn't bear to say "sexual" or "indecent". 'Of a minor.'

'Oh, yes,' Mr Gibson said. 'That's right. You're the sex offender. *Alleged*, that is,' he added, quickly. 'We don't want to be getting *too* far ahead of ourselves there, do we?'

No, Tom thought, we don't.

'What previous have you got?'

'Sorry?' Tom said, looking back at him blankly.

'What previous *convictions* do you have, Mr - er -'

'Lewis,' Tom said, again. 'None.'

'None?' Mr Gibson echoed, incredulously. 'Well, anyway, not to worry. I'll get all that, antecedents and so forth, from the CPS. So, Mr - er - er-'

'Just call me, Tom,' Tom said, wishing he was dead.

'Right. OK. Thanks, Tim.'

When he finally managed to get a grip - on who the hell Tom was and what the fuck was going on - the solicitor explained about the court hearing in the morning, which was what he called a bail application. He said that *theoretically*, as an alleged offender, Tom had a right to bail; it was for the prosecution to show why bail shouldn't be granted and, *theoretically*, the seriousness of the offence was not something the court should take into account; *theoretically*, even a murderer, even a *child molester*, could get bail. That was the *theory*.

But, in practice, everything was different.

'So you're saying I won't get it?'

Mr Gibson shrugged. 'It's hard to say. You might. Then again, you might not.'

That was a great help. Tom was so glad he'd asked. 'What happens if I don't?' he enquired, dry mouthed.

'You'll be remanded in custody. Taken to prison,' Mr

Gibson explained, apparently having concluded that, since he didn't know what "previous" was - and appeared to believe he didn't have any - Tom was congenitally stupid.

Tom swallowed. Somehow, he'd never really thought about that before - all those people banged up for offences for which they hadn't been tried - which, for all anyone knew, they hadn't even committed. The prospect of joining them was less than appealing. Suddenly realising he might not see Susannah or Miranda again, until they could visit him in some stinking gaol, he felt physically sick. Just for a moment, he really thought he was going to throw up.

Maybe the solicitor thought so too. At any rate, standing well clear, he said, 'Don't get too downhearted, Tim. There's a realistic prospect you'll get bail - with conditions, of course. But it's in your favour that you're employed, that you're in a stable relationship, that you've just become a father. It's not entirely hopeless, you know.'

Through the watches of a long night spent alone in his cell, Tom struggled to believe that.

When he stood in the dock, the following morning - filthy, unshaven, stinking of his cell - he felt he looked every inch the part. Criminal, pervert - take your pick; at that moment, he felt he might be either or both. And if he felt the part now, he daren't think how he was going to feel after a few days, or weeks, or months, or - God forbid - *years* inside. How was he going to face it? And if he couldn't, what was the alternative? He didn't know. But right now, he felt anything - *nothing* - was better than that.

He looked round the court room, dreading to see a face he knew, a witness to his humiliation. But when he saw Van sitting there - head up, looking fierce, defiant, almost *proud* - he could have kissed her. Then again, given where kissing Amy had landed him, maybe not.

He struggled to follow the proceedings. Some guy - presumably a solicitor - he'd never even seen before seemed to be acting for him. Christ knows what had happened to the duty solicitor, Mr Gibson. Maybe he'd smoked himself to death. A diminutive woman, apparently acting for the prosecution, vigorously opposed Tom's application for bail. If she were to be believed, no woman was safe while he was at large.

Faced with opposition like that, Tom didn't expect much from Mr Gibson's replacement but he acquitted himself surprisingly well and when, against all the odds, the magistrate told him his bail application was granted, Tom very nearly wet himself with relief. He didn't even mind being told not to commit any *further* offences whilst he was on bail; the fact of his having committed the one with which he was charged apparently being taken for granted.

When the hearing was over and he'd been debriefed by Mr Gibson's stand-in (who pointed out that his boss had been on night duty and did have to sleep at some point) Tom caught up with Vanessa who was waiting for him in the lobby.

'Thanks for coming,' he said.

She didn't answer. She just put her arms around him and hugged him. It felt good but it was kind of scary too. The fact that Van was comforting him - rather than taking the piss out him - only served to underline his being in the deepest of deep shit.

'Did you see Susannah?' he asked, as she released him.

'Yes.'

She didn't have to say any more; he could tell the news wasn't good.

'And?'

'She knows, Tom.'

'You told her?'

'No. The police did. They got to her first. Bastards.'

'Shit.'

He didn't even want to think about that conversation - about what the police had told her, about her disbelief, her embarrassment, her horror, her shame. How could she ever forgive him? If the consequences of his recklessness, of his *stupidity*, had only been confined to himself, he thought he could have borne them with comparative ease, for nothing hurt him so much as the conviction - the certain knowledge - that he had hurt her. If there was one thing he'd have given his life not to do, it was that.

'How did she take it?'

'Well, she was pretty…taken aback.'

He didn't need to be told that was putting it mildly.

'The police didn't exactly soften the blow for her. They'd obviously made it sound as bad as possible. But it'll be OK,' she assured him, in response to his agonised groan. 'Once she's adjusted to the idea. Really. You'll see.'

'Christ, Van,' Tom said, sinking his head in his hands. 'I hope you're right.'

'Why didn't you tell me?'

Tom had never seen Susannah like this before - really angry, really hurt, really disappointed in him - and it scared the shit out him, more than anything else that had happened in the last thirty-six hours.

'I didn't want to worry you,' he said. He recognised that, as lame excuses went, that one wasn't just on crutches, it was in a wheelchair.

'Well, it's too late for that now. So, you'd better tell me the truth. You'd better tell me what happened.'

So, he told her. He told her the truth. But as he'd already discovered, the trouble with the truth was it just didn't sound plausible. At any rate, it didn't sound anywhere near as plausible as Amy's story - the one everyone, or almost everyone, seemed so keen to believe. But Susannah was different. He loved her and he trusted her. He had faith that *she* would believe him, even if no one else did. Because that was what love was all about, wasn't it? Trusting someone, believing in them, keeping faith with them. No matter what.

When he'd finished, there was a long pause, while the realisation sank in.

Then, aghast, he said, 'You don't believe me. You think - Christ, Susannah! You think I'm guilty!'

'What do you expect me to think, Tom? How many times did I warn you, you were getting too close? But you wouldn't listen.'

'I know. It's all my fault, I know that. I shouldn't have touched her. It was a bloody stupid thing to do. But you can't think I - that I touched her like that!'

'Why? I'm a doctor - a *paediatrician* - remember? Have you any idea how many kids I've seen who have been touched like that?'

'I know but -'

'But what? You're different? Are you? Are you, really? Do you think I haven't seen the way you look at her, Tom? The way you light up, when she looks at you?'

He groaned. She had every right to be angry with him, he knew that. But he was tired and overwrought and his patience was very nearly exhausted. And he was so sick of answering questions, of trying - and failing - to explain.

'You think she lights me up inside? You're right. She does. But not in the way you mean. There's only one woman who lights me up like that, Susannah, and that's you. I thought you knew that. I love - *loved* - Amy but like a daughter not -'

He stopped. A new idea had occurred to Susannah - he could see it in her face - and it would have been difficult to determine which of them it horrified, which of them it sickened more.

'You can't think that of me,' he said at last, cut to the quick, wounded to the very core. 'You *can't*.'

'I don't know what I think, Tom. I just know I want you to go.'

'You want me to leave?' he queried, stupidly. What else could she have meant? But somehow he couldn't quite believe it. He didn't want to be sent away; he wanted to be held and comforted, to be believed and forgiven.

'Yes, I want you to go. And I don't want to see you again, Tom. Ever.'

Now he got it.

For a minute, he couldn't move or speak. He was simply too stunned, too winded. How was it that just when he thought things couldn't conceivably get any worse, they always did? He'd expected her to be angry - he knew he deserved that - and he'd expected her to say some pretty harsh things to him but, at bottom, he'd always expected her to believe him. He'd been so sure of that, he'd never - not for a single moment - considered the possibility that she'd *leave* him. He'd thought they loved each other better than that. He could think of nothing, short of death, that would have separated him from her and it hurt - it hurt like hell - to find she didn't feel the same. As he stood, staring back at the hard and angry lines of her face, he felt hers was a worse betrayal even than Amy's.

'Please, Susannah,' he said, at last. 'Don't do this. I'm lost without you. Please. I'm begging you.'

He would have taken her hand - he hadn't dared touch her before - but she snatched it from him.

'I can't help you, Tom. Just get your things and go. I don't care where you go or what you do. Just don't be there, when I come home.'

Chapter 9

In a kind of daze, he went upstairs to the special care baby unit. He couldn't just go, as Susannah had bid him, couldn't just disappear from his daughter's life - as well as hers - without even saying goodbye.

Miranda was sleeping. She was a tiny, oblivious bundle and if, as he stared down at her, Tom had been capable of feeling anything at all, he'd have envied her.

'You can pick her up, you know,' the nurse said. 'If you want to.'

Tom shook his head. 'It's all right. I don't want to disturb her.'

'They're sound sleepers at that age; you're not likely to wake her.'

But despite that encouragement, he couldn't touch Miranda now. Not now he knew what Susannah thought - what the nurse would think too, no doubt, if she knew. Now he knew even Susannah was capable of believing such evil of him, how would he ever be able to touch his daughter again?

Not that it was going to matter. Miranda wasn't going to miss his touch, because he'd never be a father to her now. Even if Susannah let him see her, she'd be five or six, at least, by the time he was free. He'd be a stranger to her. She wouldn't know him and wouldn't want to know him - and who could blame her? He'd be an ex-con, a *sex offender*. Susannah was right: she was better off without him. They both were.

When he left the hospital, he wandered around quite aimlessly, for a while. But he was hurting so much inside, everything made him want to cry - the sight of couples, other people with their kids, getting on with their ordinary, un-fucked-up lives - and he didn't want to do that in public, in front of everyone, right there in the street. So he went home. Except it wasn't home, anymore. It was Susannah's place.

'Just get your things and go,' she'd said.

But he couldn't be bothered to pack. He didn't want his things. She could do what she liked with them. Burn them, for all he cared. He shoved a few clothes into a bag, picked up the keys to his flat and walked out, locking the front door behind him. He hesitated for a moment, then pushed his house keys through the letterbox. He wouldn't need them again.

When he let himself in, the flat felt as cold and airless as a tomb. It didn't feel like home anymore - because it wasn't - and it had a disturbed kind of feeling about it that the police had left behind them like a bad smell. He'd been there with them only the day before, but it felt like a lifetime ago now. He kicked the front door shut behind him, dropped his bag on the floor and then, for a long while, just stood there motionless, staring sightlessly in front of him.

Eventually, he kicked off his shoes, went into the bedroom and lay down on the bed, fully clothed. He lay there for a minute or two, until he started thinking this was the bed he'd shared with *her*; this was where they'd made Miranda. The thought choked him and, swearing, he hauled himself up again and went and threw himself down on the bed in the spare room.

No one ever slept there.

He lay on the bed, listening to someone ringing the doorbell - over and over - and waiting for them to go away. If he could have been bothered, he'd have shouted at them to fuck off and leave him alone. But it didn't seem worth the effort.

After a while - a long while - the ringing stopped. He'd just started to believe whoever it was had gone away, when he heard the sound of the letterbox being opened. Then a familiar voice yelled, 'Tom, if you don't open this fucking door right now, I'm going to get the police to do something useful for a change and kick it in.'

There was a pause.

'I mean it,' she said. Then, after another pause, 'Right. Fine. Have it your own way. It's your front door.'

A second later, concluding she really did mean it, he opened to her.

'About bloody time. What's the matter with you, Tom? Are you deaf or just stupid?'

'Go away, Vanessa.'

'Not a chance,' she said, pushing past him and tripping over a pile of unopened mail that was lying behind the front door. 'What the fuck's all this?' she demanded, scowling. 'Don't you open your post?'

'Not anymore.'

She muttered something underneath her breath but, having heard enough to gather it wasn't complimentary, Tom didn't ask her to repeat it.

'What do you want?' he asked, instead.

Ignoring his question, she surveyed his person from head to toe, in disgust. 'Tom, how long is it, since you shaved, or showered, or changed your clothes?'

He shrugged.

'Well, my friend, you stink. So, may I suggest you do all three. Right now.'

'What for? What's the point?'

'Never mind what the fucking point is, just do as you're told.'

By the time he'd done as he was told, she'd made him something to eat.

'I'm not hungry,' he said, realising for the first time as he said it that, even if he wasn't, his body was.

'Tough. Eat it, anyway.'

He sat down and stuffed some of whatever it was into his mouth. Despite everything, it tasted good and his stomach growled. He'd barely eaten in days. Well, lately, there hadn't been anything to eat, except a packet of marzipan long past its sell-by date. And somehow, he hadn't fancied that. It was lucky Vanessa had thought to shop, before she came.

'You're a lousy cook,' he said, as he cleared his plate.

'No doubt. But don't talk with your mouth full.'

She handed him a cup of coffee, sat down opposite him

and said, 'How long have you been holed up here?'

'Since I saw you last. How long is that?' He hadn't left the flat, or seen or spoken to anyone, since he'd moved back into it and he'd lost track of time.

'That was five days ago, Tom! No wonder you're such a bloody mess. What were you going to do, just starve yourself to death?'

He shrugged. He hadn't had a plan.

'So what happened with Susannah?'

'Isn't it obvious? She didn't believe a word I said. The police have got her convinced I'm some sort of pervert, so she told me to fuck off out of her life. Forthwith.'

'I'm sorry, Tom. But look, I'm sure it'll -'

'Please, Van, don't tell me it'll be all right in the end. Because it isn't and it won't be. OK?'

'OK. Sorry.'

After a pause he said, 'Have you seen her?'

'Yes, but she didn't tell me anything. Only that she hadn't seen you and that I'd probably find you here. I'd gone to her place looking for you but, of course, you weren't there. Then I started phoning you here but, as I discovered while you were in the shower, you'd unplugged your phone. You have such consideration for your friends, Tom.'

'Sorry.' There was another pause. Then, almost grudgingly, he said, 'How is she?'

'Fine. So's Miranda. They went home yesterday.'

'Oh. Great.'

He thought of them, going home together for the first time. He thought of Susannah, rocking their daughter to sleep in the nursery they'd made for her, feeding her, changing her, loving and caring for her - without him. Tears of a fruitless self-pity stung his eyes and, swallowing hard, he pressed them away with the heel of his hand.

When he'd regained control of his voice, he said, 'What about Amy? Is she back at school yet?'

'No,' said Vanessa, who'd noticed his emotion but was pretending she hadn't. 'And if she's an ounce of decency, she won't be back. She'll be too ashamed to show her face.'

'Don't be too hard on her,' Tom said, not meeting Van's eye. 'She's just a kid, after all.'

She stared back at him, aghast. 'I don't believe you, Tom! Have you gone soft in the head or something?'

'No, but...listen, Van, there's something that's been bothering me, something I wanted to ask you.'

In the five days he'd spent locked alone in his flat, he'd had a lot of time to think. But somehow, instead of revealing the truth, reflection seemed only to have obscured it. Once, he'd felt sure he knew exactly what had taken place that night between himself and Amy. But gradually, as the days had passed and he'd reviewed the evidence against him, he'd begun to doubt himself. After all, what evidence did he have - other than his own memory, his own recollection of events - that *he* was right and *she* was wrong? And wasn't memory, notoriously, the most unreliable, the most selective and the most partial of witnesses?

He loved Amy; he'd acknowledged as much to Susannah - and, loving her, how could he be really sure - how could he be *certain* - his feelings stopped short of sexual desire? Over the years, Van had told him a lot of complicated, unlikely-sounding stuff about his subconscious and something she called "repression". He'd never understood or credited half of it. But now it somehow came back to haunt and make him doubt himself. How could he - how could *anyone* - know the truth about anything, even themselves, for certain?

Consciously, the thought of making love to Amy appalled him. But what if there was a secret, hidden part of himself - a part he couldn't bear to acknowledge - that wasn't appalled, that *relished* the idea? What if he'd thrust her away not because the thought of touching her in that way horrified him but because he wanted to so much, he was afraid he wouldn't be able to stop himself? Was it a sin to be tempted or only to fall?

And what if he *had* fallen? What if, after all, he *hadn't* thrust her away?

'Well?' Vanessa demanded. 'Out with it. I can't answer, if you don't ask.'

Tom took a deep breath and, still not meeting her eye, said, 'Is it possible I did the things Amy claims but, because I can't face having done them, I've - what do you call it - *repressed* the memory? What I want to know is: is it possible I've got some sort of selective amnesia and that I'm guilty, after all?'

'No, Tom.'

He looked up at her then, with a frown. 'What do you mean, "No, Tom"? Is that it? It's not exactly a *reasoned* argument, is it?'

'Well, what do you expect me to say to such a ridiculous suggestion? If you'd done what she claims, the memory of having done it wouldn't stay repressed, once you'd admitted the possibility of your own guilt. You've done that; so now, if you'd done what she claims, you'd know it.'

'I hope you're right, Van,' he said. But despite that expression of doubt, he was inexpressibly relieved, not just by *what* she'd said but also by the *way* she'd said it. Even now - even when he'd confessed his own doubts - Van believed he was innocent and, somehow, that made it so much easier for him to believe it too.

'Of course I'm right. You didn't do what she claims, Tom. And if you weren't such a hopeless case - if you had *any* belief in yourself - you wouldn't waste your time, or mine, asking such ludicrous questions.'

For the first time in what seemed a very long time, Tom smiled. 'I'm grateful for *your* faith in me, at any rate,' he said. He thought, but didn't say, he wished Susannah had had half as much. 'It means a lot to me.'

She shrugged away his thanks. 'Just try to remember to have *some* faith in yourself, Tom. The likelihood is you're going to need it.'

There was a long pause. Then, reluctantly, she drew a letter from her pocket and held it out to him.

'I think you ought to open this,' she said. 'I found it amongst that pile of mail on your doormat. It's from Genghis.'

Tom took the letter from her hand, glanced at the direction and tossed it down on the table.

'Aren't you going to open it? I think you should.'

'What for? I can guess what it says. In view of the criminal charges against me, having regard to the reputation of the school and the interests of the pupils, there being no alternative and with regret - etcetera, etcetera - I'm sacked. Right?'

She nodded. 'I'm sorry, Tom.'

'Don't be. I'm not. It hardly matters to me now.'

After another pause, she said, brightly, 'Well, that's that out of the way, then. Now get your coat.'

'What?'

'Get your coat. You're going for a walk.'

'Oh, no! No, Van. Really. I *really* don't want to.'

'I don't care what *you* want. Get your coat. After everything I've done for you, the least you can do is walk me home.'

'Isn't that what you psychologists would call emotional blackmail?'

'It's what anyone would call emotional blackmail. But I don't care. Just get your coat.'

Vanessa was right, of course. As always. He hadn't wanted to talk to her or anyone. He hadn't wanted to shave or shower or change his clothes. He hadn't wanted to eat and he certainly hadn't wanted to go out. But having been made to do all those things, it was remarkable how much better he felt. He still felt lousy - but lousy was a great deal better than he had been feeling.

When he let himself back into the flat, after seeing Van home, there was something different about it. He didn't know what it was but he could just sense it.

He went into the kitchen and found her sitting at the table, where Van had sat.

She got to her feet, when he came in, almost nervously.

'Hello, Tom,' she said. 'You weren't here so - so I used my key. I hope you don't mind.'

He almost laughed at that. She believed lies about him; she dismissed him from her life, tossed him aside like a used

condom; she denied him his child; in short, she ruined his life -
and never so much as a by-your-leave. But when she used the
key he'd given her, she wanted to know if he minded. If that
made any kind of sense, he was living in the wrong dimension.

'What do you want?' he asked, for the second time that
day. Wasn't that just typical? No one, for five days. Then
two of them, at once. Like buses.

'I took Miranda home from hospital, yesterday.'

'I know. Van told me.'

He waited. He knew she hadn't come all this way to
tell him that. Whatever she wanted, he was sure he wasn't
going to like it. The only consolation was he didn't have
anything left for her to take. It seemed to him, she'd taken it
all already.

'Well?' he demanded, the suspense making him
impatient. 'You didn't come here just to tell me that. So why
don't you tell me why you did come?'

He noticed her hands were trembling and she was
twisting one around the other in an agitated manner, unlike
anything he'd ever witnessed in her before. Looking hard in
her face for the first time, it seemed to him she was close to
tears. Good. He hoped she was suffering. He hoped she was
fucking miserable.

For a moment, she just carried on staring at him. Then
her face crumpled. 'Oh, Tom!' she cried and the next moment
she was in his arms, sobbing onto his neck.

He didn't know how she came to be in his arms, which
of them had embraced the other; he knew he oughtn't to be
holding her, that he ought to thrust her away, like the hated
object she was, but he didn't. Instead, he pressed her to him,
hungrily, greedily, as if his life depended on it. So what, if she
knew he needed her? So what, if she even guessed how much?
The truth was it was much too much for him to let pride stand
in his way.

'What is it? What's the matter?' he asked, putting her
from him, so that he could see her face. 'What's happened?'

'Nothing,' she said, the tears streaming down her
cheeks. 'It's just...I don't know what to say to you, Tom. It's

my illness -'

He felt himself blanch. Her illness was back. Her illness was back and she was going to die. There was no inexplicable reprieve. How could he ever have believed in something so impossible? If such things ever happened to anyone, they certainly didn't happen to *him*. He'd thought he had nothing left to lose but, of course, he had. And this was it. So what, if she'd left him? She'd been alive and well and that was something - that was very nearly *everything*. But he only realised that now. And now it was too late.

'Oh, Tom, no!' she cried, seeing his stricken look. 'I didn't mean - I'm perfectly well!'

'You're well?' he gasped, his mind reeling.

He couldn't keep pace with the speed at which things were changing - or, at least, at which they appeared to be. Suddenly, it seemed everything was in a state of flux and he wished to Christ someone would tell him what the fuck was going on.

'Then, what -?'

'I only meant it's my illness that's made me crazy. It must be. How else could I have come to believe such terrible things about you?'

He stared down at her, entirely doubting his ears. If she had said what he thought she said, no doubt it didn't mean what he thought it meant. At the moment, it seemed nothing did.

'You mean you believe me? You don't think I'm guilty? You don't believe I assaulted Amy?'

'Of course I don't believe it, Tom! I *know* you're innocent.'

Perhaps he was dreaming. He pinched himself - hard. But she refused to go away.

'I'm so sorry, Tom. How can you ever forgive me for doubting you?'

'Oh, Susannah!' he exclaimed, believing her at last. 'I could forgive you *anything*.'

He pulled her back into his arms and held her hard against him, as if he would meld her to him. And this time, they were both crying.

'So,' he said, some while later, 'what made you change your mind?'

'I don't know. Maybe it had something to do with going home and finding you weren't there. I can't tell you how that made me feel. All your things were there but you weren't. It was as if you'd died. And I missed you, indescribably.'

'Me too,' he said, squeezing her hand.

'And when I thought about you and what the police had said, somehow, suddenly, it seemed so ludicrous. So *impossible*. I couldn't understand how I'd ever believed it, even for a moment. I can't say what made me change my mind; it just happened, suddenly and completely. It was like a revelation, as if one minute I was blind and the next minute, without warning, I could see. Does that make any sense?'

'I think so.'

'Have you ever had that experience, Tom? Have you ever been convinced of something and then been equally - more - convinced of its opposite, without being able to say what made you change your mind?'

He laughed. 'Only about twenty times a day!'

That might have been a slight exaggeration but he certainly knew what it was like to find himself in the wrong - and to wonder quite how he'd managed to put himself there, yet again.

Looking down at the hand that was holding hers, she said, 'Will you ever be able to forgive me?'

'I've told you already, there's nothing to forgive.' And there wasn't, was there? After all, why shouldn't she have doubted him, when he'd doubted himself? 'But I'm afraid you still have something to forgive me for. There are a couple of things I need to tell you, Susannah.'

He told her then about the letter from Genghis, telling him he was sacked.

'So, if you take me back, you'll be keeping me, until I find something else or...' He didn't finish the sentence. He couldn't bring himself to say, "until I'm sent down". Instead, he said, 'I could sell the flat, of course.'

'If you want to. But there's no need. You know I earn enough to keep both - to keep all three - of us. There's no need to worry about that now. Anyway, I quite like the idea of your being a kept man. And I can always take payment from you in kind. So,' she said, when he didn't smile, 'what's the other thing?'

That was more difficult to broach. He minded losing his job - of course he did - but it didn't make him feel ashamed. Not like the second thing he had to tell her.

'It's something the police found, when they searched my flat.'

'You mean the so-called "pornographic material"?'

'They told you?'

He hadn't foreseen that. Didn't suspects have *any* right to privacy? He supposed they didn't. He supposed he had no right to expect his affairs to be treated as confidential or even handled with reasonable discretion. It seemed he'd forfeited such rights, the moment he'd committed the crime of becoming a suspect.

'I think you can safely say the police told me anything and everything they thought would reflect badly on you, Tom. So, do you want to tell me what this "material" was?'

If he was honest, he didn't want to but he knew he had to. If he didn't tell her, he knew she'd find out anyway. By the time his case came to trial, if not before, *everyone* would know.

Why had he bought - why had he *kept* - that bloody magazine? He wished to God he'd thrown it away. He was disgusted with himself.

In such matters, Tom was cursed with a strong puritanical streak. As a single man, he'd considered masturbation as much a necessity as it was a pleasure and, so long as that activity was the sole preserve of his right hand and his imagination, his conscience was quiet. His problems began when he was tempted to supplement his imagination with the sort of material - innocuous though many people would have regarded it - that he'd surrendered to the police.

He couldn't help liking women's bodies, nor could he deny deriving a great deal of pleasure from looking at them - especially when they were unclothed. But he knew that liking something didn't necessarily make it right. The exchange of pleasure for pleasure was one thing - a fair and equal exchange - but the exchange of pleasure for *money* was another. He couldn't avoid the conclusion that such an exchange was fundamentally exploitative and demeaning - of both parties. He'd always felt that way but he was human and, now and again, the pleasure to be had from looking had grown too strong to be resisted and had overcome his scruples.

He told himself now, for the thousandth time, he'd done nothing wrong, nothing to be ashamed of - but it made no difference to the way he felt. Whose life, he asked himself, scrutinised in every intimate detail, could bear examination without raising a blush? No one's could. But, somehow, knowing that didn't make him feel any better.

He'd told the police he hadn't looked at that magazine, or anything like it, for months. That much was true. But he couldn't pretend to himself or Susannah (if she asked) that he hadn't looked at it since he'd stopped being a single man. He didn't want to have to admit that to her, not just because he was embarrassed and ashamed but because - more than anything - he dreaded hurting her. Of course he might lie, in order to spare her feelings, but he doubted she'd believe him. If he discovered she had a magazine, full of pictures of naked young men, he doubted he'd believe her if she swore she never looked at it.

'I'm sorry, Susannah,' he said, when he'd made his confession. 'I wish I'd just thrown the bloody thing away. I don't know why I didn't.'

Of course, he *did* know and so, no doubt, though he hadn't told her in as many words, did she. Which is why, for a moment, he didn't quite believe his ears when he heard her say, 'For God's sake, Tom, is that *all*? Is that *really* what all this fuss is about?'

He struggled hard to keep the smile of relief off his

face.

'But don't you mind? I mean, I think I would, if they'd found a similar magazine - full of naked men - at your house.'

'Yes, but they didn't, did they?'

'No.'

'Exactly. There you are, you see? The trick is not to get caught.'

He grunted. 'Well, it's a bit late for that.'

Now he'd got Susannah back and had told her the worst, he wanted more than anything to see Miranda. It was a need so strong it was almost physical - not that he'd have dared admit that now, even to Susannah.

'Where's Miranda?'

'At home, with Mum. She's come to stay for a few days.'

God, Marion! He'd almost forgotten her. He felt himself blushing at the mere thought of the things she was going to hear about him - if she hadn't heard them already.

'Have you told her?'

'Who? *Miranda*?'

'No, idiot! Marion.'

'Well, yes. I didn't have any choice. I had to explain why you weren't there.'

'What did she say?' he asked, dreading the answer.

'Most of it doesn't bear repeating. I've never seen anyone so angry, so *outraged*. Honestly, Tom, you can't imagine.'

Unfortunately, Tom thought he could - only too vividly. In the early days of their relationship, he knew Marion had been convinced he'd let Susannah down, in the end. And now he had. But even Marion couldn't have envisaged anything as bad as this. Even she couldn't have imagined he'd get himself arrested for the sexual assault of a minor - of his own pupil. Taken all in all, he guessed outraged was an understatement; murderous was probably nearer the truth.

'She was absolutely beside herself,' Susannah went on,

as if to confirm the worst. 'It was all I could do to stop her coming round here herself.'

Tom was mightily relieved she'd managed it. Suddenly, the thought of going home - even though Miranda was there - had become a lot less appealing.

'But it's all right, now. She's calmed down. And I expect she'll forgive me, in the end.'

'Forgive you?' he echoed, in some confusion. 'For what?'

'For having doubted you, Tom,' she said, as if it was obvious and he must be some kind of cretin not to have realised. '*She* didn't doubt you. Not for a minute.'

'She -? But -? Bloody hell!' Tom exclaimed, amazed and extremely gratified. What a wonderful woman Marion was. How had he ever been fool enough to dislike her? Really, it beggared belief, even for him.

'When I told her what the allegations were, she said she'd never heard anything so ludicrous. If I hadn't already come to my senses by then, I think she'd have lynched me. She couldn't believe I hadn't stood by you. Neither can I, now. Doubting you seems like a kind of temporary madness. I'll never understand it. I'm just so glad I'm over it.'

'Trust me, Susannah,' he said, pulling her into his arms once more, 'you're nowhere near as glad as I am.'

'I'm not saying you're guilty, Tim,' Tom's solicitor assured him. 'That's not for me to decide. But even leaving aside the complainant's - that is, Miss Martin's - account, there's still a fair amount of circumstantial and corroborative evidence against you.'

'Such as?' Susannah demanded, in a tone that made Tom extremely thankful she wasn't speaking to him.

This was the first time he'd seen Mr Gibson, since that night in the police cells and, strongly suspecting their second meeting would be no more satisfactory than their first, he would much have preferred to endure it alone. But Susannah had insisted on coming too. She'd done a lot of insisting, just lately. Tom was half amused and half exasperated to find that, having changed sides, she displayed all the usual zeal of a turncoat. Once, she'd believed in his guilt. Now she believed in his innocence. And from the moment of her conversion, she'd been on little short of a crusade to compel the rest of the world to share it. By suggesting to Susannah that there was a strong case against him, Mr Gibson obviously didn't realise the extent to which he was taking his life in his hands. But Tom didn't doubt he'd find out, before too much longer.

'What evidence *can* there be,' she demanded now, 'other than the word of that neurotic, hysterical girl?'

Tom wished to God she wouldn't ask. He didn't want to hear the evidence against him yet again - he'd rehearsed it himself, so many times, he knew it off by heart - and he especially didn't want Susannah to hear it. But there was no way of avoiding it now.

He tried hard not to listen as, one by one, Mr Gibson checked off the facts that condemned him. There was the frequency with which he was known (he hadn't denied it) to have met alone with Amy, at his flat. There was the sinister interpretation the prosecution placed (quite naturally, in Mr Gibson's view) on the fact of his having pressed a supply of condoms onto her. Out of the corner of his eye, Tom saw

Susannah shoot him a startled look; he'd somehow omitted to mention that to her. There was the fact that his belt had been unfastened, when he'd chased Amy out onto the street; not, Mr Gibson stressed, that that was so much the problem, as Tom's having repeatedly assured the police it had been fastened when he'd answered the door. Then there was his admission, made too late to do him any good - and in fact, in Mr Gibson's view, doing him far more harm than good - that he'd put his hand on the complainant's breast. Tom was very careful not to look at Susannah, at that point. That was something else he'd somehow forgotten to mention.

When, at last, Mr Gibson had finished, there was a silence. If Susannah's faith in him wasn't quite dead and buried, Tom thought, it must at the very least be in intensive care.

'And then,' Mr Gibson resumed, noting the lengthening silence and keen to drive his point home once and for all - nothing was more inconvenient than a client (unless it was a client's *partner*) with unrealistic expectations of success - 'it doesn't help our case that Miss Martin is so very attractive.'

Tom winced. He'd never enjoyed the sight of blood and he was all but convinced he was about to see the colour of Mr Gibson's.

'How *precisely* is that relevant?' Susannah enquired.

Only a fool, Tom thought - only a prize imbecile - would fall for that smile. But, of course, that didn't necessarily exclude his solicitor.

He listened, as Mr Gibson explained - with all the appearance of expecting to live out his natural lifespan - that the jury would be more likely to believe that Tom had lost control of himself and been overcome by desire for an attractive girl, rather than for one who was plain - or just plain ugly.

'I fear the jury will be only too alive to the obvious temptation. At least, the men amongst them will,' he concluded, with a spectacularly ill-judged laugh.

Tom watched as Susannah ground a couple of millimetres of enamel off her teeth and then said, 'So, logically, if a plain woman alleges she's been raped, she's less likely to be telling the truth than a more attractive one?'

'I don't make the rules, Miss Barton.'

'Doctor,' Susannah snapped.

Mr Gibson looked momentarily confused, as if she'd made a sudden, unexpected appeal for medical assistance.

'Susannah *is* a doctor,' Tom explained.

'Ah, I see. I beg your pardon, *Dr* Barton. But, as I was saying, I don't make the rules. I'm simply telling you what experience teaches me to expect. And then there's the problem of your personnel file, Tim. I've obtained a copy of it from your employers - I should say, your *former* employers - and I'm sorry to say it doesn't make for very happy reading.'

Tom might have guessed that much but, just for good measure, Mr Gibson went on to outline the problems, as he saw them. There was Tom's drinking; it appeared (though, admittedly, not recently) that he'd frequently turned up for work, smelling strongly of alcohol and had more than once been suspected of imbibing during school hours. There was his sickness record and his time keeping, which (again) though much improved of late, still strongly suggested a marked lack of reliability. Then there was his disciplinary record, which (even leaving aside his former contempt for the school's strict no-smoking policy) appeared to indicate he'd broken just about every rule in the book, at one time or another. And then, to cap it all, there was his previous history of what Mr Gibson called "mental breakdown".

'I'm afraid, Tim,' he concluded, sadly, 'that none of this is likely to endear you to judge or jury.'

'But even if any - or all - of it were true, it doesn't *prove* anything!' Susannah objected.

'Perhaps not,' Mr Gibson conceded, 'but it does tend to paint a picture of the sort of character we're dealing with. And you may be sure the prosecution will make plenty of hay with it.'

'Then stop them! You're supposed to be *defending* Tom, aren't you? Don't you give a damn about the truth? Doesn't the judge? Doesn't *anyone, anywhere* in this whole process? Is everything simply to be carved up for convenience? Tom's innocent! Why can't you understand that?'

'What *you* don't seem to understand, Dr Barton,' Mr Gibson replied, as if addressing a particularly unfortunate imbecile, 'is that the process, as you call it, isn't about guilt or innocence. It isn't about the truth. It's about what can be proved and what can be disproved. And my advice is that the prospects of securing Tim's acquittal - whether *in fact* he is guilty or innocent - are decidedly remote.'

'So it's hopeless then?' Tom said, thinking - desperate though that made him feel - that, if that were the case, he might just as well throw in the towel now and plead guilty. After all, if he confessed to and expressed contrition for a crime he hadn't committed (thereby saving the system the bother of proving it against him) he'd get a more lenient sentence - at least that was what Mr Gibson had told him. He didn't want to plead guilty (since he wasn't) but if conviction was a foregone conclusion, there really wasn't much point in paying Mr Gibson the small fortune he was demanding for preparing what would be an utterly hopeless defence.

Perhaps Mr Gibson read his mind for, all at once, matters seemed to take on quite a different hue. As a solicitor, he might not have had much of a clue about anything else but he was always alert to any hint of a threat to his fee - and he leapt to its defence now with an alacrity that, as his client, Tom couldn't help but covet.

'Oh, no, Tim. It's not *hopeless*. Not hopeless, at all! Never say die, you know. *Nil desperandum* and all that. I'm duty bound to give you the downside, you know. But I've a top man, a highly respected barrister - Mr Chadwick - working on your case, as we speak. So all's not yet lost. Not by a long way.'

'You think we can win then?'

'There's always a chance. But we'll have a much better idea, when we've got Mr Chadwick's opinion.'

Tom wondered (not for the first time) quite why he had to pay for *two* opinions - and why Mr Gibson bothered burdening them with his, if everything ultimately depended on Mr Chadwick's. Either the system was totally mad - an unfettered licence to print money - or he was. And just for once, Tom felt inclined to give himself the benefit of the doubt.

'We've an uphill battle,' Mr Gibson confirmed, 'that much I don't deny. But never fear, Tim. We shall make a fight of it yet. And Mr Chadwick's the man to come up trumps for you, if anyone can.'

Tom would have loved to believe that. But, taken all in all, somehow he wasn't inclined to hold his breath.

'I'm sorry, Susannah,' he said, as they walked away from the solicitor's office. One way and another, he seemed to be doing a hell of a lot of apologising just recently.

'It's not your fault,' she replied, distractedly. 'You're not responsible for the *injustice* of the justice system.'

'I didn't mean that. I meant, I'm sorry I didn't tell you about the condoms and the way my hand...'

He couldn't possibly say the words, even (perhaps especially) to her, so he made do with a gesture towards her own breasts.

She gave him a grim smile. 'Forget it, Tom. Though I wish you had told me first, so I didn't have to hear it from *him*.'

Tom had the distinct impression Susannah didn't like Mr Gibson very much.

'But I understand. At least, I understand how in making a grab for her, you might accidentally have touched her breasts. But how on earth did you end up supplying her with *condoms*?'

'You'd need to have been there,' Tom said, knowing beyond a shadow of a doubt he'd never manage to explain - to Susannah or the jury.

'I wish I had been. I think there's just half a chance I'd have advised you against it.'

But of course Tom had known that, which is precisely why he hadn't told her.

'Sorry,' he said, yet again.

After that, they walked for some time in silence and Tom felt a dark and familiar depression begin to settle around him. After their meeting with Mr Gibson, the prospect of prison seemed so near, so real, so immediate, it was almost tangible.

At length, Susannah sighed and he took her hand, as much for his own comfort as for hers.

Looking up at him then with a puzzled frown, she said, 'Tom, why does Mr Gibson call you Tim?'

He groaned. 'Just don't ask, Susannah. Please. I'm depressed enough already.'

Later that evening, Tom was lying on the sofa, not altogether comfortably, with Miranda sound asleep on his chest. Despite the substantial crick he had in his neck, he daren't move for fear of waking her and he lay, to all intents and purposes, imprisoned beneath her. He thought, smiling down at her, that she must be the tiniest dictator in Christendom; he could have picked her up with one hand but his whole body ached with such love for her that - though entirely unconscious of her power - she already ruled him more effectively than anyone, even Susannah.

They were holding hands - at least she was holding Tom's index finger - and, with his other hand, he was gently stroking what little hair she had and softly telling her she needed to make more of an effort, if she wanted to avoid resorting to a comb-over to hide her bald patch.

Tom was no more conscious of her observation than Miranda but Susannah had been watching the two of them for some time, with a smile on her face and a lump in her throat. Looking up at her at last, Tom was just about to ask her what was wrong, when the doorbell rang.

Neatly wriggling off the hook, Susannah went to answer it.

When she came back, she was ashen-faced and Tom was just about to ask her what was wrong for the second time, when he saw she wasn't alone.

'This is Lucy,' Susannah said, in a voice that wasn't quite like her own. 'She's from social services. She says she needs to have a word with us. About Miranda.'

Tom wasn't sure how he guessed, how he just *knew*. Maybe it was something to do with being a suspect, maybe that was how he'd come to see himself. Maybe that was why being treated with suspicion almost seemed natural, almost seemed *right*. He ought to have expected this, maybe a part of him *had* expected it.

He stood up and put the still-sleeping Miranda into Susannah's arms. He did it without thinking. But when he realised what he'd done and why, a joke occurred to him about being the one left holding the baby. The only trouble was even he didn't think it was funny.

It was impossible to be angry with Lucy; she was so reasonable, so very nearly apologetic. She explained that she understood, of course, that nothing was proven against him - yet. But in cases involving the alleged sexual assault of a minor there were, naturally, concerns for the safety and well-being of the accused's children. Assuming he had any. She was sure Tom could understand that.

And of course, he could. He understand only too well. This was simply another instance of his being guilty until proven innocent. But by now, he'd got used to the judicial system and that endearing, seemingly-unconscious way it had of mimicking Alice's looking-glass world - punishment first, conviction second.

Lucy said she understood that "Mum" had gone back to work, already.

'I had no choice!' Susannah exclaimed, hotly resenting the implied criticism. 'Tom's lost his job because of these ridiculous allegations against him. We do have to eat, you know!'

'Quite. But the present arrangements do mean Dad is alone with Baby all day.'

'So?' Susannah said, somehow making the word sound more like a three-second warning than a prompt.

Wincing, Tom tried to take her hand - he knew the look

she was wearing now and dreaded where it might lead - but she shook him off.

'I'm afraid,' Lucy replied, noting their little exchange, 'my department doesn't consider it in Baby's interests to be alone with Dad at *any* time.'

'So you want me to stop working?'

'Not necessarily.'

'Then what?' Susannah demanded, genuinely baffled. Then, looking suddenly horrified, she exclaimed, 'You can't mean to take Miranda into care!'

'That is one option. But,' Lucy said, looking at Tom, 'I trust that won't be necessary.'

'It won't,' Tom said. He wasn't going to risk that for anything. 'I'll move out. That's what you want, isn't it? First thing in the morning. Now, if you like.'

'Now would be best, Mr Lewis.'

'Fine,' Tom said, avoiding Susannah's eye. He knew, without looking, that she was regarding him with a mixture of disbelief and disgust. 'No problem.'

'Really?' Susannah enquired. 'And if you move out, what am I supposed to do? Take Miranda to work with me? Or just leave her here with a good book?'

'We'll work something out,' Tom told her, gently. 'I'm sure Marion will help. Please, Susannah. It's best this way.'

She glared at him then, as if she hated him.

There was a pause, while Lucy noted that look. Then she said, 'Naturally, there's no objection to Dad having *contact* with Baby. We're not inhuman. But it will need to be supervised - and to take place within my department.'

'You mean at social services? So Tom can't even *visit*? Even when *I'm* here?'

'I'm afraid not.'

Even Tom felt angry then. The suggestion that he couldn't be trusted even when Susannah was there was an insult to both of them. He wondered if they deliberately hired women to say such things to people, on the grounds they were (slightly) less likely to get a punch in the face. By now, he promised himself, Lucy's male counterpart would have been sprawling bloody-nosed on the carpet.

When Lucy had gone, Susannah stood and watched Tom pack. She was quietly seething and he was silently counting down the seconds to the inevitable explosion.

'I can't believe you did that!' she exclaimed, at last.

'Did what?' he asked, knowing full well.

'Just gave in like that! What's the matter with you? Can't you see how wrong this is? How absurd? If I didn't know better, I'd think you wanted to leave us!'

Before he answered, he reminded himself that she wasn't really angry with him; it just felt like it.

'You know that's not true. I don't want to leave you, Susannah - you or Miranda. But I'd rather do that than risk her being taken from us. There's just no point in fighting a battle you can't win.'

'Who says we can't win? How do you know, if you don't even try?'

'Because Amy's father is a judge. He has more power than we do, Susannah. It's as simple as that.'

'You think he's behind this?'

'Who else?'

And if it was the judge, the fact was Tom didn't even blame him for it. Not really. Sure, the judge had plenty of faults but no doubt he loved his daughter, in his way - he'd fought hard enough for custody of her after all - and what mightn't he do, driven by that love? If anyone ever touched Miranda in the way he was alleged to have touched Amy, Tom wouldn't just do everything he could to make the culprit's life a misery - he'd kill him. Judged by that standard, Amy's father was the model of restraint.

'I don't suppose every accused gets a personal visit, like the one we've just received,' Tom went on, in response to Susannah's doubtful look. 'I'd say someone's decided to make me a special case. And who has a better motive than the judge? And if he can do that, what else can he do? What *can't* he do?'

If Tom was right, Susannah dreaded to think what that meant for his trial and, looking back at him, she saw that thought had occurred to him too.

'Oh, Tom!' she cried and - with heartrending predictability - burst into tears.

'Don't,' he said, gently drawing her into his arms. 'You know I hate it, when you cry.'

'I can't help it,' she sobbed, clinging to him. 'I thought - whatever happened - we'd be together until the trial. But now...I can't bear it, Tom! It's so unfair.'

He knew exactly how she felt. They'd both counted on the time before his trial - before he went to prison - to be together. Now, suddenly, even that had been taken from them. Tom hated to think they'd probably already spent their last night together, maybe for *years* to come. It had come and gone, before they'd even recognised it for what it was.

'I know, Susannah, I feel the same. But let's not think about that now. I don't know if you've noticed but Lucy's sitting outside in her car, waiting to see me leave. So, I'm going to have to go before too much longer.'

She groaned and clutched him closer to her.

'But of course,' he said, softly brushing her cheek with his lips, 'you could always take me to bed first, if you like. After all, it might be our last chance for a while. And I don't mind keeping her waiting, if you don't.'

As Tom had predicted, Marion was only too glad to help, though she was beside herself with indignation at what she called the "outrageous affront" to pair of them, which had necessitated it. She'd have written letters of complaint not just to social services but to her MP and - it wouldn't have surprised Tom - to the Queen herself, if he hadn't finally managed to persuade her it would do more harm than good. Tom knew when he was beaten - and he knew when it was time to admit it and play dead.

Despite her somewhat excessive zeal (like mother, like daughter, Tom thought) he was grateful for Marion's support - both moral and practical - and not least because the fact that she was there to look after Miranda left Susannah free to spend the occasional night with him, at the flat. So despite the best efforts of the judge (if indeed it was him) thanks to Marion they hadn't spent their last night together. At least, not yet.

Extremely welcome, eagerly anticipated and thoroughly enjoyed though Susannah's overnight visits were, they didn't stop Tom missing her like crazy and - deprived of her influence and having nothing better to do than sit at home all day and brood - it wasn't too long before his old habits began to reassert themselves.

Sitting around the flat all day, he got to thinking he could murder a fag. More than once, he walked over to Ravi Patel's and loitered there, trying to persuade himself to give in to temptation, until Ravi finally told him - very politely - that if he wasn't going to buy anything, he'd be very much obliged if Tom would get the fuck out of his shop.

Then, of course, he missed Susannah in more ways than one and it wasn't long before he was wondering how, in Christ's name, he'd ever endured life as a single man. The fact that he *had* was enough to give him a whole, new-found respect for himself, because he was seriously struggling to do it now. If Ravi hadn't already made his views clear, Tom thought he might well have taken to loitering next to the magazine rack - though he'd never have dared buy anything. Not now.

Given that he was lonely, bored, miserable and frustrated, he didn't think it was unreasonable to allow himself the occasional drink or even occasionally (provided Susannah wasn't around) to go so far as to get thoroughly drunk. The fact was, the occasional whisky did wonders in dulling if not his pain then at least his perception of it. Rediscovering that fact finally enabled him to understand, to *remember*, how it was that he'd endured his life before Susannah had come into it - and soon it was as if he'd never left that life behind him. Soon, he was drinking much too much, not just now and then but every day. He was getting up late, forgetting to eat and generally treating himself with a thorough-going contempt he'd scarcely have shown for his worst enemy. At first, he was careful to keep these little lapses (as he thought of them) from Susannah - he didn't want her worrying - but it wasn't long before even that didn't seem to matter much any more.

Susannah wasn't blind or stupid. She knew precisely what was going on and did her best to steer Tom gently back in the right direction (it was hard to nag, when he had so much to bear already) but her efforts were to no lasting avail. Tom really meant to cut down every time he promised her he would but, night after night, he found himself buying another bottle and telling himself he really would stop pissing about, he really would make a concerted effort - tomorrow.

Taking shameless advantage of Susannah's good nature, he'd have drifted on like that indefinitely, if he hadn't ultimately managed to behave so badly that even *her* patience was finally exhausted. For Susannah, the final straw came when Tom turned up at social services to see Miranda - he had (very graciously) been granted one hour's supervised contact a week - looking unkempt, obviously hung-over and smelling so strongly of alcohol that no one in their right mind would have struck a match within twenty feet of him. Tom had plenty of faults but Susannah had never been ashamed of him before - and she hadn't needed to see the look on Lucy's face to decide that enough was finally enough.

Of course, she couldn't tell Tom what she thought of him - she couldn't give him the benefit of her unexpurgated opinion - in front of Lucy, so she bit her tongue and bided her time and, like a fool, Tom thought he'd got away with it. It wasn't until she came to the flat, later that evening, that he learned the extent of his mistake.

He hadn't been expecting her and he was surprised and (initially, at least) delighted to see her. He just wished she'd let him know she was coming; he was more than half-pissed already and not entirely sure he was still capable - though, obviously, he was more than willing to give it a go.

Having given her to understand as much, he received such a tirade of abuse in reply that (keen though he was to put his capabilities to the test) he quite frankly wished she'd stopped at home. Still, he didn't have to endure her presence for long; she scarcely stuck around long enough to outstay her welcome, short-lived though it was.

Fixing him with a look, the like of which he prayed he'd never see again, she delivered herself of a few choice words expressive of her extreme disgust with him and - promising him he'd seen the last of both her and Miranda, unless he changed his ways *and* was sharp about it - she left him to stew.

Having slammed the door behind her, with an aspersion he very quickly learned to hope she hadn't heard, Tom spent an intensely unpleasant couple of hours, alternately cursing her and himself, before he finally admitted that (as usual, damn her) she was right - and emptied his whisky bottle into the lavatory.

Somehow, he realised, he'd managed to forget that, although he'd returned to the single life, he wasn't a single man. He had Susannah and he had Miranda and whatever his other privations might be, that was what - that was *all* - that really counted. How could he have been fool enough to jeopardise the only thing that really mattered to him? He'd very nearly lost them once already. Soon, he'd be in prison and they'd be lost to him again. And in the interval, it seemed all he could do was his best to drive them away. He thought he'd been in pain before but, faced with the prospect of losing them through nothing but his own reckless, selfish stupidity, he suddenly realised he hadn't known what pain was.

He was engulfed with shame and remorse but he couldn't go to Susannah - to plead with her, to throw himself on her mercy - because Miranda was there. So he had to make do with the telephone. It wasn't an easy call to make - he'd made so many promises he hadn't kept, in the past - but somehow, she seemed to know this time was different (perhaps she heard the fear - the absolute terror - in his voice) and she was so sweet to him, when he'd finally finished grovelling and promising to mend his ways, that it very nearly made up for the roasting she'd given him. Indeed, she was so undeservedly forgiving that she promised to reward his good behaviour, the next time she stayed overnight at the flat, with what was just about Tom's favourite thing.

So, though he'd never have anticipated that as the outcome, when he put the phone down, Tom was fairly slavering at the mouth. He really wished he knew how Susannah had got to be so much better at his favourite thing than he was, when it stood to reason *no one* had had more practice than he had. He supposed it must just be a gift. But if he'd been half as good at it as she was, it was certain he'd never have been able to leave it alone.

For the next few days, at least until he saw Susannah again, he denied himself a drink of any kind. He wasn't thinking of permanently taking the pledge (Christ, things weren't *that* bad) but he did want to show her he meant what he'd said - this time. As a further sign of good faith, he set about cleaning the flat from top to bottom so that, just for once, Susannah wouldn't complain she felt like she ought to wipe her feet on the way out. When he'd done that, as a means of staving off boredom - and temptation, he decided it was time to get fit. He started jogging again and, thinking that prison was no more for the weak-limbed than it was for the faint-hearted, bought himself a set of weights. He wasn't exactly expecting any of the other inmates to take a fancy to him but he thought it best to be prepared - to be in a position to stand at least a *chance* of fending off any unwanted attentions - just in case. And then, of course, there was everything he'd heard about the popularity of sex offenders inside. Remembering that, he realised he'd be lucky if he still had any private parts left to defend, by the time his sentence was up.

Spurred on by that thought, he worked hard all week and, when he turned up at social services the following Saturday, Lucy looked at him as if she barely recognised him. Well, he was sober, freshly-showered, clean-shaven, well-groomed and still glowing from that morning's exercise - and she'd never seen him like that before. Come to think of it, Tom wasn't sure Susannah had either. She didn't comment on his transformation; she just looked at him and smiled - in a way that made him more impatient than ever to get her back to the flat.

He spent his permitted hour with Miranda, under Lucy's watchful eye. He looked forward to these visits all week but they were never an unmitigated success. Somehow, as a putative sex offender, there didn't seem to be much he could say or do - and certainly no conceivable way in which he could touch his daughter - that wasn't ripe for misinterpretation. He felt so self-conscious and inhibited in consequence that, much as he'd longed for the visit all week, he invariably began wishing it was over, almost before it began.

At the end of his allotted hour, he followed Susannah and Miranda out onto the street (it was a technical breach of the rules, so he just had to pray Lucy wasn't watching) hoping to persuade Susannah to favour him with a visit, sometime soon. She hadn't been anywhere near him all week - he guessed she was giving him a taste of how things would be, if he dared let her down again - and he was getting desperate. He dropped a few hints (the sort that would have made plutonium look lightweight) but she didn't pick them up. Perhaps she thought he hadn't suffered long enough.

He was feeling pretty disappointed but then, as she was about to leave him, she kissed him in that way she had that somehow seemed to turn him inside out (for the life of him, he couldn't think why she didn't *always* kiss him like that - but for some reason, she seemed to think it too good for everyday use) and then he was almost certain he knew what was coming next.

'I'll see you, later,' she said, when she'd finished with him - just as he'd dared to hope she would.

Then she walked away, leaving him standing there on the pavement, staring after her, so full of gratitude he was almost choking - and with such a raging hard-on he had more than half a mind to sprint after her and tell her later wasn't soon enough.

But he didn't. He made himself wait and - while he was waiting - he promised himself that (as he didn't really deserve it, anyway) he wouldn't sulk if she'd forgotten about his favourite thing.

Of course, in the event, he had no need of such exemplary self-control. She hadn't forgotten - and since he'd been as good as his word, so was she.

It was a good job Susannah gave Tom his favourite thing when she did because, only a week or so later, he'd have been completely incapable of appreciating it as it deserved.

It all started with a newspaper report. Tom never read the local paper, since the average instruction manual was more entertaining. But oddly enough, when he caught sight of his own face staring out from its front page, his interest was piqued. To say the least.

He'd been standing at the checkout in Ravi Patel's (actually buying something, for once) when - with a quick glance over Tom's shoulder, to make sure there was no one in earshot - Ravi had said, 'You *have* seen this haven't you, Tom?' and slapped the paper down in front of him, on the counter.

Tom had opened his mouth to say, 'Seen what?' - and felt his eyes start from his head and his voice die, strangled in his throat.

'Sorry,' Ravi said, seeing Tom hadn't known. 'But I thought - best to warn you.'

Through his shock - which felt something like the application of a stun gun to his testicles - Tom felt himself nod and mutter a hollow-sounding thanks.

'Take it with you,' Ravi said, stuffing the paper into Tom's bag, along with his groceries. 'You never know, maybe you can sue the bastards for defamation or something. I hope so. Serve them right.'

Tom looked from Ravi to the huge pile of papers still waiting to be sold and gulped, longing for a convenient hole into which he might crawl and quietly die.

'Don't worry, Tom,' Ravi said, reading that wish or something very like it. 'Everyone who buys that paper here, I point to your picture and I say, "See him? I know him. You take it from me, he never did those things they're saying he did." So, you don't let it worry you, Tom. Everyone knows the papers are full of lies. Journalists - all those type of people - pack of cunts. Everyone knows that.'

Back at the flat, Tom took some comfort from what Ravi had said (and far more from his obvious, well-meaning friendship) but it was scant enough, when he found himself exposed to the world at large as a pervert and a paedophile. Of course, the paper didn't actually use those words - but it didn't require a very high degree of literacy to read between its lines.

"Disgraced teacher", Tom read, "sexual assault", "underage girl". Just in case his photograph wasn't enough to enable everyone to identify him, his name and address appeared in the report's opening paragraph, in letters that seemed to him at least six feet high. He struggled to follow the logic that afforded his accuser anonymity (as if, somehow, *she* were the one stigmatised) but allowed *him* to be publicly branded and shamed, even before his conviction. Somehow that seemed doubly wrong, an affront to both of them. If, by some miracle, he was ultimately cleared, would the paper report that, he wondered? And if it did, would anyone read that report, with half the attention - or half the relish - they'd devoted to the account of his disgrace?

And then, of course, the paper didn't content itself with simply repeating the allegations against him. Anything and everything else it could find to his discredit was laid bare before the world. He had a history of "mental health problems", it reported, was strongly suspected of "alcohol abuse" and had (quite rightly, if somewhat belatedly) been summarily dismissed from his job. In addition, social services had thought it best to remove him from "the family home", amidst "concerns for the safety of his baby daughter".

Tom knew he oughtn't to care, because what was said about him wasn't true. He knew the truth; those he cared about - those who really mattered to him - knew it too. But, though it ought to have been, that knowledge wasn't enough. The lies - the distortion of the truth - still hurt, because he knew most people would believe what they read. Most people would never know the truth. For most people even an acquittal

- even a not guilty verdict - wouldn't be enough to clear him. Something of the stigma of Amy's allegations would always remain. And knowing that, how could he fail to feel the mark of Cain was upon him?

'You can't stay in for the rest of your life, Tom. You'll have to go out sometime.'
　　'Says who?'
　　'Commonsense, for one thing. Don't you think you might - just maybe - be getting this a tad out of proportion?'
　　That was easy for her to say. She wasn't the one with her name and face plastered all over the newspaper.
　　'Hardly anyone reads that thing, anyway. I mean, what's the circulation going to be? Fifteen thousand, if that.'
　　Tom groaned. How would *she* like having her pants (metaphorically speaking) taken down in front of a crowd of *fifteen thousand*? How much of a consolation would *she* find it, that the crowd wasn't twenty or thirty thousand, instead?
　　Ever since Tom had had his pants (metaphorically) taken down, he'd been refusing to show his face outside the flat, despite Susannah's best efforts to convince him (first) that the vast majority of people wouldn't have seen the report and (second) that, of those who had, the vast majority would have forgotten all about it by now.
　　'People have their own lives and their own concerns, Tom,' she said, not for the first time. 'Trust me, no one's that interested. No one cares that much, even about something like this. Anyway, who's going to recognise you from *that* photo? I can't imagine where they got it from, it makes you look like Herman Munster.'
　　Tom was relieved to hear that much, at least. In amongst everything else, he had somehow found time to worry that he really *did* look like that. He'd never considered himself the handsomest of men but, Christ, judging by that picture, he ought to have been wearing a bag on his head.

Even if Susannah was wrong - and, looking more like a member of the Munster family than either of them cared to admit, he *could* be recognised from his photograph - Tom was eventually forced to concede that he couldn't spend the rest of his life holed up in his flat. Since Susannah (quite unreasonably) refused to shop for him, he had no choice but to face the outside world again, if he didn't want to starve to death. It was, he found, possible to stomach only so many home-delivered take-aways and, in the end, even he grew sick of eating pizza and chicken biryani for breakfast.

As Ravi stayed open till two in the morning, sometime after midnight (and so safely under the cover of darkness) seemed the best time to venture forth - at least for the first time. And of course, as he hadn't been out, he hadn't been jogging for days, so it seemed entirely reasonable to *run* there and back.

He couldn't stop himself (when he'd finally mastered the street door and emerged triumphant into the night air) from glancing round, to check if he'd been spotted. Of course, he was being ridiculous. At that time of night - or, more correctly, *morning* - there wasn't a soul about. So, when he set off at a good pace and had the distinct feeling he was being followed, he knew he had to be imagining it. Even he wasn't paranoid enough to suppose he was being followed by someone who wasn't there.

Then quite suddenly - as if from nowhere - someone was running alongside him. Tom barely had time to register the fact, before the newcomer said, 'Excuse me, mate,' and laid a heavy, detaining hand on his shoulder.

Without thinking Tom slowed and, the next moment, feeling an intense, excruciating pain spreading outward from the centre of his face, he realised he'd been punched hard on the nose. Instinctively, his hands went to his face, so he was in no position to parry the second blow, which was delivered almost immediately to his stomach. He groaned - as what felt like all the available air left his lungs in a rush - and doubled up in agony. As he did so, his assailant aimed a kick at the side of his head, which landed with a sickening crack, squarely on his left temple. A split second later, Tom was on the ground, only half-conscious and utterly defenceless.

Through a kind of a haze, he registered the words "fucking *pervert*, fucking *child molester*" being screamed at him. He tried but failed to lift himself up. Then, suddenly, his whole body was rigid with pain. In the same instant, he felt himself retch and realised he'd been kicked in the balls. By the time the second kick landed, his hands were firmly clamped between his legs but they made no real difference. No one could have convinced him it was possible to feel more pain than he was feeling already.

How long he lay there afterwards, he had no way of knowing. Every part of him protested its agony. But his balls, still cradled protectively in his hands, clamoured loudest of all. Even so, it was bliss - sheer bliss - compared to how he had felt.

It was only when he sensed himself being lifted and a calm, soothing voice asked, repeatedly, if he could tell them his name that he realised someone had called an ambulance.

He guessed, at some point, he must have told them his name because when he finally came to properly, he was lying in a hospital bed and Susannah was there.

Seeing he was awake, she called the doctor over, introducing her to Tom as "Sarah".

When Tom had confirmed he knew who and where he was - and why - Sarah told him he had a broken nose, a cracked rib, a couple of broken fingers and (like he couldn't have told her) a pair of swollen, badly-bruised bollocks. It all looked a great deal worse than it was, she assured him (she didn't say anything about how it *felt*); sorry as they were feeling for themselves, his balls would be back to normal in a few days and his ability to father children was unaffected. Well, that would be a comfort, Tom thought, if he ever had sex again - which, given the way he felt at the moment, seemed pretty unlikely. Because of the blow to his head, she told him, he'd be kept in for a few hours for observation but, all being well, would be free to go home later that day. Tom couldn't wait.

'How do you feel?' Susannah asked, when Sarah had

left them alone.

If his face and his ribs - and everything else - hadn't hurt so much, he'd have laughed.

'Fucking fantastic,' he told her, taking her hand in his - the one without the broken fingers. 'How do you think?'

After a pause, he said, 'I'm not sure I like the idea of having my private parts examined by one of your colleagues. I hope we don't meet socially.'

'I shouldn't worry, she probably wouldn't recognise you with your pants on.'

'Thanks. That's a great comfort.'

Of course, once they'd got the jokes out of the way, she wanted to know all about the attack but he couldn't bring himself to tell her. He was ashamed of the truth, of being beaten up for being a pervert and a child molester - even though he wasn't one - so he tried to pretend he'd just been mugged.

'Then you don't think it had anything to do with that newspaper report?'

'Of course not. How could it? Like you said, no one was going to recognise me from that photo and, anyway, it was dark. It was probably just some smack head,' he said, with only half an idea that was the word he wanted.

'Maybe,' she said, obviously unconvinced. 'But he didn't actually take anything, did he?'

'Well, no...but he probably got scared off.'

'By what? Your screams?'

'No! I mean, he probably got *interrupted*. After all, someone called an ambulance, didn't they?'

'Yes. Though it seems rather strange they didn't leave a name.'

'Well, people don't want to get involved - at least not any more than they have to. Anyway, whoever it was, whatever his motive, one thing's for sure - that's the last time I go jogging. I always suspected exercise was bad for your health - and now I know it is.'

By the time Susannah had finished her shift, Sarah had

pronounced Tom fit enough to go home, provided Susannah went with him.

Of course, Tom was glad of her company. But as he lay on the sofa with a pack of frozen peas firmly clamped between his legs, he couldn't help thinking this was an awful waste of an overnight visit.

A few days later - when he could finally walk without looking and feeling too much like John Wayne, after a hard day spent riding the range - Van came to see him.

He was almost as surprised as he was pleased to see her. He'd phoned her a couple of times but hadn't actually set eyes on her for weeks and (though he'd never have told her so) he'd missed her. Somehow, life just wasn't the same, without someone to take the piss out of him.

'To what do I owe this honour?' he asked, easing himself into the chair opposite hers. (Sitting could still make him wince, if everything wasn't exactly where it ought to be.) 'I was beginning to think you thought I'd died.'

'No, I heard the assassin failed. Bloody amateur. Nice black eye, though. It suits you.'

'Thanks. I'm thinking of getting the other one done to match.'

'Why not? You've never been one to do things by halves.'

Yes, Tom thought, smiling; he definitely had missed her.

They exchanged news; not that Tom had much to tell. He'd been forcibly separated from his family, vilified in the press, beaten to a bloody pulp and had just received a date for his trial. So it was all pretty much the same old same old with him.

'Amy's back at school,' Vanessa said, when he told her about the trial. 'I can't believe she's got the bloody nerve. I'd like to wring her neck.'

'It's just as well you don't teach her then.'

'You're not kidding. I don't know how you stood her. Matt says -' She stopped and came as close to blushing as

Tom could imagine she ever got.

'Who's Matt?' he asked, sensing the answer to that question was the key to her almost-blush; though he was damned if he could see how, considering Van was just about as gay as they made them.

She pulled a face, expressive of exasperation with herself, and said, 'He's your replacement. Sorry, Tom. I didn't mean to mention him.'

He laughed. 'Why not? Why shouldn't you?'

He asked but he knew why: she hadn't meant to mention his replacement because she didn't want to hurt his feelings, didn't want to rub his nose in his total expendability. And he laughed because he didn't want her to know that, somewhere deep inside, it *did* hurt. Now he thought about it, he realised that, of course, he would have been replaced. But somehow, he hadn't thought about it until now. *His* life might have fallen apart but, naturally, everything and everyone else carried on just as before. How silly, how *arrogant* to have overlooked that fact - to be surprised by it - even for a moment.

'So, what's he like?'

'All right.'

'Is that it? Come on, you must be able to do better than that.'

By the time she'd finished, Tom really wished he hadn't asked.

'Right. So, he's everything I'm not. He's young and good looking and hard working and clever and organised and funny and the kids love him and Genghis thinks the sun shines out of his arse and -'

'You did ask,' she reminded him.

'So I did. But a *true* friend would have lied to me.'

'I did lie. He's far more impressive than I made him sound. But I didn't want to make you jealous.'

'I'm not jealous!'

Raising an eyebrow in his direction, Van said, 'Now who's lying?'

When she'd gone, Tom smiled to himself to think just how easy it is to be replaced, even in a true friend's affections. Van was obviously as fond of Matt as she'd ever been of him. No wonder he hadn't seen much of her lately. Absence supposedly made the heart grow fonder but, not for the first time, Tom suspected the truth was that out of sight was out of mind. He understood. He just hoped Susannah wasn't going to find it so easy to forget him, when he was languishing in gaol.

And that thought, suddenly catching him unawares, was more than enough to wipe the smile off his face.

'You won't forget me, will you, when I'm inside?'

'Oh, Tom! How can you ask me that?'

'Why not? You're human, aren't you?'

'I won't forget you.'

'Good. But I just wanted to say, I'll forgive you if you do. If you find someone else.'

'I won't!'

'OK. Great. But if you *do*, let's at least remain friends, OK? I mean, I'd like to think I could rely on that much. Whatever happens.'

By now, Tom had more or less accepted conviction and prison as an inevitability. Mr Chadwick's opinion was still awaited but Tom was beyond expecting miracles; he knew he was going to prison and he knew he was going to be there for several years. Realistically, no matter how Susannah might deny the possibility, how long would it be before he found himself replaced in her affections? It was - it must be - only a matter of time. She'd miss him for a while; then she'd get used to being on her own; then she'd find someone else, someone just like Matt - someone younger, funnier, cleverer, better looking than him.

And if he lost her, of course, he'd lose his daughter too; a new lover for Susannah meant a new father for Miranda. Tom might *be* her father but he'd already learned that being a father to her was a different matter altogether - that was something he could all too easily be denied, another role in which he could all too easily be replaced. And she wouldn't even miss him. How could she miss a father she'd never known?

He could already imagine those cold, rainy Saturday afternoons spent in the park or the zoo or some other cheap and un-cheerful public place, with a social worker indiscreetly shadowing their every move - because, of course, he was a sex offender and couldn't be trusted. He could already see the way Miranda would look at him - this stranger - with a mixture of fear and repulsion and shame. He could already hear her say, 'Do I *have* to, mummy? I don't like him!', and hear Susannah reply, 'He's your father, Miranda. It's one afternoon a month. That shouldn't be too much to ask.' Because, of course, she'd want to do the right thing and she'd want Miranda to do it too.

And even knowing Miranda dreaded them, he'd look forward to those Saturdays all month with a hunger he could already feel. And knowing his love for her embarrassed her, because she couldn't return it, he'd struggle to conceal his emotion - the extent of his need - to feign an indifference he'd end up wishing he could feel.

And then he'd take her home again and Susannah would take pity on him and ask him in, because he was lonely and unloved and - lost. But he'd refuse, not because he was proud, but because he just couldn't bear to see the way she looked at *him* - his replacement. Tom could see him too, some kind-hearted, good-natured, thoroughly decent bloke he wouldn't even have the luxury of hating.

And eventually - out of compassion, more for himself, even than Miranda - he'd stop trying. He'd stop turning up - he'd pretend he was busy or ill or just didn't give a damn - and eventually Susannah would come round to remonstrate with him. And then he'd make a fool of himself because, of course, he'd have known all along that she didn't love him anymore - but because he'd never stopped loving her, he just wouldn't be able to stop himself taking her in his arms. And feeling her flinch, he'd say, 'Please, Susannah. Don't push me away. Just for a minute. Please.' And he'd hold her and bury his face in her hair. And she'd endure his embrace and his heart would be racing at the contact and, when he finally released her, she'd look back at him with a mixture of pity and guilt because - hers wasn't.

And after that - because he just couldn't bear any more - he'd drop out of their lives altogether. And that would be that. And secretly, everyone would be relieved. And perhaps, in the end, he'd be more relieved than anyone.

And afterwards...he stopped. He didn't even want to think about afterwards, though he thought he could see what would follow and how it would end, all too clearly.

He shook himself, as if to ward off that vision of the future. Christ, he told himself, get a grip. Once he got going, he could turn self-pity into an art form; if they ever made it an Olympic sport, he'd be a gold-medal winner for sure. He didn't want to waste his time feeling sorry for himself; he wanted to make a better future - for himself and for all of them - than the one he'd imagined. He just didn't know how he was going to make it happen. And perhaps the truth was, he couldn't.

Chapter 11

'Tom, will you marry me?'

'I'm sorry, Susannah, I must be going crazy. I could've sworn you just asked me to marry you.'

'I did.'

'Oh. I see.'

'Is that it? Aren't you meant to be a bit more enthusiastic than that? If I wasn't quite so thick skinned, I'd be hurt.'

'Sorry. I'm just surprised - well, shocked really. Why now? I mean, is now the right time? After all, if I'm convicted, we'll be apart for...years, probably. A lot of things might change in that time.'

They both knew he was thinking principally of her feelings.

'That's precisely why now *is* the right time. Things almost certainly *will* change, if we let them. I know you think I'll forget you, that I'll find someone else and, even if I don't, that I'll have fallen out of love with you by the time you're free -'

He opened his mouth to interrupt but, taking his hand, she said, 'No let me finish, Tom. Of course, you're right. All that is a possible future. But it's not the future I want. If we're separated for a long time, no doubt I will be tempted to stray. As you said yourself, I'm only human after all. But I don't *have* to give in to temptation. I can choose not to and I do. I mean to be faithful to you, Tom. I mean to be waiting for you when you come home and I mean for us to be as much in love with each other then, as we are now. That's what I want. And marrying you is my way of pledging to you - and to myself - that I'm going to do everything in my power to make that future happen. That's why I want us to get married. And that's why I'm not going to take "no" for an answer. So just say "yes". OK?'

But Tom couldn't say anything just then, for a lump the size of a golf ball that had somehow got lodged in his throat.

Neither of them wanted a fuss, so it was a very quiet affair, with only Marion, Vanessa and a sleeping Miranda as witnesses.

'How did you manage it?' Van demanded. 'Did you drug her? Or hypnotise her? Or play it safe and do both?'

Tom grinned. 'I don't expect you to believe me, Van, but *she* asked *me.*'

'Now I've heard everything,' she said, with a grin almost as broad as his own.

In contrast, Marion spent most of the day in tears and, though Tom kept telling her it was supposed to be a *happy* occasion, he knew exactly how she felt. From time to time, throughout the day, when he looked at Susannah and thought how lucky he was that she was alive and well, that she had believed and forgiven him and loved him still - enough to be determined to share the rest of her life with him - his own heart was so full of love and gratitude, he could have burst into tears himself.

Given that it *was* his wedding day, social services had granted special dispensation for Tom to have unsupervised contact with Miranda (provided Susannah undertook not to leave the two of them alone together) and he couldn't put his daughter down all day; it was such a privilege to be able to hold her, without feeling his every look, his every word, his every gesture was under scrutiny. It was his wedding day and he knew it was more traditional for the groom to be unable to keep his hands off the bride but, luckily for him, Susannah understood why, just for a few hours, the first place in his arms - if not quite in his heart - was Miranda's.

They spent their wedding night at Tom's flat; Miranda stayed at home with Marion. Susannah wouldn't have been entirely surprised if Tom had wanted to keep their daughter with them - but either the idea didn't occur to him or, in the end, he just didn't have the nerve to suggest it.

It was absurd but, when it was time to go to bed, he was actually nervous. They'd known each other so long and were so familiar and intimate with one another that he hadn't suffered performance anxiety for a very long time. But something about the solemnity of the occasion made him self-conscious and more than usually anxious not to disappoint.

'I've never been to bed with a married woman before,' he confessed, as he slid in beside her. 'I wish I'd done it sooner. It's quite exciting.'

'What do you mean, "quite"?' Susannah asked, wrapping her fingers around his erection - making him suck in his breath with a sudden little gasp of pleasure.

And after she'd done that, he didn't worry about anything for a while.

He had absolutely no right to be but, despite everything, Tom was happy.

He was pretty sure he knew what the future held - he was pretty confident of spending the next few years inside - but with Susannah and Miranda waiting for him when he got out, he could bear it. Just. So, right now there was nothing he wanted but the ability to live in the moment - to relish it - and forget about the future, until it arrived. If there was a knack to doing that, he hadn't mastered it yet. But he was working on it.

As his trial grew ever nearer, Mr Gibson arranged a meeting with Tom's barrister, Mr Chadwick, at which he was to deliver his long-awaited opinion. Tom wasn't looking forward to it; he anticipated some pretty awkward questions, even though he knew Mr Chadwick was meant to be on his side.

He wished Susannah would stay at home; everything was that much harder to endure when she was there enduring it too. But as usual, she stubbornly insisted on going with him.

'You won't be able to come with me when they send me down,' he told her, exasperated. 'I will have to do that bit on my own.'

'Fair enough,' she replied, unmoved. 'I don't fancy that bit anyway.'

Mr Chadwick was exactly what Tom had expected - polished, pinstriped and public school. Judging by the way he looked down his nose at him when they shook hands, Tom had lived up to expectations too. The look seemed to tell him he was either a criminal or a fool - the only doubt in the barrister's mind being which was worse.

'Tell me about the belt,' he said, almost as soon as they'd sat down.

And like an idiot, Tom blushed.

Exchanging a glance with his solicitor, Mr Chadwick said, 'I see you know which belt I mean.'

Wishing harder than ever that Susannah had stayed at home, Tom said, 'Yes. I suppose I do.'

'So fastened or unfastened, when you answered the door?'

'Unfastened, I suppose. It must have been. I certainly didn't unfasten it after Amy arrived.'

'What you told the police was a lie then?'

'No! Not a lie, just…a mistake.'

'I see. You told the police you were certain you'd fastened your belt before you answered the door. Now you're only certain you didn't *un*fasten it after Miss Martin arrived.'

Tom had told himself he'd keep calm, no matter what happened, no matter what was said. He wouldn't let the barrister throw him; he wouldn't lose his temper. But he was feeling agitated - and guilty - already.

'Look, I put my pants on, I went to the door. I thought I remembered fastening my belt because that's what I'd normally do. But clearly this time I didn't or the witnesses wouldn't have seen what they saw. But it's easy to be mistaken about something like that, isn't it? If I asked you if you locked your front door when you left home this morning, you'd probably say "yes". But can you be really sure? And would it be a lie, if you told me you had and then went home and found you hadn't?'

'I'm not the one on trial, Mr Lewis.'

'I know you're not. But the point I'm trying to make is that I might be mistaken about fastening my belt before I answered the door. That's the kind of mistake anyone could make. But *un*fastening it after Amy arrived - that's different. I couldn't be mistaken about that. I had no reason to do it. And I didn't do it.'

'I agree it's unlikely you'd be *mistaken*,' Mr Chadwick told him, with a smile. 'But the jury won't be blind to the fact that you have an obvious motive to *lie*. You'll appreciate, Mr Lewis, that if you change your story, for whatever reason, on a point such as this - it may be a small point but it may prove to be a crucial one - it does make it very difficult to believe you on other points. I imagine you can see that, can't you?'

'Yes,' Tom admitted, with a very nearly overwhelming sense of hopelessness. 'Of course I can.'

'Good,' Mr Chadwick said, looking pleased. 'That makes my job a good deal easier.'

'How?' Tom asked, clearly having missed the point.

'You should understand, Mr Lewis, that we have a decided advantage, in that Miss Martin will be obliged to give evidence - to take the stand - whereas you will not. As I'm sure you know, the accused cannot be *obliged* to give evidence at his own trial but it's sometimes difficult to decide whether that evidence ought to be volunteered. If I had any qualms on that head in your case, you'll forgive me for telling you that you've just resolved them. You will not make a good witness in your own cause and, if you take the stand, it will be against my advice.'

'But doesn't that just mean Amy gets to tell her side of the story and I *don't* get to tell mine? How is that an advantage?'

Mr Chadwick smiled, as if the simplicity of Tom's mind amused him. Perhaps it did. 'It is in precisely that, Mr Lewis, that the advantage lies.'

Now Tom was seriously confused.

'I will tell your story for you,' Mr Chadwick explained, spelling it out as if to a simpleton. 'That way, you can't be cross-examined on it. And that way you can't be tripped up. Miss Martin, on the other hand, *must* tell her own story. Which gives us a very welcome opportunity, under cross-examination, to exploit its weaknesses. And no one's story is without them. Then, of course, there's the question of character. It's likely to undermine Miss Martin's standing with judge and jury, if we can cast doubt - as I believe we can - on her sexual mores.'

'Her sexual -? But she's a virgin!'

'Is she, Mr Lewis? And how would you know that?'

'She told me.'

Mr Chadwick smiled. 'And you believed her?'

'Of course. Why wouldn't I?'

This time, the barrister laughed out loud. 'Didn't she also tell you she was on the pill?'

Tom looked back at him, aghast.

'I mean that she was taking an oral contraceptive.'

'I know what you mean, for Christ's sake!' Why did everyone always assume he'd never heard of the pill? 'But how the hell did you find that out?'

'I told him.'

Tom turned to Susannah, in disbelief.

'At least, I told Mr Gibson.'

'Why? That's got nothing to do with this.'

'I disagree,' Mr Chadwick replied, mildly. 'I think it's highly relevant. And I intend the jury to think so, too.'

'Well, they won't,' Tom said, flatly, 'because you're not going to tell them. Amy told me in confidence. By rights, I shouldn't have told Susannah. And I wish now I hadn't,' he said, with a hot and angry look in her direction. 'Besides, the night I'm supposed to have assaulted her, she told me she'd lied. She said she wasn't and never had been on the pill. She told me then she was a virgin.'

'That's as may be, Mr Lewis. But with respect, you're missing the point. It doesn't matter whether Miss Martin was on the pill. What matters is what she told you. It will be my job to convince the jury that she told you she was using a contraceptive in order to encourage intimacy between you.'

'But that's rubbish!' Tom exclaimed. 'She only said she was on the pill because she wanted to seem grown up.'

'Exactly. She wanted you to see her as a woman - as a

potential sexual partner - not as a child.'

'No,' Tom insisted. 'That's not true.'

'Isn't that what you just said yourself? You said, she wanted to make herself seem "grown up"?'

'Yes - but not like that. She wasn't making any kind of a *pass* at me!'

'Are you sure?'

'Of course I am!'

'Isn't it true that, on at least one occasion, she came to your flat so inappropriately dressed that you were forced to give her one of your shirts to - how shall I put it - preserve her modesty?'

By now, Tom didn't need to enquire as to the source of Mr Chadwick's information. He'd never been this angry with Susannah before and it wasn't a feeling he enjoyed.

'For Christ's sake! She's just a kid, it didn't mean anything! Trust me, she wasn't dressed like that for me. If it was for anyone - other than herself - it was for Brad.'

'The boy with whom she was supposedly having this non-existent sexual relationship? The boy she was using to try to make you jealous?'

'Don't be ridiculous!'

'Is it ridiculous? Isn't it true that Dr Barton warned you many times that, in her opinion, Miss Martin was in danger of developing inappropriate feelings for you?'

Tom couldn't even look at Susannah.

'She warned me, yes,' he said, through clenched teeth. 'But I didn't believe it then. And I don't believe it now.'

'But once again, Mr Lewis, with respect, that's hardly the point. The trial isn't about what you believe. It isn't about what I believe. It's about what the jury believes. And we can control that, to a much greater extent than you might suppose possible. And that,' he concluded, with smile that Tom itched to wipe off his face, 'is what my job is all about.'

'So, you're advising me to lie, in order to get myself off the hook, is that it?'

'No member of the Bar - no barrister - would *ever* do that!' Mr Chadwick exclaimed, in apparent outrage. 'There's a whale of a difference between asserting that something is true and inviting the jury to believe that it *may* be so.'

'Is there?' Tom enquired. What, to Mr Chadwick, was "a whale of a difference" was, to Tom, a distinction so fine that it was lost on him. No wonder the barrister thought him simpleminded.

'I think,' Mr Chadwick said, ignoring Tom and turning to the solicitor, 'we really ought to obtain the complainant's medical records. If they confirm she *was* taking the pill that will tend to undermine her character and credibility with the jury, particularly as she's underage. If they confirm she wasn't, we can argue she lied to Mr Lewis with the intention of inducing him into a sexual relationship.'

Mr Gibson smiled. 'A no-win situation for the complainant, then?'

'Precisely!' Mr Chadwick replied, returning the solicitor's smile and obviously relieved to find himself properly appreciated at last.

'But what good will any of that do?' Tom demanded, feeling the situation rapidly spiralling out of control. He'd never felt so cheap, so *low*, in all his life. 'Even if we claim Amy led me on - leaving aside the inconvenient fact that she *didn't* - she's underage, for Christ's sake! I'd have no defence, if she lay down in front of me stark naked, with her legs open!'

There followed a pained and disapproving silence.

Then Mr Chadwick said, 'And that, Mr Lewis, is precisely why you will *not* be taking the stand. If you allow your emotions to get the better of you like that in court, it may well cost you your liberty.'

'Please, Tom,' Susannah said, fixing him with a pleading expression. 'I know this is hard for you - how much you hate it. But you have to do what's best for you - not just for your own sake, but for Miranda and me.'

Tom sighed, wishing someone would explain to him why his duty invariably seemed to conflict with what he wanted and - not infrequently - with what he believed was right.

'I'm sorry,' he said, dully. 'I didn't mean to sound so -

crude. I know you're trying to help me. It's just...I'm not used to trying to make things *appear* to be something they're not.'

'Remember, *we* don't decide upon the truth, Mr Lewis,' the barrister replied, 'that's the jury's job; we merely canvass *possibilities* and let them decide. And to answer the point you made, about Miss Martin's being underage, you're absolutely right. Even if we can show that she led you on that's not, strictly speaking, a defence - though the jury would, undoubtedly, be more sympathetic to you. But notwithstanding that it's no defence, we can use the *suggestion* that she lead you on to discredit her story. We can - and, if you take my advice, we *will* - suggest that Miss Martin made a pass at you, that she was rebuffed and that she subsequently concocted this whole, malicious story against you in a misguided attempt to seek revenge.'

Tom groaned - and buried his face in his hands. If it wasn't burning with shame, he thought, it ought to have been. He didn't want to go to prison. But he was beginning to wonder just how low he was going to have to sink, in order to avoid it.

'You groan, Mr Lewis, but haven't I, in fact, just summarised your own account? You say yourself that, on the night in question, Miss Martin kissed you. Mightn't that reasonably be termed a pass? You say you pushed her off. Which is precisely what I mean when I say her pass was rebuffed. You say the allegation she makes against you is false, is a lie. I merely suggest the motive for that lie is revenge.'

Tom had to admit that everything Mr Chadwick said was true but, nonetheless, it wasn't the truth. He didn't know why Amy had lied but, whatever the reason, he knew that having failed in a prolonged and concerted attempt to get him into bed wasn't any part of it.

'In any event,' the barrister continued, 'isn't what I've suggested really the only even halfway credible explanation we have to offer the court? After all, one of you is lying, Mr Lewis. Your motive for lying is obvious - you wish to avoid being punished for your crime. Miss Martin's is less obvious - which is why we need to do a little work, to make it more so.'

'You're angry with me,' Susannah said.

'No,' Tom sighed, taking and squeezing her hand. 'I was but I understand why you did what you did. I just can't go along with it, that's all.'

'But -'

'I just can't, Susannah. I can't do that to Amy. Despite what she's done, I care too much for her for that.'

'More than you care for me? More than you care for Miranda?'

Tom groaned. He wondered if she had any idea how much such questions hurt him. She couldn't have; she wouldn't ask them, if she had.

According to the barrister, his choice was to tell the truth and go to prison. Or to lie and walk free. What kind of a choice was that? As a hypothetical ethical dilemma, it might have interested Tom but, as a real life problem, it was just about tearing him apart.

He didn't want to lie - but then, he didn't want to go to prison. If he told lies about Amy to save his own skin, he was no better than she was. And was it really any less culpable, if he lied not for his own sake but for Susannah and Miranda? It was the age-old question of whether good could come from evil, whether a wrong could ever make any kind of right. He'd debated that question a thousand times. But all of a sudden, he was so weary of it - so sick of searching for an answer he never found - he could have wept. Sometimes, doing the right thing was the easy part. All too often, the hardest part was knowing what the right thing was.

Tom might have been sick of the argument - of the fruitless search for the elusive "right" answer - but it raged between them for days. Susannah simply couldn't understand why he was prepared to sacrifice everything, for the sake of a girl who'd told lies about him. He chose prison over freedom, for Amy's sake - and Susannah struggled to see that as anything other than a betrayal.

Tom understood how she felt and was utterly miserable, in consequence. But he just couldn't give way. He knew what it was like to have someone poking around in the most private and intimate corners of his life and drawing all the wrong conclusions from what they found. If it was wrong for someone to do that to him, it was wrong for them to do it to Amy.

'Come on, Susannah, you know how appallingly women are treated by the system. Why should a woman have to be a virgin - or a *nun* - to be believed, when she says she's been assaulted? You know it's wrong for a woman's sexual history to be used to discredit her in that way. You've always said so.'

'That was before you were falsely accused, by a hysterical, adolescent girl! OK, in principle, I still think a woman's sexual history should be regarded as irrelevant. But I don't want to see you penalised - I don't want to see you *incarcerated* - for the sake of that principle.'

'Then what's the use of it, Susannah? What's the use of any principle if, the first time it becomes inconvenient - the first time you need it to guide you to do what's right - you chuck it straight out the window?'

They'd very nearly stopped speaking to each other - at least, Susannah had very nearly stopped speaking to Tom - when, one evening, she turned up unannounced at the flat.

'OK,' she said, almost before he'd had chance to take in her sudden, unexpected appearance. 'I don't like it - but you win.'

'Win what?' he asked, nonplussed.

'Well, not the lottery, dimwit. You need to buy a ticket for that. I mean, you win the argument. I still say you're wrong. But it's your choice and I won't argue anymore.'

He regarded her, through narrowed eyes, strongly suspecting this was a trick or some sort of elaborate practical joke.

'Why?'

'Because, finally, Mum made me see what I should have seen for myself. She reminded me that, when I was ill, you wanted me to have a termination and I wouldn't. You wanted me to do what you thought was in my best interests. And I wanted to do what I thought was right. This is the same, isn't it? You respected what I wanted then, even though you could have lost me, even though the consequences of my choice might have been terrible for you. Well, now I have to do the same thing. I have to respect what you want and let you do what you think is right, even if - even *though* - I think you're crazy.' She shrugged. 'So, I won't argue anymore.'

'Did Marion really say all that to you?'

'More or less.'

'Bloody hell.'

'Quite,' Susannah agreed, pulling him towards her. 'So now we've got that straight, why don't we make up properly? I didn't come all this way just for a chat, you know.'

Chapter 12

'You know I'd stay if I could, Tom.'

'Of course I do.'

'I wanted us to be together, tonight of all nights.'

'I know,' Tom said, 'but it can't be helped.'

It was the night before his trial, which he and Susannah had naturally planned to spend together, but Miranda had come down with a cold and now Marion had caught it from her. Marion had tried hard to insist she could still cope but, much as Susannah wanted to do the selfish thing and pretend to believe her, she just couldn't.

'You could always come home with me...'

'You know I can't, Susannah. Don't tempt me.'

'I don't see why,' she objected, miserably. 'What could social services do now, even if they found out? The trial will be over tomorrow and you'll either be free and clear or...'

'Inside,' he finished for her.

Holding him tight, she said, 'Isn't that all the more reason to be together now, while we can?'

'You know I want to, Susannah, but I can't. It's not worth the risk. I couldn't bear it, if they took Miranda away.'

She sighed, knowing he was right and that she had no choice but to submit.

'I swear you used to be more fun than this,' she said, feigning petulance. 'It is OK to break the rules every now and again, you know.'

Smiling down at her, Tom said, 'I'll break all the rules you like *after* my trial. But right now, I'm in enough trouble. So go on, get your coat and I'll walk you home.'

When he got back, he'd barely shut the door behind him, before there was a knock on it.

Fucking hell! Who the fuck was that? He was on trial in the morning, for Christ's sake! Wasn't that persecution enough? Was five minutes' peace in his own home the night before *really* too much to ask?

As if by way of reply, the caller knocked again - louder this time.

It must be a neighbour, Tom reasoned; anyone else would have had to ring at the street door. Maybe it was that mousy woman, who used to keep calling round at all hours wanting to borrow a cup of sugar, even though he never had any. Or maybe it was that old chap, who lived on the floor above and kept accusing him of littering the communal stairs with his cigarette butts, even though Tom had told him at least a thousand times that he didn't smoke anymore.

By the time whoever it was knocked for the third time, it wasn't so much a knock as a determined attempt to demolish his front door. With a muttered curse - and every intention of throttling whoever was on the other side of it - Tom flung it open.

And in one quick movement, Amy shot inside and kicked it shut behind her.

As Mr Gibson had explained to him, in words of one syllable, so that even he could understand, it was a condition of Tom's bail that he had no contact with Amy. If he breached that condition, he was liable to be arrested and thrown in goal - regardless of the outcome of his trial. Maybe Amy didn't know that. But even if she didn't, she'd have to be insane to think she was welcome within fifty miles of him. Let alone in his flat.

He'd opened and closed his mouth at least half a dozen times, before any sound emerged. 'Are you crazy?' he managed, at last. 'What the fuck are you doing here? Are you trying to get me arrested or what?'

'Of course not! Calm down!' she exclaimed, scowling at him. 'No one knows I'm here - and they won't, if you keep your voice down. Christ, Tom, I'm not *deaf*.'

'But - but -' he spluttered, like an engine trying and failing to start. 'What do you want? How did you get in?'

'I snuck in through the street door, after that mousy woman with the sweet tooth - you know, the one who's sweet on you.'

(Tom was too preoccupied just then to ask her what the

fuck she was talking about.)

'I've been hiding out here for *hours* waiting for you. Where the hell have you been?'

'Never mind where I've been! What in the name of fuck are you doing here?'

'I wish to Christ you'd stop swearing. I've come to explain.'

'*Explain*!' he echoed, incredulous. 'Bloody hell, Amy, I don't envy you that one! You've got about as much chance of explaining yourself as - as *Hitler*!'

He wasn't just angry; he was *apoplectic*. It was bad enough that she dared to show her face at all but she was so cool - so infuriatingly self-possessed - he wanted to shake her. (Well, if he was honest, he wanted to slap her but he supposed shaking would have to do.) Of course, he couldn't and didn't do any such thing - but as he stood there, glaring down at her, with something like real hatred in his heart, the façade of her face suddenly crumbled and tears started to her eyes, almost as if he had.

'You're right not to envy me,' she said, in a voice thick - almost choked - with suppressed with emotion. 'Do you think this is easy for me? That I don't know what I've done? What misery I've caused?'

And of course, the moment she said that, he was lost. She looked so childlike - so touchingly, achingly vulnerable - it was simply impossible to be angry with her. Despite everything she'd put him through, all he wanted to do then was take her in his arms and comfort her. He knew he mustn't; he could guess what Susannah would say, if he dared do anything even half as stupid. He knew he should throw her out, right now; every instinct of self-preservation demanded it. He knew perfectly well what he *should* do - but all along, he knew perfectly well he wouldn't do it.

'Don't cry,' he pleaded, in an altered tone. 'You know I hate it.'

'Don't be so bloody mean to me, then!'

'OK. Sorry. Look, come inside and sit down and say what you've got to say. And I won't be mean. And you won't cry. OK?'

Biting down hard on her lower lip, she nodded and followed him inside.

He didn't know whether he could trust her but he knew for sure he couldn't trust himself - so he made a point of sitting across the other side of the room from her, well out of harm's way.

'So,' he prompted finally, when she showed no sign of giving the explanation she'd promised, 'tell me. What made you do it?'

She looked up at him, still with that bruised, close-to-tears look. 'Can't you guess?'

Somehow the way she asked it, it wasn't a flippant question. She asked as if she genuinely thought he might - perhaps even *should* - have guessed what had motivated such malice, such an intimate and personal betrayal.

'No, Amy. Trust me, I've tried. But I can't. I don't understand why you've done this to me. I wish I did. It hurts me - more than you might think - to be forced to think this badly of you.'

Her tears started to fall then and he was extraordinarily glad of the six feet that separated them. It cost him a supreme effort to remain where he was. But he did it.

'You hate me now. Of course you do! You'll never forgive me.'

'Perhaps not,' he agreed. 'But I wish you'd tell me, nonetheless. What did I do to make you hate me so much?'

'Nothing! I don't *hate* you, Tom! How can you think that? None of this is your fault.'

'Then for Christ's sake,' he exclaimed, his patience exhausted, 'will you please stop torturing me and tell me *why*?'

And so, finally, taking a deep breath, she did.

Looking him squarely in the eye, she told him the truth - steadily, bravely, almost defiantly - and the longer she went on the more uncomfortable he became.

Nothing was as he'd supposed it to be. It was as if the world had suddenly shifted on its axis, forcing on him a whole new perspective. All at once, everything looked different and, all at once, he could see that all the assumptions he'd made - about guilt and innocence, about motive and blame - were all utterly, hopelessly wrong. But the hardest part of all - the part he really couldn't forgive himself for - was that the truth was obvious. So obvious, it seemed to him he must have been wilfully blind to it.

He'd never have believed that, by the time Amy had finished, *he'd* be the one racked with guilt and apologising. But impossible though it seemed, he was.

She'd explained everything - or almost everything. But there was still one question she hadn't answered and, in the end, because he'd never quite resolved his doubts on that point, he had to ask it.

'There's still one thing I don't understand. What made you kiss me? It was *you* who kissed *me*, wasn't it?'

'Of course it was! I'm sorry, Tom. It was stupid of me. I was confused - upset about Brad - and just for a minute, when you put your arms around me, I thought…I'd had these feelings for you, for a long time. I knew it was wrong but -'

'You had *feelings* for me?' he asked, feeling himself blush. He oughtn't to have been surprised, after everything Susannah had said, but he was.

She nodded. 'Did you never guess?'

'I - er - no. No, I didn't.'

'Well, like I said, I knew it was wrong. You love Susannah and anyway you're way too old for me. So I didn't intend to do anything about the way I felt. You were just a fantasy, that's all.'

He was careful not to betray it but, inwardly, Tom glowed at the mere thought of being *anyone's* fantasy. It was almost enough to make up for being described as "way too old."

'But that night, when you put your arms around me and you were so kind, just for a minute I lost my head. I knew, as soon as I'd done it, I'd made a really stupid mistake and then I felt such a fool. That's why I ran. Sorry,' she said again.

'There's no need to apologise, Amy. We all make mistakes like that, especially when we're young.'

'Can you forgive me, then? I mean - for all of it.'

'I would forgive you, if there was anything to forgive. But there isn't. You're not to blame, Amy. The truth is - I am.'

Some while later, she said, 'Tom, I'm starving. It's amazing how hungry confession makes you. Will you fix me something to eat?'

'Fix it yourself,' he told her, deciding she'd let him grovel long enough. 'I'm not your servant.'

'I thought you were feeling guilty.'

'I am. But not *that* guilty.'

When she'd made herself something and was halfway through eating it, she suddenly said, 'Can I stay the night?'

'Are you insane? Of course you can't!'

'I've got nowhere else to go, Tom. I can't go home now, it's nearly midnight. The judge'll kill me.'

'That's the least he'll do, if you stay out all night.'

'He won't know. He'll just assume I'm in my room - and by the time he misses me in the morning it'll be too late, won't it?'

Imagining the judge's face when he made that discovery (on the very morning of Tom's trial, in which Amy would be the chief, the *only* real witness against him) gave Tom a decidedly warm glow. It might not have been a very noble feeling but it was no less pleasurable for that.

Acceding to her request to share his bed was, of course, sheer madness - any competent psychiatrist would have committed him for it - but he did it anyway. He didn't want to be alone, any more than she did.

Nonetheless, he made a point of putting a pillow between them and ordering her, in the strictest possible terms, to keep on the other side of it - which, for some unaccountable reason, amused her no end. But when, despite the pillow, her arm found its way around his waist, he didn't complain.

He knew he shouldn't be doing what he was doing. He knew no onlooker would understand (he'd hesitate even to tell Susannah) but he couldn't help it.

After they'd lain like that for a while, he suddenly said, 'If anyone could see us now, I wouldn't have a prayer. They'd just throw away the key.'

'No they wouldn't,' she replied, somewhat drowsily. 'There'd be absolutely nothing they could do. Didn't I tell you? I turned sixteen, last week. So...just let me know, if you're tempted.'

There was a pause.

Then he said, 'That's not funny.'

But it was too late. She was already having convulsions.

When he woke the next morning, he could scarcely believe what he'd done. He'd spent the night before his trial in bed with her; even if she was sixteen, he'd be crucified if that ever came to light.

He made breakfast and took hers in to her. She was still sleeping; putting his hand on her shoulder, he shook her gently awake. She came to with a start that, for some reason, made him think of the judge.

'It's all right,' he said. 'I've brought you breakfast.'

He sat on the bed and watched, while she ate it.

'You got through the night unmolested then,' she said, with a mouth full of toast. 'See? I told you, you could trust me.'

'Very funny. I hope you're going to take your evidence seriously. You do realise what this trial means for me, don't you?'

'Of course I do!' After a pause, she asked, 'Are you nervous?'

'What do you think? Aren't you?'

'Me? No. What have I got to be nervous about?'

He laughed and shook his head at her. 'You're a strange girl!'

'Am I?' she enquired, without apparent resentment.

'In the sense that I imagine there are few - *very few* - like you. But I wouldn't have you any different, for the world.'

She smiled, put her arms around his neck and kissed him on the cheek.

He felt himself blush, though - for once - not with embarrassment or shame but only with pleasure.

Looking into his face, she laughed. 'I've made you blush!'

'Nonsense,' he said, with as much indignation as he could muster. 'Now, for Christ's sake, get up or you'll be late.'

By the time they'd finished arguing about what she was going to wear, they were both hopelessly late.

As Tom dragged her along - half running, in the effort to keep up with him - she panted, 'Did it ever occur to you, Tom, that *you're* the one on trial? They can't start without you, you know!'

Of course, they couldn't be seen arriving together. So he left her on the corner, with strict instructions to wait at least five minutes before she followed him into the court building.

As Tom might have expected, there was an anxious little posse awaiting him, the moment he'd cleared security.

'Where on earth have you *been*?' Mr Chadwick demanded, in that tone in which angry parents address their wayward children and barristers invariably address their clients.

Tom would have loved to say, 'In bed with the complainant,' just to see the look on his face. But of course he couldn't - not least because Susannah was there.

'Sorry,' he said, instead. 'I overslept.'

'*Overslept*!' Mr Chadwick cried, looking hard-pressed to decide whether he was more affronted by Tom's stupidity or his temerity. 'Then I suggest you invest in an alarm clock! Another ten minutes and there'd have been a warrant out for your arrest!'

'Sorry,' Tom said again, this time looking at Susannah and pulling a rueful face. He wished he could tell her what had really happened. But he barely had time to grab her hand

and say, 'Don't worry. Really. It'll be all right,' before the usher dragged him off to the dock. He hoped he'd sounded convincing.

Inside the courtroom, there was almost as much consternation amongst the prosecution team as (until Tom had finally condescended to put in a long-overdue appearance) there had been amongst the defence. There were half a dozen lawyers - barristers, solicitors and legal clerks - running around like headless chickens, looking just about ready to wet themselves, which Tom had no doubt was accounted for by Amy's disappearance from home and her non-appearance (so far) in court. The collective sigh of relief when she finally *did* appear might have been registered on the Beaufort scale.

Looking around the court, Tom noted with some surprise that the press box was packed and had about it a distinct aura of expectation. He wouldn't have thought his case was important enough to have attracted such interest. He'd expected a reporter from the local paper but not from any of the *nationals*. But then again, Amy was the daughter of a judge - and that fact alone was probably more than enough to get the press slavering at the mouth. He secretly smiled to think that, just for once, they were going to get more than they'd bargained for - and, just for once, he didn't begrudge it to them.

Apart from the press, the lawyers and the court officials, the only others present were Susannah and Vanessa (who were there to lend him their support) and Genghis (who was there to relish his long-awaited, much-coveted downfall). Tom had wondered if Amy's father would be there too but he wasn't. Part of Tom was sorry for that - but the better part was relieved, for Amy's sake.

Having been kept waiting, the judge wasn't in the best of moods when matters finally got underway and he vented his spleen, in just about equal measure, on the defence (for failing to produce Tom) and the prosecution (for failing to produce Amy). Tom had to admire his even-handedness. Thoroughly unpleasant he might be but - no doubt bearing in mind the famous scales - at least he was equally so to both sides.

As Tom had been advised it would, the trial began with the prosecuting barrister, Mr Spencer, outlining the case against him. Tom had never had a very high opinion of himself but even he found it difficult to recognise himself from Mr Spencer's description. If even half what he said was true, no more scheming, perverted, despicable, *loathsome* excuse for a human being had ever crawled upon the face of the earth.

By contrast, when Mr Chadwick rose to reply, Tom found himself transformed into a model citizen, with a list of virtues which would have done the most innocent, fresh-faced and irritating of choirboys proud. Suddenly, he was a man so wronged, so maligned by the outrageous allegations against him, that the heart of Attila the Hun would have bled for him.

Tom dreaded to think what the jury made of it; probably half of them wanted him lynching, while the other half wanted him deifying. He supposed there was a bizarre, primitive kind of logic to the process - everything was reduced to black and white; black was lumped into one side of the scales and white into the other - but whether the resulting pantomime could be said to constitute *justice*, Tom rather doubted.

When Mr Chadwick had finally finished lauding him to the skies, it was time for Amy to give her evidence. She climbed into the witness box and took the oath, clear-eyed and with her head held high. Tom's heart swelled with pride as he watched her. But he'd have been lying if he'd said he wasn't scared - for both of them. He knew what a task Amy had set herself in electing to tell the truth. And he also knew that his reputation, his freedom - it was hardly too much to say his whole life - depended on her telling it and being believed.

The prosecuting barrister got to his feet once more, gave Amy what was no doubt intended to be a reassuring smile and launched into his carefully prepared examination-in-chief. Initially, it seemed everything went to plan. Amy described how she'd argued with Brad, called at Susannah's house in search of Tom and been comforted and reassured by him; all exactly as he'd told the police and everyone else a thousand times over. There was nothing to surprise either side here.

Her account of events had always mirrored Tom's, right up to the moment when one of them had kissed the other.

That moment having been reached in her evidence, Mr Spencer said, 'So, the two of you were sitting on the defendant's sofa. He had you in his arms. You were crying. He dried your tears. What then?'

There was a pause and, just for a second, Tom thought she'd lost her nerve.

Then she said, 'I kissed him.'

Mr Spencer performed a sort of miniature double take. Then, with an embarrassed laugh, he said, 'I think, Miss Martin, you meant to say the defendant kissed you.'

'No,' she replied, flatly. '*I* kissed *him*.'

This time, there could be no doubt she meant what she said and it required all Mr Spencer's considerable experience to maintain his composure. 'Surely you're mistaken. After all, that's not what you told the police.'

'No. But the statement I gave to the police was nothing but a pack of lies.'

There was no concealing it now; this time she'd really put the cat among the pigeons. Even the dullest of jurors - even the *judge* - couldn't be deceived into thinking all was well with the prosecution, when its chief witness had just announced its entire case was founded on a pack of lies. A murmur of surprise, a sort of collective intake of breath, rippled through the courtroom and, just for a moment, Mr Spencer - mouth gaping, eyes bulging - resembled nothing more closely than a landed fish.

It seemed only the judge remained unperturbed. He was impatient to get on; if the trial collapsed so be it. That would leave him with a very welcome window in his diary, which he was sure he could fill far more pleasantly than this. He hadn't played golf all week - and there was a certain little masseuse he liked to visit, whenever he could find the time, who really gave the most effective relief.

With a glance at the clock, he said, 'Mr Spencer, may we get on?' It was framed as a question but only a fool would have taken it for one.

'I - er. Yes, My Lord. Though, given this rather unexpected turn of events, perhaps an adjournment...?'

'I think not, Mr Spencer. There's been enough delay already. I believe we've tried the patience of this jury quite sufficiently, for one morning.'

'As Your Lordship pleases,' Mr Spencer replied with a respectful bow - doubtless wishing his lordship at the bottom of the ocean, in a concrete overcoat. With a supreme effort to rally what remained his wits, he turned once more to Amy.

'Miss Martin, there can surely be only one explanation for your extraordinary claim that you lied to the police. If the defendant has intimidated you -'

'I have been intimidated,' Amy broke in. 'But not by Tom.'

'Then by whom?' Mr Spencer demanded.

Long ago, his pupil-master had taught him the first rule of advocacy is never ask a question, unless you already know the answer - and he was about to discover why.

Taking a deep breath, squaring her shoulders and looking him straight in the eye, Amy said, 'My father.'

Apart from Amy, only Tom had known the answer to Mr Spencer's question, before it had been asked. Upon everyone else in the courtroom - and the press, in particular - her reply acted like the application of a set of jump leads to the genitals: Mr Spencer literally choked and even the judge couldn't quite suppress a somewhat boggle-eyed start of surprise.

Having sunk half a pint of water and been thumped on the back half a dozen times by a colleague who threw his all into the task, Mr Spencer finally recovered the power of speech. 'Are you referring to - are you alleging intimidation by - His Honour Judge Martin?'

'As he's the only father I've got, I couldn't very well mean anyone else, could I?'

Looking just about ready to faint, Mr Spencer demanded, 'Are you seriously asking this court to believe that *His Honour Judge Martin* forced you into retracting your allegations against this defendant?'

'Don't be stupid. He didn't force me to *retract* them. He forced me to *make* them, in the first place.'

This time the murmur of surprise amounted to more of a clamour.

'Order! Order!' the judge yelled, banging down his gavel, just as he'd seen it done a thousand times in the movies but too rarely got an opportunity to do himself.

Watching him, Tom couldn't decide whether he more closely resembled the Queen of Hearts - or a two year old having a tantrum.

'Miss Martin!' the judge exclaimed - the threat she posed to a brother judge had galvanised him as almost nothing else could have done and he had suddenly turned a quite alarming shade of purple - 'I must warn you to be extremely careful what you say. I will not tolerate the making of such wild allegations against a fellow member of the judiciary. Even if the member in question *is* your father!'

'But I thought you wanted to know the truth,' Amy replied, all wide-eyed innocence. 'That is why we're here, isn't it?'

The judge didn't have an answer for that one and, for a minute, he looked as if he was struggling to swallow a hornet's nest - without the benefit of so much as a glass of water. Having got it down somehow - with an understandably dyspeptic grunt - he motioned Mr Spencer to proceed.

'His Lordship is right to warn you, Miss Martin. If your allegations against your father are false, you'll face prosecution for perjury; in the unlikely event that they're true, you'll be prosecuted for wasting police time and conspiring to pervert the course of justice. So before we proceed, perhaps you'd like to take a moment to consider the position in which you've put yourself.'

'Quite right, Mr Spencer!' the judge cried, clearly wishing he'd thought of that one himself. 'I'm quite prepared to adjourn to allow this witness to consider her position. Shall we say ten o'clock tomorrow morning?'

Mr Spencer was already bowing his relieved assent when, in clear, almost ringing tones, Amy said, 'But I don't want an adjournment. I just want to tell the truth. Why are you trying to make it so difficult for me?'

All eyes turned to the judge but, with a press box packed to overflowing, what could he do? He spluttered and puffed out his cheeks and looked to Mr Spencer for inspiration - but he'd just played his only trump card and didn't have another up his sleeve.

'If the witness is happy to proceed, My Lord...' Mr Chadwick murmured, half rising. He was careful to avoid the judge's eye; he didn't need to look him in the face to gauge how highly his lordship would value that contribution. He knew he'd just made himself about as popular as a porcupine in a balloon factory. But he was mindful of the press box too - and felt obliged to make a show of doing *something* in the interests of his client.

'Oh, very well!' the judge snapped. 'Let us get on, then! But understand, Mr Spencer, we're not here to investigate this young woman's allegations against her father. You are to confine yourself to questions which will establish the reliability of her evidence against *this defendant* and not against any other person. Do I make myself clear?'

'As crystal, My Lord,' Mr Spencer replied, with another bow.

Tom thought mud would have been a more accurate simile. But he guessed the gist was that the judge wanted Amy's opportunities for telling the truth about her father kept to a minimum. Knowing Amy as he did, Tom didn't envy Mr Spencer that task; if Amy was determined to say something, he figured there was just about no power on earth that could stop her.

'You say you're here to tell the truth,' Mr Spencer resumed now, turning to Amy, 'but I seriously doubt *you'd* know the truth, if it were staring you in the face.'

For a second, Tom thought the judge was about to break into spontaneous applause but, in the event, he contented himself with an approving grunt.

'First you claim the defendant assaulted you. Now you allege you were intimidated into making that claim by your own father - a respected High Court judge. I ask you, Miss Martin, what possible motive could he - could *any* father - have for such extraordinary behaviour?'

'Fear,' Amy replied simply. 'It's always a great motivator, don't you find? My father was frightened of being blackmailed.'

'*Blackmailed*? By the defendant?' Mr Spencer gasped, wishing harder than ever he'd taken heed of what his pupil-master had tried to teach him.

'That's right. You see, like a fool, I told Tom my father beat me.'

There was another gasp of surprise. Every other moment brought a new revelation and every new revelation was greeted by some exclamation of astonishment. Really, Tom thought, if he hadn't been the one on trial, it would have been just about the funniest thing he'd seen in a long time. Clearly, he hadn't been too wide of the mark, when he'd liken the proceedings to a pantomime.

'Mr Spencer!' the judge exclaimed, as if his wig was on fire. 'I insist you control this witness! I insist you confine her to what is relevant *to this case!*'

'Isn't the truth always relevant?' Amy replied, all wide-eyed innocence once more. 'Of course, if you don't want to hear it, I can always tell it to the press instead.'

At that, the judge all but spontaneously combusted. He wasn't used to being threatened - least of all by a mere slip of a girl. But what could he do, except curse the independence of the press? He itched to silence Amy, to suppress what threatened to be an inconvenient - possibly even a dangerous - truth. But how could he, in front of a press box stuffed to overflowing? His hands were tied and the girl knew it. Damn her.

'Get on, Mr Spencer!' he barked, submitting to the inevitable with a bad grace. 'The sooner we have a conclusion here, the better for all concerned!'

'Indeed, My Lord. Miss Martin, you claim you told the defendant -'

'That my father beat me,' Amy cut in, once more.

'That's right. I begged him not to tell anyone, because I knew it wouldn't do any good. But Tom being Tom, he had to *try*. He confronted my father and told him he'd report it, if it happened again. I don't suppose my father was too worried about the police or social services - they've never done anything to help my mother or me in the past - but there was always the risk Tom would go to the papers. So my father was on the lookout for a way of discrediting - of *destroying* - Tom, before Tom destroyed him. When I came home that night and, like a fool, blurted out what had happened - that I'd kissed Tom, that we'd struggled and he'd chased me out onto the street - I gave my father the ammunition he needed. Of course, I didn't know *then* that he had a reason to hate Tom or I'd have kept quiet. But I didn't know and I had no one else to turn to and, somehow, it all came tumbling out of me. My father can be very persuasive - almost *charming* when he chooses - and, before you know it, you've let you guard down and given him what he wants. And then, of course, he isn't charming anymore. Anyway, once he'd got the facts out of me, all he had to do was twist them to make Tom look guilty, draw up a statement for the police - and make me sign it.'

'But *why* did you sign it,' Mr Spencer demanded, acutely aware he was clutching at straws, 'if, as you say, it was all lies?'

'Didn't I just tell you, my father beats me? He could make me do almost anything. I might have put up more of a fight - but then I remembered that, after all, I'm my father's daughter. Deep down, all that cunning - that ruthless determination to survive and succeed - is in me too. So why not put it to good use? If I didn't help him, he'd only find some other way of destroying Tom. The only way to make Tom safe was to destroy my father, instead. So, that's what I decided to do. I knew I'd need evidence, so I started to gather it. What I found surprised even me. I had thought I knew my father - the depths to which he was capable of sinking - but I didn't. He was far worse and his influence far greater than even I'd imagined.'

'You say you have evidence but of what, exactly?' Mr

Spencer tried hard to sound challenging but, even to his own ears, his voice had the ring of despair.

'Of all of it, 'Amy replied, simply. 'I can prove I signed the statement I gave to the police under duress. Did I mention my father and the Chief Constable are members of the same Masonic Lodge? He was more than willing to bend the rules for my father and spare me any unnecessary, impertinent questioning. The statement my father wrote was all that was ever required. I can prove my father persuaded Tom's employers to sack him, without even awaiting the outcome of his trial. That cost him a packet. The headmaster was worried Tom would sue for unfair dismissal but once my father had written the school a nice, fat cheque he soon relaxed.'

Tom glanced at Genghis. He hadn't been looking any too happy for a while and, right now, he was a peculiar sort of sickly green. Tom bit the inside of his cheek till it hurt, in the effort to stop himself laughing out loud.

'I can prove my father contacted social services,' Amy continued, 'that he claimed Tom was a risk to his own daughter and had him separated from his family. I can prove he leaked the story to the local paper and that he paid a thug - well, an off-duty policeman but it's the same thing - to beat him up. You see, whatever my father wants he gets. People believe him without question; they stretch the rules to accommodate him, simply because of who he is. And if they're reluctant, he can always write them a cheque - or have them beaten into submission.'

There was a silence. Tom looked to the judge expecting him to intervene but he was just staring at Amy, as if she were some elemental force of nature beyond his control - and the will to live would entirely desert him if she raged much longer. Tom couldn't imagine what his lordship's problem was; *he* was thoroughly enjoying himself.

'My father's influence extends everywhere,' Amy resumed. 'That's why I had to wait to tell the truth. I had to make my accusations publicly and ensure the press box was packed, or my father and his friends would have found some way of hushing it up, of getting him off the hook. It's true I could have cleared Tom's name sooner and saved him a great deal of pain but I wanted more than that. I wanted to put a stop to my father - for good. I hope Tom can understand and forgive me for that,' she said, looking up at him. 'I hope he thinks - and I hope we'll both find - it was a sacrifice worth making.'

'You claim you can prove all this,' Mr Spencer said, grey in the face and looking just about ready to drop, 'but where's the evidence? Why should the jury believe you? You say you were lying before; how do we know you're not lying now?'

'Because it's all here,' Amy replied, reaching into her bag, extracting a package and setting it down on the ledge of the witness box, in front of her. 'I've copied every letter and every document. I've recorded every phone call and every conversation. The evidence wasn't difficult to get; it's amazing how careless someone becomes, when they believe they're unimpeachable, when they believe they're above the law.'

'No one is above the law!' the judge exclaimed, finding his voice and making a contribution to the proceedings at last - albeit not one overburdened with originality.

'I'm very pleased to hear Your Lordship say so,' Amy replied, closing the trap with an alacrity that made Tom want to leap to his feet and cheer. 'A few minutes ago, Mr Spencer, you were threatening me with prosecution for wasting police time and conspiring to pervert the course of justice. I hope you meant what you said. Because you'll find all the evidence you need in that package. Against me. *And* my father.'

When, from the depths of the corner into which Amy had backed him, the judge finally announced Tom's acquittal, virtual pandemonium ensued. The press made an immediate stampede for the door - closely followed by a decidedly shamefaced Genghis - and everyone else began arguing and yelling all at once. Mr Spencer, in particular, was demanding to know who was responsible for making a bigger monkey out of him than Guy the gorilla - in twenty years at the bar, he'd rarely looked or felt a bigger chump - and it seemed to Tom that he had to fight his way across a sea of bodies to find his way out of the dock and into Susannah's arms.

Just for a few moments, their happiness in his acquittal and in each other was enough to make Tom forget everything - and everyone else - and by the time he looked round for her, Amy was gone.

Leaving Susannah to call Marion with the good news, Tom went in search of Amy and caught up with her just as she was about to step outside and face the barrage of waiting press.

'Hey!' he said, grabbing her arm and turning her to face him. 'Where the bloody hell do you think you're going, without so much as a word?'

Then - to hell with all of them - he pulled her into his arms and gave her the hug of her life.

'You were magnificent,' he told her, as he released her. 'Like some sort of latter-day, saner Joan of Arc.'

She laughed, blushing from the compliment as well as the embrace. 'I hope I don't suffer the same fate! What's the penalty for conspiring to pervert the course of justice? I suppose it isn't being burnt at the stake; no doubt they'll consider that too good for me.'

'They wouldn't really prosecute you, surely.'

She shrugged. 'Who cares? I don't. Not as long as I take my father down with me. And they can't very well prosecute me without prosecuting him, can they?'

'I suppose not.'

'Anyway, it's my bet they won't prosecute either of us. Despite all the evidence I've gathered, they'll say there isn't enough to convict him. The best we can hope for is he'll be pensioned off or found some sinecure somewhere, out of the limelight. Isn't that what usually happens, when people like him - judges, politicians and their like - are finally found out?'

'I can never make up my mind,' Tom said, gazing down at her with an admiring smile, 'whether you're wise or only cynical.'

'That's because you're not wise enough to know the difference.'

'No doubt. Anyway, what are you going to do now? I mean, after you've run the gauntlet of the press.'

He didn't like to think of her having to face her father alone. He wasn't sure it would improve matters if he went with her but he was willing to try; it was, after all, the least he could do. But of course, she didn't need him; she'd got everything arranged already.

She reached into her bag once more, pulled out her passport and an airline ticket and waved them gleefully, in his face.

'It's independence day,' she said. 'At least for me. I'm leaving home and Claremont - and flying off to the States to live with my mum.'

'But your father's got custody, hasn't he?'

She laughed. 'Sure. But I can't see him objecting - not after what I've just done to him. What?' she demanded, watching the smile that was spreading across his face.

'I was just thinking...when all this began, I'd never have believed any good could come of it. But somehow, it has.'

'Of course it has! Didn't I always tell you, the end justifies the means?'

He hugged her again as they said goodbye and, when he let her go, it was reluctantly.

'Keep in touch,' he called after her, as she walked away in that halo of sunshine she carried around with her.

'I will,' she promised, turning back to him one last time. 'I'll never forget you, Tom. You know that.'

'I really misjudged that girl,' Van said, suddenly appearing at his elbow and nodding towards Amy, who was standing at the top of the courthouse steps, surrounded by journalists. 'I don't think I'll ever be able to look her in the face again.'

'You won't have to,' Tom replied.

As he explained why, he breathed an inner sigh of relief that he hadn't launched the full-scale assault on Amy's character and reputation that Mr Chadwick had advised. If he had, he wouldn't have been able to look her in the face now either.

'Well,' Van said, when she'd heard him out, 'it's going to seem pretty strange back at school without you, or Amy, or Genghis - not that I'm sorry to see the back of *him*.'

'You think the governors'll sack him?' Tom asked, only just stopping himself from rubbing his hands together in glee.

'If he hasn't got the decency to resign first. They can hardly turn a blind eye to him taking a *bribe* - even if the money did swell the school's coffers, rather than his own.'

'I hope you're right,' Tom said, beaming. Really, things just kept getting better and better.

'And once Genghis has gone, I'm almost sure to be appointed acting head and, you never know, if I play my cards right, I might even land the job permanently this time. So, how do you fancy your old job back? I'm sure I could swing it for you. After everything you've been through, Tom, it's the least the governors could do.'

'Aren't you forgetting about Matt? Claremont doesn't need *two* philosophy teachers, does it?'

In response to her torn, agonised look, Tom laughed; just for once, he'd thought of something she hadn't.

'It's all right, Van. I'm grateful for the offer but I don't think I do want my old job back. I think I just want to be Miranda's dad for a while and, later on, maybe I'll go back to that PhD I started - once, in another lifetime - and somehow forgot to finish.'

As they finally left the court building together, Tom felt Susannah slip her hand into his. He looked down at her and found her regarding him through narrowed eyes, which - to his relief - had a smile in them.

'Is there anything you want to tell me, Tom?' she asked. 'About last night? About you and Amy?'

'Yes. But not now; I'm too happy. It wouldn't do any good to scold me now.'

'When does it ever?' she asked, smiling and shaking her head at him.

'You always do me good,' he assured her, pulling her into his arms. 'You always have and you always will.'

As he moved to kiss her, something compelled him to look up and standing there, right across the road from him, larger than life - larger than ever - was the hospital chaplain. He was looking right at Tom, almost *into* him somehow, as if he thought everything - Tom especially - was a joke of such cosmic proportions, he could barely contain himself. As their eyes met, he winked and gave Tom a flash of that keyboard grin. Because like he said, he'd always been a sucker for a happy ending.

'Look, Susannah!' Tom cried, pointing. 'Across the road. There's that chaplain I told you about. The one who scared me half to death, the night Miranda was born.'

She looked and looked back at him, blankly. 'Where?'

What was she, *blind*?

'You're joking! There! Right *there*, for Christ's sake, blotting out the sun!'

He looked back again. But impossibly, even the grin had disappeared.

THE END

Printed in the United Kingdom by
Lightning Source UK Ltd., Milton Keynes
137373UK00001B/156/P